A STUDY IN MURDER

A HOMES & WATKINS ROMANTIC MYSTERY

Debra Snow
with
ARJAY LEWIS

A Study In Murder: Homes & Watkins Book One
Copyright ©2019 Debra Snow & Arjay Lewis

Cover Design: Marianne Nowicki, PremadeEbookCoverShop.com
Editing: Brandi Aquino; www.editingdonewrite.com

ISBN-13: 978-1732659346
ISBN-10: 1732659346

Published by:
Mindbender Press
474 South Main Street
Phillipsburg NJ 08865
www.mindbenderpress.com

PRAISE FOR A STUDY IN MURDER

"I have the good fortune to read many Holmesian pastiches. One of the best I've seen recently is Debra Snow's and Arjay Lewis's Homes & Watkins adventures. Not only do they have the flavour of classic Doyle, but they also differ with a splendid sense of humor that provides both mystery and comedy in welcome doses. Recommended VERY highly!!!"

—Marvin Kaye, Editor
Sherlock Holmes Mystery Magazine

Dedication

To our Grandparents
George and Bertha Snow
Joseph and Elizabeth Stenger
Thomas and Tulia Jenkins
James and Bertha Lewis
They helped us to create the lives we have.

"You know my methods, Watson. There was not one of them which I did not apply to the inquiry. And it ended by my discovering traces, but very different ones from those which I had expected."

—*Sir Arthur Conan Doyle*
The Memoirs of Sherlock Holmes (1893)

1. Writer's Block

Mark Watkins

*I*t was the winter of 1887, when the unexpected letter found its way to our rooms at 221B Baker Street.

Holmes had been in one of his melancholy moods of late, as often occurred when the cold weather forced him indoors. Added to this fact was that, although his services were in demand, there was nothing that challenged his unique mind.

Until that letter.

Mrs. Hudson, our landlady, brought it up with several other envelopes, as soon as the morning post arrived.

Holmes' trained eye went to it immediately, and with a quick move of his catlike reflexes, he tore it open and perused it as I examined the remaining correspondence.

Holmes rose to his feet, held the letter aloft, and turned to me to say, "Watson, the game is afoot!"

I dropped my hands from the keyboard, shook my head, and muttered, "Utter crap."

I shut down the word-processor program, then my computer, and gave up for another day.

It was pointless to even try.

I stood and my eyes fell on the full-length mirror in the room that was both my office and bedroom. The one Susie insisted I get her.

I saw her there in my mind's eye.

"I need something large enough to see if my outfit looks right."

"You always look beautiful," I told her.

"Flatterer," she said with a smile, as I kissed her cheek. *"You're just trying to turn my head."*

I was back in present time, where all that was reflected was a middle-aged man, not thin but not yet fat, about five feet seven, with sandy-gray hair and horn-rimmed glasses. I needed a shave, and wore pajamas and a bathrobe that was more wrinkles than anything else.

I approached the mirror like an adversary as I examined myself in all my glory. I'd gained weight, with a bit of a belly where there never had been one. I glared into my bloodshot eyes. Too little sleep and too much alcohol.

Susie would be disappointed in me. But she wasn't here to say so.

The buzzer for the outer door of my building went off.

Who would that be? I thought. I felt it was too early, then I glanced at the clock. It was just past 11:00 AM.

Well, early for me.

I walked to the intercom which stood on the wall, hit the button, and yelled, "Who is it?"

"Mark?" came the garbled reply, made even less intelligible by the cheap speaker. "Hey, babe, it's Jeff."

I pushed the other button, which buzzed open the front door so he could enter. If you live in Manhattan, it's like you're a prisoner. Everywhere you go you pass through secured areas and deal with surly doormen, whose attitudes often resemble prison guards. This is all for the illusion that you are somehow safer, when on any given night some crazed, strung-out addict could break into your apartment through the one spot you didn't cage.

I ran a hand through my hair and adjusted my glasses.

Fine time for my literary agent to show up. A thought occurred to me. If I wanted him to stay away, all I had to do was show him the crap I'd just written.

Probably not. Jeff was a friend, and a good one at that.

Besides, I was still considered one of the finest Sherlock Holmes writers of the new millennium. My novels were actually much better than that cliché-ridden garbage I'd just knocked off.

The death of Sir Arthur Conan Doyle, creator of the most famous of all fictional detectives, Sherlock Holmes, had been a boon to writers everywhere. There were still a good dozen or two of us who knocked out new adventures with regularity for the long-deceased detective. That is, of course, if he had ever lived.

And in my case, they sold quite well.

I'd received good reviews for each of my five novels. *Death In The Borley Rectory* even got to the *New York Times* Best Seller list, though it hovered near the bottom in its brief stay.

I'd been able to write what I considered good books, and I didn't resort to the popular trick of having Holmes and Watson meet historical figures: Freud, Jack the Ripper, the Prince of Wales, et cetera. I preferred my fiction unsullied by what I always considered a trick: the writer trying to be far too clever for his own good.

Of course, that all happened when Susie was alive.

It was easy with her there to read my work, correct my childish typing or spacing errors, and encourage me along.

Before the cancer.

The knock came at the door and I jumped. I stared at the door for a moment and didn't quite remember who I expected. I gave a quick glance through the fisheye peephole and undid the three locks to pull open the door.

Jeffrey Moss, literary agent supreme, burst into the room like a runaway subway train.

He walked past my series of built-in bookcases that lined one wall, filled with books from classics to modern. Although I often read books on an electronic device these days, I still loved the feel and smell of the real thing.

"Mark!" he bellowed, and pushed the shock of his unruly white hair out of his eyes. "Hey, is it okay if I smoke, babe?"

I nodded. Jeff was the only person Susie ever let smoke in this apartment. That rule started when we moved in back in the '90s.

God, we were just a couple of kids when we first rented this place, straight out of college. She was such a beauty then, petite, dark-haired, dark-eyed, with an intellect that made my head go soft and a body that made everything else get hard. I thought I was the luckiest man in the world.

Which, of course, I was.

There was such a sudden lump in my throat, I coughed to clear it.

"I think you know where the ashtray is," I told him.

"Sure, babe," Jeff said, and put down his briefcase on the way into my tight kitchen. I always believed that it was supposed to be a hallway that some crazy contractor made into a kitchen when the apartment got subdivided sometime in the ancient past, long before we moved in. Then, years later, the building went condo, which gave me a chance to buy my own apartment for an outrageous sum, as well as continue to pay rent, though it was now called "condo fees." It was the only apartment I'd ever had in New York City.

Jeff turned on the blower in the hood over the range, lit his cigarette, and took a long hard drag that relaxed him at once.

"Meetings all morning," Jeff said, his words highlighted with pale smoke. "Couldn't smoke at all. I tell you, a couple more laws and I'll move to Canada. I can get marijuana on any street corner, but tobacco will be illegal."

"To what do I owe the pleasure?" I asked.

"Checking up on you, babe," Jeff said, and took another drag. "I see you are still wearing your stylish outfit."

He looked at me from head to toe, and took in my pajamas, bathrobe, and worn slippers.

"I *am* wearing different pajamas since your last visit, and I did shave, last Tuesday or Wednesday," I sassed. I felt a little vexed. If I wanted to stay in my damn pajamas all day, it wasn't any of his business.

He blew a well-aimed burst of nicotine-laced vapor into the blower and gazed at the floor.

"Babe," he said quietly. "It's been two years—"

"Christ, Jeff," I responded, my voice loud. "I don't need a damn cuckoo clock—"

"I'm worried about you, all right?" Jeff shot back. His voice exceeded mine easily. In spite of his cigarette habit, all those years he'd spent as an actor still gave him excellent vocal control.

"I'm fine," I said, and rubbed my face. This was what it was like every time Jeff showed up. "Please don't start on that, 'Susie wouldn't want this' crap, okay?"

"I get it!" Jeff conceded. "I've tried to talk to you as a friend. I won't do that today."

"Good."

"Today I am here *strictly* as your agent." Jeff crushed out his cigarette. He stormed over to his briefcase, loudly put it on the table, and opened it. "Your last hardcover, *The Crime Of The Casual Crook,* was published over two years ago, and the follow-up paperback stopped being printed six months ago."

"So, no new royalties will be forthcoming," I agreed. "I've put enough away. I don't have to worry."

"Look, Mark," Jeff went on with that I-know-this-game tone he adopts when he wants to wheedle something out of me, "you know the publishing business as well as I do. Unless you come out with a book every year, you're sunk. Publish or die."

"Unless you're John Updike," I pointed out.

"Even he couldn't get away with it in this market," Jeff quipped. "Look, you struggled for so many years with books that didn't take off — good reviews but no sales."

"And you got me editing deals on those anthologies," I affirmed. "I know it, and I appreciate—"

"You finally hit it with the Sherlock Holmes books — approved by the Conan Doyle estate — and I don't have to tell you, that took a lot of negotiations."

I exhaled heavily. "I know."

Jeff was about to go into his ten-minute song and dance about how much tougher it is these days, and how there used to be a lot more money and a lot less competition and so on. I've heard it all before, and it just annoys me.

Jeff's a good agent, and the need to persuade and cajole authors is part of his job. Authors tend to be lazy animals, unless we need the cash.

He just didn't understand. Susie was more than a wife. She was my editor, as well as my number one fan.

I wrote the Sherlock Holmes stories for her.

She was the biggest Conan Doyle fan on earth. It was a delight to watch her face as she read my novels and enjoyed every morsel like a fine meal.

I'd tried to tell Jeff that the idea of writing another book, another Holmes book, would just be too hard if I couldn't see her brown eyes peer at me over her glasses, and her insights into my characterizations.

"Look, Jeff," I blurted out. "I can't do it. Not right now. I've… tried… really I have. But all I can produce is junk of the worst order."

"Babe," he continued, "you've got to keep trying. For Chrissake, you're a great writer. And a great writer should write!"

"Yes," I grumbled, and I felt my face flush hot with embarrassment. Jeff usually never praised my talents, and pushed me to always improve my technique. For him to suggest that I was a great writer was unheard of.

"You need to get out, babe. Marsha keeps telling me to have you over for dinner again."

"And invite over another one of her single friends, like the last time?" I shook my head.

"She can't help it." He shrugged. "There are a lot of single women in this city, and you are quite a catch."

"I-I can't," I said. Since Susie was gone that part of me was absent. I used to look at women all the time — not to do anything about it, just to look. Since Susie died, I didn't have the interest. "Besides, I get out — I buy groceries."

He yanked open my refrigerator, which was quite sparse.

"Okay," I snapped. "I go out to eat."

"Mark, you need to get out of this damn condo and do something. Meet people, experience life."

I tightened my jaw as I felt tears stab my eyes.

Experience life? I thought. *With Susie in the cold, cold ground?*

I wish I had just died with her. It would've been so much simpler.

"Whatever," I snarled, annoyed that it was a pretty lousy comeback for a writer.

"Tell you what, Mark. I got a deal for you."

"Look, Jeff, I just don't want to—"

"Hear me out, babe. A mystery conference is coming up."

"A fan con? Those things are such a pain—"

"It's here in town. They want *you* to participate."

"What are you talking about?"

"The Northeast Mystery Conference. They want you to be a featured speaker — and they are willing to pay."

"I don't know—"

"Think about it. It's just five days next month, here in town. You give a lecture the first night, Wednesday, and sit on a panel on Thursday."

"A panel?"

"Yeah, a panel of writers who do Holmes stories."

"Oh great!" I snorted. "Do you know how much dreck there is out there? Why do I want to be associated with that?"

"For one thing," he said, his voice far too chipper, "I know for a fact that Sheryl Homes is a participant."

I paused as his words sunk in.

"You're kidding."

"Not in the least, babe."

Sheryl Homes was my number one competitor in the genre of Sherlock Holmes books. Like me, she also had the approval of the Conan Doyle estate.

I'd read her books. They were good and a great read. In the last four years, her books inspired me on my own work. She was not yet at best-seller status, but I was sure she would be soon. Her writing just got better and better.

What I knew about her was this: she lived in New York, was married, and if her book jacket photo was any indication, was a fine-looking lady.

The chance to actually *meet* her, eye to eye? Well, from what I'd heard, she was a good three inches taller than me, but close enough.

"Okay," I proclaimed, surprised by my sudden decisiveness, "sign me up."

"That's great, you won't regret this," Jeff prattled, and he pulled out a manila envelope from his briefcase and put it on the table. "This is just what you need, babe."

"I don't know about that…"

Jeff made his way to the door, undoubtedly on his way to a meeting, or off to annoy a writer, or kiss up to the next publisher on his list.

"You go to this, you'll get ideas. Put 'em down on paper and we are on our way to another best seller. I can feel it in my bones."

We said our good-byes and Jeff went out the door with one final, "You won't regret it!"

Jeff was wrong. I already regretted it.

I'd done conventions before, and they are long, dull endeavors. The only reason I'd done them in the past was that they gave me a chance to get away with Susie to a hotel room.

The image of a naked Susie as she held a flimsy sheet from the hotel bed up to her neck appeared in my mind.

"What is it about you and hotels, Mark? At home we make love once a week. We get to a hotel and you want it twice a day!"

"It reminds me of our honeymoon."

"Hmmm. That's the right thing to say," she said, and lowered the sheet to expose her breasts. "You don't mind that I'm a hell of a lot grayer and plumper than when we got married?"

"You're beautiful. Come here and kiss me."

"Again?" she chuckled and pushed the sheet aside to expose herself completely. "Oh, all right, since it reminds you of our honeymoon."

I yanked myself out of the memory. I stood there, as my hands shook.

I wanted a drink, badly, but it was far too early in the day, and I was drinking more than I should. I grabbed the envelope Jeff left and walked into the bedroom, where my attention was drawn to my empty, rumpled bed.

Our bed.

This time, I let the tears come.

2. Frontispiece

Sheryl Homes

"The Northeast Mystery Conference is only a few days away. I can't have you backing out now," whined Gloria in my ear.

"I didn't know my ex-husband was going to be in charge of everything!" I fumed. "Have you seen the online schedule? He has me running from place to place and room to room."

"Look, you're one of the founders of the club, and you know how your husband has his hooks in the group. But why are you whining to me, Sheryl? You know I'm retiring."

"A fine time to leave me!" I barked into the phone. "Just when I need you."

"Look, dearie, you're good," she explained calmly, "but you need to find a new agent. This convention will have agents storming the place. If you show up at all these panels and stuff, someone has got to notice you—"

"I don't want another agent. I want you!" I finally admitted. "You've built my career, negotiated all my contracts—"

"And my hubby had a heart attack," she explained patiently. "Dearie, you know I love you, but I'm not getting any younger. I need to get the hell out of New York and be with my man."

I pulled the phone away from my ear and looked at the photo of the woman who had been my first agent displayed on the screen. The photo was me and Gloria from a lunch five years earlier to celebrate my first sale. Gloria was a short, slightly chubby woman, gray-haired and bespectacled. In the photo, I towered over her and was the complete opposite with my Irish coloring, green eyes, and flaming-red hair.

I returned the phone to my ear. "I guess since I'd agreed to it…"

"That's the spirit!" Gloria chuckled. "Besides, I heard that Mark Watkins will be there."

I exhaled loudly. "Probably another misogynist who is pissed off that a woman is writing *Sherlock Holmes* books."

"Not every guy is like that! Jeff Moss is his agent, and he told me that Watkins liked your work."

"Wow," I jeered, "what a great review."

"Oh, now you're just being pissy!" Gloria grunted. "You know Moss would be a good fit for you. He even knows the genre…"

"Okay, okay, I'll do the damn convention. But please don't set me up with an agent I haven't even met yet."

"There you go," Gloria chortled. "I can't see why people say you're difficult."

"Who says I'm difficult?"

"Bye, dearie."

She ended the call. I stared at the phone for a moment, a little surprised that my agent had dismissed me.

She did have a point though. I was well aware that people said I was difficult. But there were a lot of men in the club who just didn't like the fact that "Randall's little wifey" ended up being a better writer than they were.

Especially that weasel, Allen Alexander, who'd been trying to seduce me even when I'd been married to Randall. The fact that my books had done so much better than his pathetic attempts only encouraged his lust.

I could imagine that for him it was all about dominance.

I thought about everyone in the group. We had members who were just glad to come and talk about mysteries. But then we had the triumvirate: the club president, Charles Nederlander, average height with a receding hairline and that pair of half-glasses perched at the end of his Romanesque nose; vice-president Jon Kane, thin, though not skinny, with curly black hair that sported a spray of white at the temples; treasurer and my ex, Randall Lawrence, with those bedroom eyes, full head of hair, and boyish good looks I thought I would never grow tired of.

Turned out, he grew tired of me.

A financial investor and a wannabe writer, and I had the audacity to go out and write a book that did very well.

My mother suggested I not publish, that it would be too hard on Randall's ego. I thought more highly of him than that.

I'd been wrong.

Coming home and finding slim, blonde Candy Poole in my bed with him…

I looked around my large downtown condo. This had been one of the perks of divorcing Randall — I got enough to buy this place. Right on West 4th Street in Manhattan, it was an expensive piece of real estate, but Randall was quite wealthy, and my lawyer was a shark.

But I had to admit, it still hurt.

I grabbed the heavy glass paperweight off the nearby computer desk and felt an overwhelming desire to throw it across the room.

I squeezed it until the feeling passed. It would be a stupid thing to do. Toss the heavy ball of glass and it might shatter or break something else. A year since the divorce and I'd only finished unpacking completely two weeks ago.

I should have quit the stupid club. How could I move on with my life if I was still surrounded by the same people? It was odd, they all encouraged me when I started, even Randall. They all liked my early drafts of the novel. It was when I got an agent and sold the book that it all changed. And then it hit the *USA Today* best seller list, and I was suddenly the enemy.

Even with Randall.

He went out of his way to make snide comments, especially when I was writing. In defense, I ended up writing in coffee shops or when he was at work.

I was coming home from a great writing session, feeling that high a writer gets when they know they've done good work. I was excited to tell Randall about how well it had gone, share that with him. Then talk to him about his day while I made dinner, and perhaps we could crack open some wine and get naked. At the time, he hadn't touched me for weeks.

I had come through the door, quietly, because if Randall was on the phone or busy at the computer, I didn't want to distract. It was when I put my purse down that I heard the first moan.

It was obviously a woman's cry of pleasure. I froze for a moment, as I took off my coat silently. Then the idea occurred to me that maybe Randall was watching porn on his computer. I smiled as I thought it might be fun to catch him, and then make his fantasy come true.

But as I headed back in the apartment, the moans got louder, and I heard Randall moaning as well.

Could computer speakers make such realistic sounds?

I reached the open doorway to the bedroom — my bedroom — and the image of naked and buxom Candy Poole atop equally naked Randall was like a slap in the face.

They were going at it quite loudly, and I stood in shock as they both climaxed, right there, right in front of me as if I didn't matter. During his orgasm, Randall turned to look at me, with that woman on top of him, and their anatomies still entwined. He glared at me as if to say, "See how easily I can replace you?"

I left that night and never went back, except to pack. I spent the next few weeks in Westchester with my parents, but every night I would see Randall looking at me with that combination of loathing and dismissal.

Both Randall and Candy would be at this upcoming convention. I would have to see that little airhead smirk at me, knowing she was bedding my husband, while I had been alone for over a year-and-a-half. And Randall would look down on me dismissively.

But Gloria was right, I had agreed to it. I would have to be the grown-up and focus on meeting agents, doing panels, and not letting any of those people get under my skin.

I sat down and began to write. If I didn't have a life that made sense, I could at least write about Sherlock Holmes, who could always make sense from the smallest clue.

3. Printer's Errors

Mark Watkins

W eeks later, showered, shaved, and dressed well, I arrived at the Hilton New York in Midtown Manhattan.

Spring was in the air, adding delightful odors to the scent of the city. I thought about walking but opted for the short subway ride to 57th Street & Seventh Avenue. Then I strolled to the hotel on the Avenue of the Americas and 54th Street.

Inside, I passed through the large lobby that had a "pseudo-rotunda" area in the center. The ceiling was designed in an enormous circle, decorated in gold leaf or gold paint, I couldn't tell the difference.

Toward the back of the hotel, I took an escalator to the mezzanine level to collect my name badge and schedule. Coming off the escalator, I glanced into the huge convention room known as the Rhinelander Gallery. It was filled with booth after booth, all separated by pipe and drape, and bore a sign at the door proclaiming it "The Marketplace."

I headed for the registration booths laid out along the hallway. There, I got on the line for attendees, where several people were behind the counter organizing badges and helping arrivals.

A striking blonde approached in a long-sleeve, turtle-necked, red dress. It was fashionable while showing off every remarkable curve. Her hair was coiffed to frame her face, she was neatly made-up, and wore red lipstick that matched the ensemble.

"And what's *your* name, sir?" she asked in a breathy voice reminiscent of Marilyn Monroe.

"Mark Watkins," I said, and her eyes grew large.

"Really," she replied, as if I had just made her day. She looked me over and then added, "The writer?"

"Yes," I said, and tried to look modest. Of course, in my jacket and open collar, I'd dressed for the role.

"Wow!" she said with a throaty whisper. "I'm a big fan."

"Really?"

"I want to be sure to catch your speech." She rose, then glanced both ways to make sure no one was nearby. She leaned close to my ear and said, "I'm in room 1230. Maybe you could autograph something of mine later."

She leaned back and giggled wickedly.

"Wha-what do you have in mind?" I said, my mouth suddenly dry.

"I'm sure I'll think of something," she chuckled suggestively.

"I'd be… um… happy to."

"I've got to find Mr. Kane," she said. "He wanted to know the minute you arrived."

She walked out from behind the booth. "You wait right here," she said, then added, "By the way, I'm Candy."

Thinking quickly, I said, "I'm sure you're twice as sweet." Then realized what a lame line it was.

She giggled anyway. "You'll just have to find out. Let me get Mr. Kane."

She traipsed off, and I realized that although her dress was long-sleeved and high-necked, it had a big circle open in the back exposing flawless skin. I also enjoyed the view of her active posterior as she sauntered away.

"She's quite a girl, don't you think?" a man said to my left.

I turned and my eyes found the speaker. He was above average height with a strong chin and receding hairline. A pair of half-glasses hung on his nose, and his Brooks Brothers suit and tie gave him an aura of success and competence.

"Hmmm?" I said, and then glanced after Candy. "Oh yes, lovely young lady."

He reached out his hand, and I could see that he wore one of the badges for the conference. Each badge was color-coded, and his was a reddish tone that signified he was staff.

"Charles Nederlander," the man announced in a deep voice as I shook his hand. "I'm the president of the club. Been a big fan of mystery all my life."

"Are you a writer?"

"Hell, no," he conceded, "I'm a lawyer, but I admire writers and know how to put events together."

"Thanks for having me."

"My pleasure. My vice-president, Jon Kane, handles the talent," he bragged. "Did you know Willow Rose is the Friday night speaker?"

"How did you manage that?" I said, impressed. I loved her work.

"Jon's a miracle worker that way. I have to be honest. He told me that when he spoke to your agent, it didn't look like you would do it."

I shrugged.

"I'm glad," he confirmed, and then looked past me. "Oh, Candy found Jon. I'll let the two of you get acquainted."

Nederlander wandered off in the direction of the large convention room. I noticed that Candy watched him go, and I got the impression she didn't care for him.

I turned as the pair drew near. The man was taller than Charles, over six feet, thin, with curly black hair with white on his temples.

"Mr. Watson?" he inquired.

"Wat—*kins*," I corrected.

"Oh, sorry," he apologized as he gave my hand a firm shake. "It's just I've read your books—"

"And you were convinced that I truly am John H. Watson, MD," I said as I returned his grip. "Happens all the time."

"Of course. I'm Jon Kane."

"My agent told me to look for you."

"So glad you decided to join us," Kane expressed and turned to Candy. "Could you get Mr. Watkins his package?"

She gave a nod and, with a flirty wink to me, reached behind a counter.

"I see you met Charles, the financial half of this endeavor," Jon affirmed. "Don't be surprised if he asks you to sign some of his books, which are all first-editions. Personally, I think that's the only reason he's involved — to increase the value of his own collection by bringing in his favorite writers."

Candy pulled out a large manila envelope, which she dutifully handed to me. She gave it to me and then rubbed my arm in a warm gesture as she spoke. "This contains your badge, your information, and your room keys—"

"My room?" I was surprised. "But I only live—"

"Tut, tut," Jon chimed in.

Did anyone actually say, "tut, tut" these days?

"You are our opening speaker, and no expense is to be spared." He took my envelope and extracted a small map. "Here is where you'll give your speech tonight," he said and indicated the Mercury Ballroom on the third floor.

I glanced at the paper. "I'll look around the facilities."

"Excellent! Now, you are participating in the panel tomorrow at one in the afternoon, which will be in the Beekman Room" –he ran his finger to a small meeting room— "on the second floor."

I nodded.

"Now, after the panel, I set up an hour at the signing booth."

"The what?"

"The signing booth. People will bring copies of your books to be autographed. After your speech, I was sure there would be a huge demand. You have your hotel room until Monday morning."

I shrugged. "Anything for the fans."

"That's lovely!" he gushed and turned to Candy. "Didn't I tell you he was first-rate?"

As we finished speaking, a white-haired woman, wonderfully coiffed and wearing what I was sure was a Chanel suit and skirt, strode up to us.

"Jon," she declared, without a look to me.

"Ms. Cunningham. Oh this is a treat!" Jon greeted her enthusiastically. "I'd like you to meet Mark Watkins. He's doing our opening night speech—"

"Ah, about Holmes!" She turned to me. I noticed on her lapel was an eye-catching cameo in green with a gold frame. The silhouette on the pin wore a deerstalker hat and held a pipe in his mouth. It was Sherlock Holmes!

"How do you do?" I offered and pointed at her pin. "That's quite lovely."

"Isn't it?" she intoned, with a glance to it. "It's Jade and cost a fortune, I'll tell you that."

"Nice."

"I'm Winsley Cunningham, and I believe you are doing my panel on Thursday."

I glanced at Jon who nodded vigorously.

"I guess I am."

"Well, that's lovely. I happen to teach a course on the biography of Sherlock Holmes at the New School."

It was my turn to nod. Even though Holmes and Watson were fictional characters, it was a popular pastime for Holmesian scholars to make up biographies for Holmes that matched Sir Arthur Conan Doyle's writings and approximated what would be his timeline.

The most famous of these researchers, William Baring-Gould, wrote several books that were now the "accepted" biography from which others based their writings. I found Baring-Gould a great resource and his books a good read, but making Holmes that real always seemed a little creepy to me.

"That's great," I said. "I look forward to being on your panel."

"You'd better be good tonight!" Winsley warned. "I've been telling them to have a Holmes speaker for years." She gave Kane a withering look. "I always thought it would be me…"

Jon gave an embarrassed cough. "Don't pressure the man, Winsley."

I jumped in. "It's fine. I hope to live up to your expectations." I extracted my plastic card key from the envelope. "I guess I'd better check my room."

"Good," Jon said. "Please arrive about a half-hour early to the ballroom so the sound man can put your microphone on. Well, you're all set then. I have to get back to..." He gestured toward the convention room.

"I need to speak to you, Jon," Winsley insisted.

"Can we talk as we walk, Winsley?" Jon offered, and he was off in the direction of the convention room with Ms. Cunningham right on his heels.

"I want to know when Randall will be here," Winsley commanded as they wandered off.

"Oh, Mr. Watkins," Candy called.

I turned to look at the blonde. As she handed me a business card, she touched my shoulder to draw near and whisper in my ear, "My cell number is on the back."

I turned the card over and hand-scribed was a ten-digit number with a little heart drawn at the end. "I see."

"If you have some free time today, you should take a look at the Marketplace."

I smiled. "I looked in. Seems impressive."

"If you do, make sure you have your badge on. You can go to any of the lectures or presentations — it's an all-access pass."

"That's great." I attempted a joke, "Is it any help with women?"

She giggled again. "You don't need any help. But you call me if you need anything. And I mean... *anything*... at all."

She took one perfectly manicured finger — red nail polish, of course — and put it under my chin.

I was sure I turned beet red, which amused Candy even more. She leaned forward and put her lips to my ear.

"I just loved your book, *Adventure Of The Wailing Banshee*," she murmured. "You captured the Holmes and Watson relationship so well."

My smile faded, though my embarrassment did not.

"Thank you," I blurted and waved my plastic key. "See you later… uh… Candy."

I walked away.

The title she named surprised me. It was indeed a very good Holmes book. I know, I'd read it.

But I didn't write it.

Sheryl Homes did.

4. First Edition

Sheryl Homes

I arrived at the Hilton on that spring day, stopped out on Avenue of the Americas to look up at the imposing structure, with my small wheeled suitcase by my feet.

The subway ride uptown had been no problem, but now I stopped and drew a deep breath knowing what I was about to face.

It would be an entire day of "friends of Randall," which meant having to face my ex-husband and his snide comments, seeing people who would do the same, and the pièce de résistance: talking to the annoying blonde bimbo he'd brought into my bed.

I would be a perfect lady and not rip her dyed hair from her head one strand at a time. That would be, of course, after I lifted her in the air and body-slammed her onto the concrete floor.

It was nice to know that I was perfectly under control!

I let go of my homicidal longings and went into the building, knowing exactly where I was going. I had helped arrange the location and I was quite familiar with how the hotel ran conventions. I also had the foresight to get my packet of information ahead of time, and all that was needed was a quick stop at the main desk to pick up my room keys, which I did.

As I rode up the escalator to the mezzanine level, I swept the crowd that was milling about so I would be on guard if approached by friend or foe.

And my eyes fell on a good-looking man.

He wasn't at all the traditional hunk you see on the cover of a romance novel, but then, who is? He was average height, so I had a good three inches on him. He had a full head of brown hair that was gray in the temples and he had strong features, but more than that, he looked kind.

With a start I realized it was Mark Watkins.

I looked him over again, pleased with what I saw. He was a little chubbier than the last photo I had seen of him, but it made his features fill out nicely. I also thought he would be taller. I'm five-ten, and it is a real turn-on to meet a man I can look eye-to-eye.

But he had an energy around him that pulled my attention. Which was not bad, not bad at all.

As my escalator reached the top, I decided I would go over and introduce myself. I liked his books, and if Gloria was right, he enjoyed mine. Maybe I could get him to write a "pull quote" on my next Holmes book. That would be good as well.

Just as I made up my mind to do so, I noted he was talking to Charles Nederlander, who started to walk away. I hesitated when I saw that Charles was replaced by Jon Kane and the bane of my existence, Candy Poole.

I decided it would be better to approach when he wasn't surrounded by my foes, and I moved into the crowd and looked away, though I am sure Candy saw me. After all, I was a head higher than almost everyone who was in that room.

I slouched to blend into the crowd better, and moved to the elevators on the far side of the convention lobby, so I could observe.

Watkins talked to Jon and Candy, and Candy kept doing little possessive things as they spoke — touching Mark's arm and moving into his personal space. What was she playing at? Had I ever mentioned I found Mark Watkins attractive in front of Candy? I don't think so. In fact, I didn't know I found him attractive until I actually laid eyes on him.

Just then Winsley Cunningham arrived, and I was glad I'd moved to a safe distance. The last thing I needed was to hear her complaints about Randall. I had enough of my own. Finally, Winsley and Jon moved off, and Candy gave Mark a card and drew close to whisper in his ear as he began to turn red.

I'd had enough.

Mark apparently was another stupid man who thought with his sex organ instead of his brain, and Candy was working her wiles so that he would follow her around like a love-struck puppy. Really, I had hoped the famed Mark Watkins would be a higher form of life, but who was I kidding?

I decided I'd best unpack and get ready for my jog from panel to panel.

I reached the bank of elevators just as a voice called out, "Well, *there* is one red-hot redhead."

I turned with disgust to see a familiar face approach. Allen Alexander, or as I called him, "the man with two first names." He wore a green and gold tweed suit that looked as if he'd mugged a clown. With his greasy hair parted in the middle and slicked back, as well as his pointed features, he was a walking caricature.

I sighed. "Hello, Allen."

"Looking good, Sheryl. Have you been working out?" He drew close. He was my height, but in this case, it was not appealing.

I gritted my teeth. "Yes, so I could punch out creeps who bother me with lame lines."

He stepped back and held up his hands. "Whoa, Sheryl, take it easy. I was just giving you a compliment."

"Which is only a little less creepy than any other suggestions you've made over the past few years. What do you want, Allen?"

He moved in close again, as if wanting to impart a secret, or perhaps to peek at my bosom from a better angle. "Did you hear Mark Watkins is the speaker tonight?"

I sighed and wanted to step back so he wasn't in my personal space, but it only doubled my anger that I even had to, so I stood my ground. "Yes, I know. I also know that you think he ripped you off."

"Yeah? Well, *Death In The Borley Rectory* is a complete copy of my book, *A Crime Of Passion*. It follows my plot line completely."

I shook my head. "*Borley Rectory* takes place in a different *year* than yours, and it takes place — oh that's right — at a *rectory*. Meanwhile, your book took place at Buckingham Palace."

"You can't convince me otherwise," Allen ranted. "I could understand that one, but when he stole my notes—"

I exhaled heavily, as I fought the desire to clock this lunkhead. "How could he have stolen your notes?"

"All I know is he comes out with *The Case Of The Casual Crook*, which was my story completely."

"Allen, seek help. You are insane, do you know that? Insane."

"Maybe I am, but I noticed he stopped writing Holmes books the same time I did. Coincidence?"

I looked at the floor and wondered if I was ever going to get away from this creep. "Look, Allen. You had one Holmes book that was published—"

"Didn't do as well as his knock-off," Allen whined.

"Well, if he did steal your book, the winner was the reading public, because they got to read a work by a gifted writer and a skilled craftsman. Talents you will never be accused of possessing."

"Man," Allen said, exasperated. "You're pretty cranky. You're not having your period, are you?"

I had reached the limit and could feel a black rage rise in me. I turned away to face the elevator. "Leave me the hell alone."

"Whoa, Sheryl, stay calm. This conference is for the Northeast Mystery Club, and you know I *am* a member, right?"

"Of course you are," I noted snidely.

"And we are sharing a panel on Thursday."

This made me turn to face him. "You're kidding! You wormed your way onto my panel?"

"Wormed-shmurmed. I published a Sherlock Holmes story—"

"Unauthorized," I spat.

"Public domain," he shot back. "And as an *expert*, I am putting my two cents in," he sneered, and with a wave turned to go.

"Your two cents wouldn't buy a penny. You are no expert, and having slogged my way through your novel, you are certainly no writer." I threw my shoulders back and got into the elevator, which took me to the 12th floor.

According to the paper holder the front desk had given me, my room was 1234. The holder contained a pair of the flat plastic key cards the size of a credit card. This was the standard practice.

Out of the elevator, I walked a bit down the hall, where I unlocked my room and stepped in.

It was a nice room with a good-sized bathroom and closet at the entranceway. This opened to a bedroom with a king-sized bed and a writing desk near the phone.

I put my small suitcase on the metal stand I took from the closet and began to take clothes out of the case and put them in drawers or hang them up.

I also checked my supply of latex gloves, shoe covers, and plastic zipper bags, putting a couple of pairs of gloves into my small handbag along with my magnifying glass. I also made sure my fingerprint powder and other necessities were undamaged.

If you are going to write about detectives, I've always felt you should be prepared to play the part.

I would need some distraction, because I might end up spending all of my downtime here in the room if my encounter with Allen was a preview of what was to come.

I looked at the bed and was suddenly overwhelmed by a depression so profound I needed to sit down. Thirty-four years old, unmarried, no children, and it looked like there would be none.

I knew that would be okay, biological clock aside. It's just I never thought it *wouldn't* happen.

Watching my parents my entire life, I just expected I would settle down, marry, and have a child or two, like my mother did with me and my sister, Jenny.

My mother was an artist, created amazing paintings, and several times a year traveled for art shows, while Dad struggled to figure out how to prepare meals and run the house while she was gone.

But they loved each other and were committed to their marriage, each other, and us. It had been a great way to grow up.

Suddenly, my phone was in my hand, and I was pressing the button for my mom.

"Hello," came out of the tiny speaker.

"Mom, it's Sheryl," I gulped.

"Yes, dear, how are you?"

I found tears were in my eyes. "I need a pep talk, Mom. I'm at the convention and all of Randall's friends are here. I don't know if I can take it."

"Is that slut with him?" my mother fumed.

This was a surprise. My mother never used words like "slut" and I found I laughed out loud.

She always knew the right thing to say.

I told her about the convention and how I felt so alone, and she listened and then gave the appropriate encouragements. Ten minutes later, I finished the call, feeling much better.

I retrieved my envelope and pulled out a small magazine. It was emblazoned with "Northeast Mystery Conference" in fancy lettering. There was a logo of the letters seen through a stylized magnifying glass.

I went through it and read up on the five days of lectures, speeches, book signings, and panel discussions. There were some Holmes ones including: *Heard Vs Carr: Who Wrote New Holmes First; Conan Doyle and Holmes, A Study in Opposites; Was Moriarty Actually Neitzsche?*

But there were other mystery writers and characters, with a panel on Sue Grafton's Kinsey Milhone, Rex Stout's Nero Wolfe, and even a comical look at the famed Philip Marlowe in book and film.

It was going to be a rather thorough program. I hoped so. I had been in on the early plans before I became *persona non grata*.

I double-checked the time for Mark Watkins' opening night lecture and noted I was listed for a panel discussions with him the next day.

I wondered when I would actually make the acquaintance of Mr. Mark Watkins.

5. Backlist

Mark Watkins

In the afternoon, I traveled uptown to my condo to retrieve clothes and toiletries, then I wandered about the hallways of the hotel to locate the correct conference rooms.

Once I was sure of which rooms I would visit tonight and tomorrow, I decided to take some time to explore the booths in the big convention room, like Candy had suggested.

I went to the mezzanine, and with my badge proudly displayed, went into the large open ballroom: "The Marketplace."

It was more impressive than my cursory glance had given me earlier. Using pipe and drape, the room was divided into numerous booths for the individual vendors.

It was amazing just how much *stuff* there was. One stall was filled with books and DVDs; the next was beautiful handmade weapons: swords, knives, and even a cudgel.

One of the booksellers had mint-condition magazines that dated back to the 1920s. Lurid drawings emblazoned the covers of such provocative periodicals as *Real Detective* and *Murder Magazine*. In the time these stories were published, they were scandalous, but by today's standards, they were pretty tame.

The good guys always won, crime didn't pay, and the murderer was always captured.

Then again, who was I to judge? The most necessary part of any Holmes story was that the master detective always caught the malefactor, much to the chagrin of Inspector Lestrade of Scotland Yard.

I found a booth marked by a sign: "YE OLDE MYSTERIOUS TOBACCO SHOPPE." The man behind the table displayed a marvelous supply of tobaccos and pipes of every sort and shape. There was a perfectly handsome, hand-carved, curved pipe.

I read the small sign under it:

Ser Jacopo Calabash

Reg price $475

Conference special $380

I decided I would not take up smoking this year.

"Watkins, eh?" the man behind the table said.

I glanced at my name badge and then into the eyes of the merchant. He was heavy set, tall, and muscular, with a head of wild hair, and one eye that looked off to the right at all times.

"That's me," I responded.

"You the writer?" the man wondered, and gave a grimace I hoped was supposed to represent a smile. "Doing the opening lecture tonight?"

"Right on both counts," I disclosed and held out my hand.

His right arm stayed by his side, and he crossed over his body with his left to give my hand a quick shake.

"Pardon the arm," he explained. "Had a stroke a year ago. Still doesn't operate quite the way it used to."

I nodded sympathetically. This explained his grimaces and misaimed eye.

"You speak quite well, though."

"Got lucky there," he clarified, and again grimaced in that rather frightening way. "Didn't affect my speech at all. Can you beat that?"

"Lucky," I commented.

"Yeah, but I had to leave my old occupation because of it."

"Really? What did you used to do?"

"Security."

I smiled. "I was a security guard for a while."

"Yeah, I read that on one of your book jackets or something," he said. "I wasn't that kind."

"Oh?"

His left hand mimed typing on a keyboard in midair. "Yeah, I was cyber security, software 'n stuff. Of course, now I focus on tobacco."

"Do you like it?"

"Nothing but the best!" he said, and walked over to the display in front of me. "So, you gonna talk about Sherlock Holmes tonight?"

"It is my area of expertise," I insisted with a modest shrug.

"Well, here, take that pipe with you." The man gestured to the Calabash pipe.

I picked it up and turned it over in my hand.

"Well, I-I'm actually going to rebuke some of the standard ways Holmes has been portrayed in film."

"Perfect! That pipe can illustrate your point."

I glanced down at his name badge, which had a green background to signify that he was a merchant and bore the name John Stewart.

"Wait," I considered, "you want me to use your pipe to suggest Holmes would never use it? Isn't that bad for business?"

"It'll get the product right in their faces. I guarantee it will sell it. G'wan, take it."

I turned the pipe over again. It would indeed make a good prop.

"Where do you want this, Stew?" a female voice announced.

I turned to see an Amazonian woman approach with a plastic bin on her shoulder. She was at least six feet tall, though John still had an inch or two on her. But she was a striking and phenomenally well-put-together lady with curly, short, brunette hair. Her outfit was tight leather pants, a black tank top, and a leather vest that showed her amazing physique, as well as very developed arms.

"Right back here is fine, Hypno," Stewart told her, as he indicated one of the tables.

"Hypno?" I questioned.

The statuesque woman gave me a dismissive glance.

"My full name is Hypatia Norris," she offered, with a throaty voice. "But John likes to call me Hypno—"

"Or sometimes just 'Hips,'" John snorted. "She helps me out. Couldn't run the place without her."

"You couldn't find your dick without me," Hypno mocked with a smirk as she put the bin behind the table.

"This is Mark Watkins."

Hypno turned, and a broad smile grew on her face. "Oh, *you're* Mark Watkins." She looked like the cat who'd swallowed the canary. "Glad to meet you."

I was surprised by the sudden shift in attitude. "Uh, thanks."

John said, "I'm loaning him the Calabash for his speech."

Hypno nodded and looked at me solemnly, and without a word, she reached into a bin and brought out the same pipe.

"Take this one instead," she said as she held it out. For some reason, she seemed exceptionally pleased with herself, as I reached out and took it. "But don't lose it. It is a *very* expensive pipe."

"I'll be careful, thanks," I acknowledged. I turned it over and noticed a small red "X" on the bottom. I considered pointing this out to Hypno but decided she chose one that was damaged or something.

She returned the other Calabash to the display stand by picking it up with tissue paper.

"Gotta keep it clean," she noted, and wiped her hands with the tissue. "I've been picking up these bins from the loading dock."

"Oh, of course," I said.

"Yeah, this is a nice place," John disclosed, "but the ballroom loading dock is way down a long hallway."

"Which is not very clean," Hypno pointed out.

I nodded. "I'll bring the pipe back after my speech."

John shook his head. "Sales floor closes when you start. Bring it back tomorrow when you come for the book signing. You'll be right over there."

He indicated a booth in the corner. It was empty now, except for a table and chairs. But there was a hanging sign that read: Author Signing.

"Oh, great. Well, nice meeting you, John, and… uh… Hypno."

She raised an eyebrow and went back to work.

"Yeah, good luck with that speech," John declared with a wave to me and a sidelong look to the woman.

I wandered up the next aisle past a booth filled with jewelry. There was a display of "Elfin" necklaces, which I guessed were for the phenomenon known as "Cosplay," though I did wonder what it had to do with a mystery conference.

"See anything you like?" the proprietor asked, as he looked at me through a pair of glasses that made his eyes look huge from the magnification. He was a rotund man with a bushy beard and a waxed mustache that would have made him a terrific Santa Claus, except that his hair was flaming red.

"Just looking for now," I deflected, and turned my attention to a display case filled with cameos imbued with silhouettes of famous detectives and celebrities crafted by the hand of a skilled jeweler. Next to it was a row of inexpensive ones that appeared to be copies made in China for a much smaller price.

There were a few Holmesian cameos, another I immediately recognized as Alfred Hitchcock, and finally a striking image of Edgar Allen Poe.

"Nice," I admired, indicating the cameos.

"Yeah, the cheap ones are the biggest sellers at this conference," the man griped. "Hey, aren't you Mark Watkins?"

"Yes."

"Saw your photo in the program. You're the lecturer tonight," he said. "I'm Norm Blake."

He adjusted the fisheye lens on his face and looked at my badge, just as a skinny, long-haired blond man walked up with a plastic bin, which he stuck under the table.

Norm glanced at his younger friend, who was tall and wiry. "Thanks, Cliff."

Cliff gave a nod and looked at me.

"Hey, you're that writer guy," he reported.

"Guilty as charged," I chuckled.

"You'd know who he is if you'd read his badge," Norm stated, and gave a hearty laugh. "He's also going to give a lecture on Sherlock Holmes tonight."

I pointed at the expertly crafted cameos, which bore price tags starting at about a hundred dollars.

"These are amazing. You can really see the difference between these and the cheaper ones."

"I hope so," Norm bragged. "Those are the ones I crafted."

"Yeah," Cliff added. "He even does it here at the booth. Which means, I have to be the salesman."

"Really?"

"It's more of a hobby, I guess," Norm expounded. "But doing it here at the booth, people come by just to watch."

"Yeah, he's really good," Cliff praised.

Norm shrugged. "I just really like making 'em."

"Your workmanship is outstanding," I complimented, and bent forward to take a closer look at the display.

"Thanks. Please let other people know." He gave a knowing smile. "You know, the paying customers."

He again gave his hearty laugh, and Cliff smiled as well. Then Cliff reached into the back pocket of his jeans, pulled out a business card, and offered it to me.

I smiled and took it.

Then I peered down at an open bin by his feet. To my surprise, on the top of several display cases lay a Calabash pipe, very similar to the one in my pocket.

"What's that?" I asked, pointing to it.

"What?" Norm said and looked to the bin, adjusting his glasses as he did.

I picked up the Calabash, at the same time I pulled my recent acquisition from my pocket.

"That doesn't look like the sort of thing you'd carry," I said, as I held a pipe in each hand and turned them over. They appeared identical.

"My idea," Cliff said. "I keep telling him you gotta expand."

"I figured why not try it?" Norm shrugged.

"How much does it run?"

"About two hundred," Cliff said.

A lot cheaper than John Stewart, I thought to myself.

"Good to know," I said, and replaced the pipe, making sure I took the one with the red "X" on the bottom, which I slipped back into my jacket pocket.

"Well, we only have a few," Cliff stressed.

"He's right. Let me know if you're interested in owning a second one — I mean, since you already got that one."

"I've got your card," I claimed as I held it up.

"And you know where I'll be," he said and gave a wave as I continued along my way. Cliff got back to unloading display cases from the bins.

The marketplace only had a few people milling about as it was the first day. My speech would actually be the real "kick off."

Of the people there, most were dressed in casual attire, some in fantasy costumes that went from the interesting to absurd. This explained why Norm had brought the elfin jewelry with him.

A man pushed past me in impressive makeup and armor. I paused to wonder what a *Star Trek* Klingon warrior had to do with mysteries, but I just shrugged and kept walking.

Another fellow went past me in a Holmesian Inverness cape with the traditional deerstalker hat. He, at least, seemed to belong at this conference.

I couldn't help the creeping feeling that maybe I was the one who didn't belong here.

6. Imprint

Sheryl Homes

I watched some TV, showered, and dressed in my good green silk one piece jumpsuit, I chose it because the silk hung on my body luxuriously. But, my legs and arms were covered, yet the sleeves and pants flared at my wrists and ankles. This created an ensemble that looked dressy, yet casual at the same time. I munched a few whole-grain bars in lieu of dinner, then headed to the auditorium. I just couldn't face eating dinner with others, and worrying about who might spot me like Allen had.

I took the elevator down and walked into the auditorium through a side door. It was completely dark, except for a couple of stage lights. Apparently, I had arrived far too early. But the set-up looked good with a large screen and a podium. The screen had the logo of the conference projected upon it.

Then I heard something.

Voices.

I stayed in the shadows and approached the stage carefully. If it was Watkins having a pre-show tête-à-tête with Candy, I didn't want to interrupt, but I was curious about who, besides myself, had shown up so early.

I crept silently down the far right aisle until I could peek between the curtain and screen. There were two shadowy figures backstage who appeared to be in an animated conversation.

"I have to pick it up where?" I heard the taller silhouette complain.

"I explained it. It's not that difficult," cooed the shorter shadow.

I pricked up my ears. Was that Candy I heard?

"It's ridiculous that I have to jump through these hoops. I've paid you. You were supposed to bring it to me—"

"Keep your voice down," the female ordered.

"Well, I don't like it," I heard the taller silhouette say.

"It's what we agreed to," cooed the shorter shadow.

They continued in hushed tones, and I couldn't follow what they said. My impression was that the man sounded cross and Candy vehement.

It was then I heard the door at the top of the room creak open.

Backing out the way I came was not an option, so I rushed forward. The concrete walls were covered with a black curtain meant to dampen sound. There was about a foot between the wall and the drapery, so I slipped behind it and peeked through the gap in the curtains.

"Who's there?" Candy shouted.

"Hello," a voice announced, entering the room. "It's me, Mark!"

"Mark!" Candy responded with delight. "You're early."

I peered through the gap carefully as Mark reached the stage and climbed up a short staircase to meet Candy as she came out from backstage to meet him on the podium.

The man she'd been speaking to was nowhere to be seen.

"Wanted to make sure I was on time," Mark said. "Is the sound technician here?"

"Not yet, but any minute now," she told him and brought a finger under his chin in another possessive move. God, that woman was using every trick!

"I like your suit," she breathed.

Crap! Watkins was falling for it. Are all men so easy? I guess I like it when I can get a man's attention with a few well-timed maneuvers, but I sure hated how easily *she* was doing it.

"My wife picked it... I mean... thanks," Mark said, suddenly tongue-tied.

I guess he hadn't meant to say his wife picked his suit. I knew she'd passed away a couple of years ago, but did Candy? Maybe she would back off?

"I thought I heard voices when I came in," Mark told her, and he glanced backstage.

"Just me," Candy assured, and her fingers moved through his hair, twining it, then releasing it. She took a deep breath, as if touching him had excited her.

"I... uh... took your advice and went into the Marketplace," Mark went on.

"Find anything good?"

"A guy loaned me a fancy pipe for the speech tonight."

She seemed thrilled by this, and a big smile grew on her face. "That's really nice. So what are you doing after?"

"After?" Mark asked.

"Your speech, silly," Candy told him, and moved closer so that she was pressing her chest against him. "I'm free for the evening."

Mom had been right. Candy was a slut.

"I was going to get dinner," Mark fumbled, then finally got the not-at-all-subtle hint. "Uh… would you care to—"

"Join you? I'd love to. I heard there's a great Italian place up the street," she prattled as her index finger traced a line around his ear.

"Oh… uh… you mean Patsy's? Hard to get a reservation," Mark hemmed and hawed.

I felt a bit like a voyeur, annoyed that she was leading him on. Then the thought struck me: *why* was she leading him on? Last I knew the bimbo was banging my ex. Had they broken up? Had Randall finally gotten his tiny brain working and given the blonde bitch the heave-ho?

"Ho" being the appropriate word choice.

"I'll take care of that." She gave him her best smile. "Since I know you're already here, I'll go make a call."

She jiggled down the stairs, and with a wave headed up the aisle and out. He watched her pert little rear end as she left.

I tried to calm my annoyance that a man whose work I respected could be turned into a quivering mass of hormones by a pretty face. Okay, maybe it was my personal animus against that *specific* face.

I wonder how pretty she'd be once I ripped her eyes out.

I really needed to get a handle on this violent streak that had blossomed lately.

"You Watson?" a voice grumbled on the stage, and I turned back to peer up at Mark.

A large man stood at the edge of the screen. Had this been the man Candy spoke with in the shadows?

"Uh… Wat-KINS, yeah," Mark told him.

The heavy man walked into the light. He was dressed all in black and carried a small black box connected to a wire and tiny microphone.

"Nice to see one of the speakers gettin' someplace early," he grunted. "I'm Joe. I'm your sound man."

"Mark."

"You know how to snake this under your clothes?"

"Sure."

I watched him hand Mark the microphone body pack.

The sound man went on. "I'll take you to the green room."

The pair of them wandered out through the backstage. I listened for a moment, and then moved silently from my hiding place and headed for the side door where I came in. I needed a drink before I could sit through this lecture because I was already in a sour mood.

Seeing another woman go into full-out seduction mode as Candy had, and seeing Mark's reaction and the heat in his eyes had been disconcerting. It had been a long time since I felt that heat, and now I had to admit a part of me missed it.

I went to the bar on the mezzanine level and ordered a double.

7. Query

Mark Watkins

I waited in the small meeting room down the hall that acted as the "green room" as they say in show-business vernacular.

Joe watched me put the mic on under my suit and checked the connections once it was in my pocket.

After I was ready, Joe left, and I sat at the large table in a comfortable chair and found a bottle of water in a small refrigerator.

I reviewed my notes, rereading a couple phrases out loud to make sure I didn't fumble over the words.

Joe came in again, pulled the microphone box from out of my back pocket, and flipped a switch.

"You're on!" he said. I followed him out of the room and through a door to the stage wings.

In front of the podium stood Jon Kane, who was speaking into a wired microphone on a stand. "It gives me great pleasure to introduce our opening-night speaker, a man whose best seller, *Death In The Borley Rectory,* is still considered one of the finest Sherlock Holmes stories, Mark Watkins."

He turned to me and gestured. I stepped forward and pulled the impressive pipe out of my pocket as I reached the podium.

The room was packed. In fact, some people stood along the curtained side walls, as all the chairs were full. The crowd applauded loudly, and I felt a bit overwhelmed. After months of hardly venturing out of my apartment, here was a room crammed with people who wanted to hear me speak.

The clapping faded, and I held the pipe aloft.

"If all you saw were Hollywood films," I began, "you might think that a pipe like this and a few props were what made Sherlock Holmes the greatest detective of all time."

I went on with my prepared speech. The audience was electrified. I'd made sure that my presentation was filled with jokes, and I was pleased most of them got laughs. I threw in one that I knew would get a groan. It did, but it only put the audience on my side even more.

I spun a great tale that tied Holmes to his modern equivalent: the forensic departments of the police that used partial fingerprints and DNA to help catch criminals.

For a finale, I hammered home the point that evidence, logic, and deduction was what made Holmes a great sleuth. I finished by saying how the techniques Conan Doyle envisioned, so revolutionary in their day, were now the standard by which all detectives pursued solutions.

The crowd exploded into fresh applause and rose to their feet as one man, clapping their hands together enthusiastically.

In the back I saw Candy clap and yell her approval, and felt a flush as an imagined picture of her without the red dress — or anything else — flashed through my mind.

I held up my hands for silence. The crowd grew quiet and returned to their seats.

"I will be happy to take a few questions," I offered, relieved that the hard part was over and I could relax.

A male voice rang out first.

"So, where do you get your ideas?"

I didn't need to see his face to know it was Allen Alexander.

I knew him well — a nut who thought I'd stolen his stories. I swallowed my annoyance and went on. "Inspiration comes in many forms. You have one idea that connects with another, and then another, until a tapestry begins to appear. Sometimes, it is through hard work, and other times an idea hits the writer like a bolt of lightning."

I smiled, as he didn't have a comeback.

"Holmes' inimitable mind and logic also is a great inspiration," I continued. "It allows the writer to get in that 'space' where a combination of unique circumstances can be seen in an entirely new light."

"Is it your assertion," a female voice rang out, "that Holmes' logic was his *only* ability? Don't you consider his intuition as part of the mix?"

I turned and gazed into the darkness where I thought the voice originated.

"I think we'd all agree," I said, unable to see who asked the question, "Holmes himself would disregard anything that reeked of emotionalism or sentiment. He often told Watson that he was a brain and nothing more."

"And yet the most important part of any Holmes story are the times sentiment come into play."

"That's a point," I agreed. "That is what made Sir Arthur Conan Doyle such a fine storyteller. He would bring characters in to express the emotional part of the tale, while Holmes strove to be above it all."

"Are you suggesting Holmes express *no* sentimentality?"

"There are the moments when Holmes' mask slips, towards Irene Adler in *Scandal In Bohemia*, or when he shows his genuine affection for Watson. But I disagree with the biographies that suggest Holmes married Miss Adler during his time in hiding after the death of Moriarty. We must remember, it is his cold, hard logic that always solved the puzzle."

"So," the woman went on, "it's just a puzzle to be solved. I've always believed that there was more to Holmes than that."

The woman approached the stage, and the light fell on her. Tall, lean, with red hair, and wearing a striking green silk jumpsuit that hugged every curve of her well-shaped frame. Her face was not classically beautiful, but it was handsome and strong. Her green eyes seemed to glow with an inner fire as powerful as the one that colored her hair.

There before me stood Sheryl Homes.

8. Remainders

Sheryl Homes

I was back in the bar, nursing another drink while trying to calm down. I'd certainly stuck my foot in the hornet's nest this night.

Great, it wasn't enough that most of the people at the Northeast Mystery Club hated me; now I'd insulted their first speaker, and it was someone I had recommended they get.

I should've shut up, just listened. He'd made some great points and basically told Allen to jump into a lake, which I *did* enjoy.

But my questions were valid, and the points important. But I could've asked them a little less forcefully.

But when I saw Candy looking at him with that gleam in her eyes, it pissed me off. Also, the drink I had before the lecture had relaxed my inhibitions.

And possibly my common sense.

The situation with Mark had gone from bad to worse, and the question and answer session degenerated to an argument between the two of us.

Apparently, he was of the opinion that anything I thought about Holmes was just plain wrong. Meanwhile, I discovered that he was an opinionated bastard who could only see his own narrow view.

To think I had actually looked *forward* to meeting him.

"Nice job, Sheryl," I heard a voice say. "You showed that cocky sleazeball who knows Holmes."

I glanced over to see Allen lift a drink in my direction in a toast.

"Get lost, Allen," I hissed, and took a delicate sip of my Cosmo, though I wanted to down the whole thing at once.

"You did have some valid points, dear," a woman's voice said, and I turned to see Winsley Cunningham next to me at the bar. "I thought you really added to the excitement. However, you might have been a little less… vociferous."

I moved closer to Winsley and noted she wore a hat that looked like she found it inside an Agatha Christie novel. On her jacket, her jade cameo of Sherlock Holmes reflected the dim light with a jewel-like quality. She had a martini glass in front of her, from which she took delicate sips.

"You're right, Winsley, I have to learn to control myself a bit."

"It's never too late to act like a lady," she attempted.

I hung my head. "It might be for me. I should find Mark and apologize. Do you know where he is?"

"I believe he went off to dinner with Candy," she said, and then her attention shifted as Charles Nederlander stepped into the room. "Excuse me."

I sat at the bar alone and wanted to bang my head against it in the hope that it would knock some sense into it. So, Mark did go off with her just like they'd mentioned when I eavesdropped on them. Great, I couldn't control my temper, and that tart would spend the night telling him what an awful person I was. I took another sip and hung my head in misery, as I heard Winsley bring Charles close to our part of the bar.

"Really, Winsley, this isn't the place to discuss this," Charles told her in a hoarse whisper.

"Randall promised he would be here tonight," Winsley fired back. "I was supposed to get answers from him."

Randall didn't come to the opening night? That was odd as this convention was his baby. On the other hand, I was glad he missed the chance to see me make an ass of myself.

"I'm not his keeper," Charles murmured as he ordered a drink.

"No, you're his partner," Winsley insisted. "And I am your biggest investor. I would suggest you *become* his keeper and make him meet me as he promised. I will have my own accountants go through the dealings of your entire company with a fine-toothed comb. Do I make myself clear?"

"Very, Winsley. Look, why don't I buy you a drink and we can talk—"

I glanced up to see Charles put his arm carefully to Winsley's back and guide her away from me to a nearby table. They continued to talk quietly, but I could no longer hear them over the noise of the bar.

I ordered some bar food, so that I would have something in my stomach and stopped at the second drink. I also found I wondered about Randall's absence.

I had been one of the founders of the New York chapter about five years earlier, with Charles, Jon, and Randall. This was before I wrote my first Holmes book. I had gotten the crazy notion that since my maiden name sounded the same, I might have some insights.

I guess it had been a good choice. I had been selling steadily and getting attention with critics and readers alike. But then Candy, who was a member of the club, showed up in my bed with her parts wrapped around my husband. The divorce drove a wedge between me and the others.

At this point, Mark Watkins probably sympathized with Randall, after I'd come out as the bitch-goddess tonight and shot down his Q&A.

Having finished eating, and knowing I had several panels in the morning, I decided it was time to head upstairs. Fortunately, no one had bothered me while I ate, but after the show I had given, everyone was probably avoiding me.

I headed to the elevator and took it up to the twelfth floor and my room. Once in there, I pulled a bottled water from the minibar to counteract the alcohol I'd consumed, but I needed some ice.

Making sure my plastic key was in the pocket of my jumpsuit, I took my plastic ice bucket and wandered out into the hall. There was a small alcove near room 1230 that had the ice machine. I heard the machine going and knew someone was filling their bucket. As I walked through the open doorway, a man turned from the machine, and without standing up completely or looking where he was going, almost walked face-first into my bosom!

"What are you doing?" I shrieked.

He fell back in surprise, his ice bucket slipped from his hands, and frozen cubes went flying.

On the floor sat Mark Watkins.

I was overwhelmed with mixed emotions. I wanted to apologize. I wanted to yell at him for not being aware of where he was going. My sarcastic side won.

"It would be you!" I sniped, not liking my own tone. "I guess they stuck all of us on this floor."

"I was just getting some ice," Mark explained as he got up and gave a glance at the mess. "I'm not the one who snuck up on you."

"I didn't sneak!" I fumed. Why did this man always make me so angry!

"Well, I didn't know you were there," he stated, and put his bucket back under the machine to refill it.

"Is that an apology?" I pressed.

"I have nothing to apologize for. You startled me."

"You should be more careful."

"Look, Ms. Homes," he said with that tone of voice you use when talking to a child, "we are only here for a long weekend. It would seem we are of two different minds. Perhaps it would be best if we just avoided each other."

He grabbed his ice bucket and began to go. Suddenly, I felt like a heel.

"Wait," I said and gently caught his arm. "I'm… sorry about… about what I did during your speech."

He turned to face me. His eyes met mine, and I was surprised. There was something about his eyes that made me feel like he was caressing me.

I went on, but my mouth felt clumsy. "I really just wanted to ask some questions, and then it escalated. I behaved badly. It was a good speech and I had no right…"

I trailed off and released his arm; my eyes moved to the floor. What could I tell him? That I'd acted like an ass? That seeing him with that blonde bimbo made me want blood?

"That's nice of you to say," he replied, and I could hear actual compassion in his voice.

"I mean it." I lowered my head to gaze at him.

He looked at me with a combination of understanding and acceptance, and I had a feeling I'd not had for over a year. I felt warm. Worse, I felt all gooey inside. I wanted to pull him into a hug.

"Well, we're both on a panel tomorrow," he stated and smiled at me. "Perhaps we can try again."

"That's a good idea." I felt like I was grinning like an idiot.

"Good night, Homes," he added with a nod.

"Good night, Watson," I said. Then, realizing my mistake, I slapped my hand to my head. "Wat-*kins*. I meant Wat-*kins.*"

"It's fine," he chuckled and walked past me. I found I watched his rear end and had to admit, for a middle-aged guy, he still had a damn fine butt.

I was about to get my ice when Mark stopped and knocked on 1230.

Candy opened the door.

I slipped into the doorway of the alcove, but I could still see Candy at the door. She was wearing a negligee that wasn't completely transparent, but mostly, all red silk and short to show off her legs and taut little body. Behind her, I could see flickering yellow candlelight, casting shadows of the furniture in the dark room.

Mark went in, as my blood ran cold. I put my bucket under the chute and yanked it down to get ice. In my vehemence, the bucket filled instantly and excess ice fell out and around the room as I cursed under my breath.

I went back to my room, and instead of my planned water, I pulled a bottle from the minibar and gulped down an airplane-sized bottle of tequila.

The bastard made me like him, possibly even made we *want* him! How dare he do that when he was about to go bang that homewrecking hellion.

I cursed and vented until I wore myself out, then I undressed and went to bed, hating Mark Watkins the entire time.

9. Galleys

Mark Watkins

My room was spinning as consciousness returned. I tried to sit up, which made me incredibly nauseous, so I lay back again.

"Candy?" I moaned and lifted my head just enough to peer around the room.

The drapes were open a crack and sunlight poured in to illuminate my computer bag on the desk. I lay back and tried to figure out just how my bag ended up on Candy's desk.

I fought the vertigo, slowly rose and glanced about, taking in the whole room. I could see my small overnight bag next to the television.

My body did not quite follow the directions from my brain, but I got myself to stand and moved slowly into the bathroom, where I found my toiletries laid out on the sink.

This wasn't Candy's room; this was *my* room.

I paused to try and figure out how the hell I got here.

I thought back to the last thing I remembered. The final images that came to mind were Sheryl Homes as she looked at the floor apologizing, then I recalled Candy in her lingerie as I went into her room. Then I had a cognac Candy poured for me, and I soon found it hard to speak, and with Candy's encouragement, I lay down on the bed.

After that, nothing.

I looked at myself. I only wore my boxers and socks, but nothing else.

I poured a cup of water from the sink and greedily drank it. I used the facilities, while leaning against the wall to stabilize myself.

In the closet, I found my good suit neatly hung on a hanger. Looking in the pockets; my wallet and cell phone were where they belonged; also my cash and credit cards; nothing was missing.

My house keys were not in the jacket pocket. I looked over to the nearby dresser. They were there in plain sight next to the two hotel key cards I had received in my "welcome" package.

My headache grew worse and I returned to the bed to lie down, still unable to recall how I got there.

I rolled over to glance at the clock by my bed, which read 11:59.

As the light poured in my window, it could only mean that it was almost noon. By my reckoning, I had been out for over twelve hours.

The panel I was scheduled to appear at started at one.

Groggily I rose, grabbed the phone, and called room service to bring up a pot of coffee and a continental breakfast.

Then I gingerly moved to the bathroom, put on a shower, and got under it. When I felt dizzy, I slammed the water to cold, which was a shock to my system but cleared my head pretty effectively.

When I got out of the shower I felt a little better.

As fast as I was able to, I got on a shirt and pants, which made me decent enough when I heard the knock at my door and the cry of "Room Service."

I opened the door to the waiter, who carried a small tray into the room, then gave a dirty look at my computer bag as it took up the desk. I instructed him to put the tray on the dresser.

"Shall I pour, sir?" he said.

I shook my head, added a sizable tip to the slip he handed me, and he was off.

I poured the coffee, slopped some cream into it, and drank it.

By 12:40, after two cups of coffee, I was feeling more like myself but still cotton-headed. The only comparison I could think of was the feeling I would get the morning after I had taken a cold remedy. This left me sleepy, dopey, as well as several other whimsical dwarves.

I successfully got completely dressed, forced down a muffin, grabbed one of the key cards, and was out the door with ten minutes to get to my panel.

I was grateful I'd located the conference rooms the previous day, as I made my way to the second floor. The ache in my head had settled to a dull throb.

"Hey, Watkins," a snide voice said as I approached the door to the meeting room.

I groaned. "I'm having a bad day, Allen. Please don't make it worse."

"Whassamatter, can't take it when someone asks you a few tough questions?" he said, smiling like the cat that ate the canary.

"Not interested," I retorted.

"Oh, I was just glad to be there. I have to hand it to you, you ripped off a pretty good speech from somewhere."

"You're too kind," I snarled.

"But, man, did Sheryl Homes take you down a peg. She really proved that you don't know squat." We entered the room and he whispered, "I think she'll be my new best friend."

He went around me and up the two steps of an elevated platform, where the other members sat behind a table. With care, I walked up the steps and moved to the last remaining seat.

Right next to Sheryl Homes.

She gave me a glance and her expression grew hard.

"Have a good time last night?" she muttered in an undertone.

I peered at her in puzzlement.

"I saw you go into Candy's room," she went on, still in a low voice. "And now you show up here with a hangover."

I'd thought I'd carried myself so well! I challenged her, "What makes you think I have a hangover?"

"Simple! First of all, I watched you last evening, and your natural tendency is to move quick and decisively. Today, your movements are slow and deliberate. Secondly, your eyes are a bit bloodshot, though it would take a trained observer to notice. Finally, yesterday you were dressed immaculately. Today you got ready in a hurry and carelessly."

"Careless in what way?"

"For one thing," she said, and her voice dropped to a whisper, "your fly is open."

Once again, I turned beet red, and with a glance to my left and right, I zipped myself as subtly as I could manage, hoping the tablecloth on the table in front of me hid the move from the audience.

"I could go on," Sheryl sassed, pleased with herself, "but I believe we'll be starting soon."

She was correct. The room rapidly filled up with people. I was sure many of them were at my lecture the previous night, and as Ms. Homes was here, they came to see if our battle would move into round two.

I looked at the other end of the table to see Allen Alexander smirking at our little exchange.

I bit my lip, adjusted my glasses, and tried to focus on the matters at hand.

I thought after our meeting at the ice machine she might be nicer. And yet, for me there had been a moment, when she looked down at the floor and murmured her apology that she looked so beautiful and so vulnerable, that all I wanted to do was take her into my arms.

Why did I keep seeing her that way? Next to me sat the *real* Sheryl Homes, a know-it-all that no man in his right mind would give a second thought.

Then again, her observations had been dead-on.

And *very* Holmesian.

The moderator rose, and I recognized Ms. Cunningham. She was in another Chanel-style suit and looked very classy. I couldn't help but notice that the Holmes cameo was absent from her lapel.

"I am Winsley Cunningham, and I am a charter member of the New York branch of the Northeast Mystery Club," she said. "I teach the history of Sherlock Holmes at the New School. I am grateful to have such a turnout—"

She quickly introduced the members of the panel, which besides Homes and me consisted of the editor of the *Sherlock Holmes Mystery Magazine*, a writer who wrote a semi-religious adventure that had Holmes seeking proof of the divinity of Jesus Christ, and the final member was Allen.

We each were to open with a statement, and then the floor was open to questions. It was basically an hour-and-a-half Q&A.

Ms. Cunningham approached Holmes from a scholarly point of view and recommended several works that gave both Holmes' and Watson's biography and timeline.

The editor, a short man with a towering intellect, spent his introduction explaining the sort of stories his magazine sought. This was listened to with rapt attention, as many of the attendees were writers who wanted to sell their own Holmes stories.

The Christian writer brought the idea of blending faith with Holmes' intellect.

Allen got up and stated that Holmes stories were a challenge, as a writer had to get the feel and the atmosphere correct, as well as giving the characters the ability to grow further than Conan Doyle allowed.

Since I had read Allen's published work, I thought he should follow his own advice instead of writing the claptrap I'd read in his awful book.

I stood, my headache ignored as I faced the audience and gave the briefest of summaries of my speech from the previous evening and sat down.

Ms. Homes stood last and brought up the subject of Holmes' intellect working at its best when combined with his intuition.

Hands sprang up and Ms. Cunningham recognized a young man in the first row.

"My question is to Ms. Homes. Is stressing the importance of Holmes' intuition an attempt to 'feminize' the great detective?"

"Not at all," Sheryl said. "Although there is a lot of talk about 'woman's intuition' even in this day and age, I think men are as capable of listening to their inner voice as well. Holmes was a man who did this without the fear of it making him weaker or less manly. I, for one, have heard the suggestion that Holmes and Watson were gay and I disregard it."

"Yet Holmes never married," another person spoke out.

"That depends which biography you read," Ms. Cunningham said.

"And be that as it may, Watson married — and more than once," Sheryl explained.

"Most biographers agree that Watson married three times," Ms. Cunningham put in. "And historically, women often died young during the Victorian Age. Especially in childbirth."

"Although Holmes eschewed emotionalism," Sheryl went on, "it doesn't mean he was less aware of things on an emotional level."

"That's a contradiction, isn't it?" I chimed in.

Sheryl gave me a withering look, which pleased me. I finally had my chance to interrupt her.

"I think," Allen pontificated from the far end of the table, "that Mr. Holmes is the epitome of contradictions, which is part of the concept."

"True, that is what makes his character so interesting," Sheryl said. "On one hand he suggests that he is nothing but a mind, and yet he wallows in depressions, plays the violin with great passion, and loves his friend Watson to the point where he was willing to lay down his own life for him."

"What does that have to do with intuition?" I shot back.

With a cursory glance to me, Sheryl continued, "It's interconnected. Holmes feels and is aware so deeply, yet he hides it behind the facade of his intellect."

I had to admit she made some good points, but I hardly felt charitable, so I pressed her further.

To say it went downhill from here, yet again, would be an understatement. Without going into details, we each argued with the other's opinion, and soon it escalated until no voices could be heard but Ms. Homes' and my own.

On the one hand, it did keep Allen quiet, though I kept seeing him smirking, which annoyed me even more and made me press my points harder.

Finally, Ms. Cunningham, who was pretty spry for an older woman, got between the two of us and told us both to shut up and let someone else speak.

We did, and fumed at each other all the while.

The time passed and more questions were asked, mostly focused on Sheryl and me. I think the audience enjoyed our interplay, and they offered questions aimed to get us going again. Then I would make a point and Sheryl would attack it, or she took a position and I would dismiss it.

Finally, after a few more arguments and snide comments aimed at one another, the session came to an end.

The fellow who wrote the Christian stories all but leaped out of his chair and ran out of the room in his haste to get away from us. Ms. Cunningham made polite noises and left in a huff. Only the editor took a moment to shake both our hands and thank us for "the liveliest panel I've been to in years."

Allen stepped to the doorway and said, "Thanks, Ms. Homes. It was a pleasure to see someone who is a *real* writer tell our overblown comrade a thing or two!"

And he left.

The room was empty and Homes and I remained in our seats, each waiting for the other to make the first move.

"Well," Sheryl broke the silence. "I suppose you have that tramp waiting for you."

"Candy is a lovely girl," I defended, though it was halfhearted. I couldn't shake the odd feeling about what had occurred the previous night.

"So *you* think," Sheryl fumed, still not looking at me. "But I've known her longer."

"Afraid of an attractive woman?" I taunted.

"Not at all. In her case, it's personal," Sheryl said, and she faced me, her green eyes afire. "Did she mention she slept with my husband?"

"Your... husband," I repeated.

"Ex-husband now!" Sheryl rose and walked to the door as I remained in my seat, my jaw agape.

She reached the door and stopped. "Maybe I should thank you. Last I heard, Randall and Candy were still an item. I can't wait to see his face when I tell him who she was with last night."

I stood as she stormed out.

I sat back down and thought it through.

Candy slept with Randall Lawrence? She'd neglected to mention that little fact.

I headed out of the conference room, which was beginning to fill with members of the next panel, and made my way to the mezzanine. I went quickly to the welcome booth, only to find Jon Kane manning the counter, with a middle-aged lady who wore a badge that named her "Alice."

"Mark," he said, his voice registering delight. "Great speech last night! How did the panel go?"

"Sheryl Homes and I almost came to blows," I reported, "but the editor of *Sherlock Holmes Magazine* said it was the liveliest panel he'd ever been to."

"Well, that's something! Marvin tells it like it is," he said, an eyebrow raised. "How can I help you?"

"I'm trying to find Candy."

"Not here right now," Jon said and grabbed a clipboard, which he scanned quickly. "She's supposed to be helping set up a PowerPoint display for tonight's speaker."

"Oh," I said weakly, then I pushed on. "I heard Candy was involved with Sheryl Homes' ex-husband?"

"Randall?" Kane said and frowned. "I wouldn't know. Randall is a charter member of the club — one of the founders. I knew that he and Sheryl got a divorce about a year back."

"Amicable?"

"I understand it was quite messy," Jon said. "As far as Candy, we are both on the conference planning board, but I honestly don't know her socially."

"Ah! Well thanks, Jon," I said.

"Oh, Mark!" Jon looked at his watch. "Isn't it time for your book signing? I have you on the schedule."

I slapped my head, not a bright move with the remains of my headache. "You're right! I've got to go!" I turned and headed into the vast conference room.

As I drew closer to the signing booth, I saw a short line that waited for me.

I passed the "YE OLDE MYSTERIOUS TOBACCO SHOPPE" booth and stopped quickly. I suddenly realized I didn't have the pipe I borrowed from him. I'd left it on the podium the previous evening, when Sheryl Homes interrupted my speech.

Hypno was running some kind of pick through her hair as I approached.

"Hey, Mark," John greeted, and indicated the line that waited for me. "Seems like you are pretty popular."

"Thanks," I said. "I'm sorry, I uh — seemed to have left the pipe in my room."

"Not a problem," John dismissed, his one eye on my face and his other aimed in the distance. "I sold the other two I had in stock. But I do have a customer for the third, so bring it to me no later than tomorrow."

"I will," I told him and headed for my line. The first person, a thin, dark-haired young man, watched me sit and pull a pair of pens out of my pocket. "Sorry I kept you waiting."

"No problem, Mr. Watkins."

"Who should I make it out to?"

He told me his name, and as I wrote he said, "So what's with you and Ms. Homes?"

I almost gouged his copy of *Death In The Borley Rectory* I had started to autograph.

I paused, then finished with my signature. "Nothing. We just see Sherlock Holmes in different ways."

As I handed back his book, it was my fondest wish that I would not hear about Ms. Homes again for the rest of the conference.

10. Kill Fee

Sheryl Homes

I sat in the bar of the hotel, with a glass of white wine in front of me.

After the previous evening, Mark Watkins had not been the only person with a hangover. The shot of tequila I had for a nightcap was certainly not needed after what I had previously imbibed.

And once again, I had gone full bitch-goddess on the man.

What on earth was wrong with me? One minute I'm staring at his ass, the next minute I'm trying to verbally emasculate him.

Was it because it had been a long time since I'd actually wanted a man? And coupled with the fact that he preferred "blonde and brainless" to me?

The bar at that time of day was not busy, but I was sure it would pick up later.

So I sat, annoyed at myself and my life. Someone slid in next to me, and I prayed it wasn't Allen, or this time I really might get violent.

"I'll have what she's having," a mellow male voice told the bartender.

It was Mark Watkins.

My smile fell, and I felt my cheeks flush with embarrassment as I focused on my drink.

"Are you stalking me now?" I grumbled. "Like Allen?"

"I just got out of the signing booth, Jon Kane took his time to relieve me. Then, I tried to locate that pipe I had last night."

"What happened to it?" I said while staring straight ahead, in an attempt to look disinterested.

"I left it on the damn podium and now it's gone," he complained. "I gave the sound man my number." The bartender placed a glass of wine in front of him, and Mark exhaled as he picked it up. "I don't want to bore you with that. I just thought… maybe… we should talk,"

Mark took a sip of wine, but I couldn't meet his eyes. If I did I would just yell at him or cry or do something stupid. Why did he create these feelings in me? I *never* acted like this or felt like this, not even with Randall when it was good. "Excuse me, don't you have to find Candy?" I seethed.

He sighed. "Well, I tried," and he began to rise.

I panicked. "Don't," I apologized. "Please."

He returned to his seat, and I could feel his stare like a weight.

I continued to gaze at my drink. "I don't know what it is. I keep wanting to just *talk* to you. Yet, every time I do, I get *so* angry."

"Maybe we should just accept the fact that we don't like each other," he confided.

"Maybe," I divulged, and met his eyes, those amazing eyes that made me melt. "It's just… I mean… I was so looking forward to meeting you."

"What?"

"I mean it. I loved *Death In The Borley Rectory*. I couldn't put that book down."

This made him smile. "Well, *Adventure Of The Wailing Banshee* is a great read. I thought you did some wonderful character revelation on Holmes, and yet nothing to cause a serious Holmes scholar to get angry."

I gave a short laugh, one that removed the layers of tension that had sat on my heart for the last two days. "I couldn't do anything that would go against the 'Canon!' For Sherlockians it is sacred."

He laughed as well. It was masculine, but at the same time full and deep. "That's what makes our jobs so difficult. We have to write a new story that won't in any way conflict with what *has* been written."

We began to talk — honestly talk. I pointed out several things I loved in his books, and he told me of moments that were his favorites in mine.

We each ordered another drink and moved to a table that offered a little privacy as we spoke about what we liked and disliked about Holmes stories.

He became animated as we spoke, and I could tell that Holmes wasn't merely an interesting character or a way to sell a book, but one of his passions, like it was for me.

"How did you ever come up with that plot twist at the end of *Casual Crook?*" I asked.

"Well, that was Susie's idea and she was—" He stopped cold.

"Are you all right?" I asked, confused by his sudden change.

"Forgive me," he glanced away, his eyes wet. "I guess you know... about my wife."

He had such pain in his eyes I couldn't bear it, and I looked back at my drink. I spoke quietly, "I heard she... passed away."

"Yeah, and I was surprised that this is the first time in two years I forgot about it for a moment."

I couldn't stop myself. I reached out and took his hand in a comforting gesture. "That must have been a tremendous loss for you."

He exhaled. "It was a loss for the stories as well. I haven't written a word since. Well, not a word I would show to anyone."

"You will. You have to let yourself grieve."

"What about you?" He changed his tone, wanting to move to something safer, and he let my hand go. "I understand you're divorced — and I've heard it was rough."

Suddenly, my anger flared again. "I suppose Candy told you all about it."

"What?"

I felt my face grow hot. "And you had a good laugh on me, the pair of you."

"Whoa, slow down, Sheryl. There you go again—"

"What does that mean?" I could feel my jaw grow stiff, as if to ward off a blow.

"You're jumping to conclusions! I heard about your divorce from Jon Kane after you told me about Candy and your husband."

"Ex-husband," I spat, and then I realized he was telling the truth. The first time he'd heard about it had been from me. I took a deep breath and looked to the exit. "You're right! There I go again. Maybe I shouldn't have sat down with you."

"You could always have a drink with Allen Alexander. As of yesterday, he's your biggest fan."

I pointed my index finger in his face. "Don't say that, even as a joke."

"Sorry," he confessed, and I could see he was.

"He's insane," I added.

This made Mark snort. "Don't I know it."

I lowered my voice. "Add to that, he has been trying to get in my pants even before the divorce." I gave a shudder. "Ew, just the thought makes my skin crawl."

Mark turned to me and fixed those kind eyes on me. "I honestly didn't know about Candy and your ex-husband."

I was ready to let it go, but I felt I was owed one more dig. "Yes and you slept with her. I can't really expect you to listen to my side—"

"Well, about that—"

"What's the matter, couldn't get it up?" I sneered.

For only a second, I saw a flash of anger appear on his face, and I had to admit it both scared and excited me. Mark seemed like this sweet guy, but there was a fire in him, one that he controlled very well.

"Actually, I don't know what happened last night," he expressed in a quiet and sincere tone.

"What?" I blurted in shock.

"I admit I went to her room, and it did seem as if... well... something was about to happen."

"What does that mean?" I nagged impatiently.

"She was in lingerie, all right?" he bickered, a bit annoyed.

"I know, I saw her."

"That's right," he agreed and gave a nod. "When things... started, I... uh... blacked out."

"Blacked out?" I repeated.

"And woke up at noon today in my own room. Like you pointed out, I was terribly hungover, yet I only had two glasses of wine last night. Oh yes, and one glass of cognac in her room."

I reached into a side pocket on my outfit and extracted a tiny notebook along with the short stub of a pencil. I glanced around the room, moved close, and lowered my voice. "Do you think you were drugged?"

"What are you doing?" he wondered.

"I take notes. Go on," I shrugged.

He considered it for a moment, and then went on. "Well, drugged... seems like the only logical explanation I can come up with."

"But why would she do that?"

"I have no idea. And I have been unable to locate Candy today to ask her about it. However, I'm pretty sure that I did *not* sleep with her."

"You merely wanted to," I said, and scribbled a few things in the notebook.

He looked down at his hands, and I could see the pain on his face. "Sheryl, I have spent the last two years in my apartment avoiding people. To have an attractive woman throw herself at me —"

"Good for the ego," I agreed and looked up at the ceiling wistfully. "She probably pursued you because she knew I was a fan."

"You're a fan of me?"

"Yes, I always brought up your name at Northeast Mystery Club meetings, despite the ravings of Mr. Alexander. In fact, you were the inspiration to write my first Holmes book."

"Then why did you go after me so vehemently last night, and again today?"

"I saw you in the lobby yesterday. I was about to come over and introduce myself... but that... that... person was there with you."

"Candy?"

"Yes. And Jon Kane and Charles Nederlander. Ever since the divorce, I'm considered *persona non grata* by that entire group. You see, Randall was one of the founding members, and Charles is his partner in his financial business."

"What does your husband do?"

"Ex-husband. He's an investment counselor, and Charles takes care of the legal end. He's a lawyer. Jon Kane is the insurance part of the team but plays a minor role. They've closed ranks to shut me out."

"Which explains why you get stuck running from panel to panel, according to the program."

"Randall's idea of a joke," I muttered.

"Nice guy."

I sighed and put my notebook away. "I felt like they were getting to you before I even had a chance to say hello, and it made me so angry." I looked at him, trying to appear contrite. "I guess I took it out on you." I reached out for my glass and finished off my drink in one long swallow. "So I acted like an ass and pissed you off," I admitted as I put my glass down.

"Look," he said, "why don't I buy you dinner?"

I looked at him as if he were insane. "Why would you do that?"

"A lot of reasons. First of all, I think both of us are a little fragile right now. We both lost important relationships."

"Mine was for the better."

"Second, it gives us a chance to get started again on the right foot."

"What about you and Candy?"

"That's the third reason. I want to try and figure out what would be her motivation to drug me."

"So you can find her and try to sleep with her again?"

It was his turn to sigh. "Look, it was nice to have an attractive blonde interested." He raised those eyes to me. "But, in the clear light of day, I've just left behind twenty-five very good years. It's hard to know what I want right now."

"What you need is to want to live again."

His mouth fell open in stunned amazement. I guess I had hit the nail on the head. And I understood — really understood. I had been hiding as well, just like him, but in a different way.

"Ms. Homes?" a voice said.

We both turned.

A tall man in a rumpled suit stood next to our table. He had a large mustache and a shaved head and was built like a linebacker.

"Yes," I replied, surprised. I slipped my notebook back into its hiding place.

The man flashed a leather wallet with a gold shield. "I'm Detective DeStadler. May I ask you to come with me?"

"Why? What is this about?" Mark demanded.

He looked back and gave a nod to a large African-American man dressed in a similar cheap suit, who I assumed was his partner.

"I'm afraid it's about your husband, Randall Lawrence," DeStadler stated as his partner drew near.

"What the hell has he done this time?" I said, annoyance creeping into my voice. "Look, we're divorced. I am not responsible—"

"It's not what he's done, ma'am," DeStadler said, his mouth a hard line. "It's what was done to him. He's dead."

His partner added, "Murdered."

11. Deadline

Mark Watkins

I accompanied Sheryl to the police station.

Actually, I didn't have a choice. Once DeStadler learned I was Mark Watkins, he insisted I accompany them as well.

We rode in the back of an NYPD police car that had been waiting to transport us. It was a bit disconcerting to be in the back with the door locked.

As if we were being arrested.

It was a short trip west to the station house on 54th Street between Eighth and Ninth Avenue. It was housed in a rather gothic structure. When we arrived, we were separated and I was shown to an interrogation room on the second floor.

DeStadler's partner offered me a cup of coffee, and it was soon brought by a uniformed officer.

It was dreadful.

I sat alone for over forty-five minutes, staring at myself in the large one-way mirror.

I wondered if they were watching me.

I was also concerned about Sheryl, what she was going through, and if she was all right. It was an odd sensation. A few hours ago, if she'd been taken for questioning by the police, I would've been pleased and hardly surprised.

Now, I felt *protective* of her.

About an hour after our arrival, DeStadler and his partner came into my room.

"My partner, John Elvis—"

"Elvis?" I repeated.

"No jokes," the large dark-skinned man warned. "I've heard them all and they ain't funny."

"I guess you should be grateful your parents didn't name you 'Presley,'" I offered, unable to help myself.

"Right," he replied deadpan.

"We need to speak to you about a few things," DeStadler asserted.

"How is Sheryl? Is she all right?" I worried.

DeStadler sat at the table across from me, as his partner, who I now envisioned in sideburns and a spangled jumpsuit, remained standing.

"How well do you know Ms. Homes, Mr. Watkins?"

I blinked. "Well, I don't really know her at all."

"You seem very concerned over someone you hardly know."

"Yes, well, I'm a fan… of her books."

DeStadler nodded. "You write, too. Is that correct?"

"I used to," I lamented, and looked at my hands.

"Why'd you stop?"

"My wife passed away. I wrote the stories for her."

DeStadler nodded. "That's rough."

I nodded back, my jaw tight.

"Apparently, you and Ms. Homes had words" –he extracted a notebook from his pocket and flipped to a page— "last night and again this afternoon, is that correct?"

"We each have different ideas about Sherlock Holmes."

"The detective?"

"Yes, Ms. Homes and I both write novels that feature Holmes and Watson."

"So she's your competitor?" Elvis growled from where he stood.

I took a deep breath. "I don't have a competitor. I don't write anymore." I felt my temper rise. "That part of my life is over."

DeStadler met my eyes. "Do you own a firearm, Mr. Watkins?"

I wondered where this line of questioning was going.

"Yes, I do," I affirmed. "In fact, I possess a carry permit."

"Now, why does a writer have a carry permit?" Elvis challenged.

I guessed that he was supposed to be the "bad cop."

"I didn't always make a living off of writing," I explained. "I needed a job that gave me time to write and offered a good salary. I became a security guard. I found I could make more if I was trained with a firearm. I got certified and still maintain my carry permit."

"So, it's still active?" DeStadler coaxed as he thumbed through his notebook.

"That permit was hard to get and expensive. I've kept paying the yearly fees, and I go to the range now and then to keep up my skills."

He looked at his notebook. "And do you still own a nine millimeter Beretta 92S semiautomatic?"

"Yes, I do," I affirmed.

"What kind of condition is it in?"

"Good," I claimed. "I take it out, clean, and oil it every few months."

"Where is it now?"

"In my condo, in my bedroom," I said and rattled off my address.

He nodded and wrote it down. "Do you know, when you applied for your permit, that you were fingerprinted, and that your prints were put in a national database?"

"I know I was fingerprinted." I gave a shrug.

DeStadler nodded again. Then, casually, he reached into his pocket and withdrew a plastic bag emblazoned with the words "EVIDENCE" on it. He placed the bag on the table and looked up at me.

In the bag was a curved Calabash pipe.

Just like the one I had last night!

I believe I must have gone pale as my shock was profound.

"You recognize this pipe, Mr. Watkins?" DeStadler queried.

"We found that at the murder scene," Elvis added with a smirk.

"We were able to get fingerprints off it," DeStadler hinted. "Do you know whose?"

"I had a pipe like that. It was loaned to me." I could feel sweat on my brow. "I used it at my speech last night."

"Well, this pipe has two sets of prints: Mr. Lawrence's and yours."

"*My* fingerprints?"

"Yes and this pipe, with *your* prints, turned up in the room where Mr. Lawrence was found."

DeStadler held out his hand and Elvis put a folder in it. He began to lay out glossy eight-by-ten photos, facedown so only the backs showed.

"I have no idea," I avowed. "The last thing I remember, I left it at the podium in the ballroom. Someone must have taken it."

I had this terrible feeling that there was a large object hanging over my head, and it was suspended on a very tiny thread.

DeStadler continued to lay out photos. "Can you tell me where you were last evening between midnight and 2:00 AM?"

"No," I said. "I mean... I was asleep... at the hotel."

"Anyone to verify that?"

I sighed. "I was with a girl... in her room... but... I blacked out."

"Run that by me again?" Detective Elvis intoned.

I quickly told the story of going to Candy's room, and how I ran into Sheryl at the ice machine. Then I told how I blacked out and woke up in my own room the next day.

Both men listened intently.

"So this woman lets you into her room, she's dressed provocatively, and she slips you a mickey?"

"A mickey?" I said and frowned. "I thought that term was only used in 1940s detective novels."

"Okay, she drugged you," DeStadler fumed.

"That's the only conclusion I've come up with," I proclaimed.

"Don't explain how that pipe ends up in the victim's apartment," Elvis pointed out.

"Someone placed it there," I suggested.

"And who would do that?" DeStadler stressed.

I thought about it. "I have no idea."

"Do you have any enemies?"

I shook my head. "Not a one."

Allen Alexander flashed in my mind, but I dismissed him. I really didn't think he possessed that level of skill. And why would he kill Randall Lawrence?

DeStadler turned over several of the pictures. They showed a man in his late thirties, very pale, with a head full of curly hair. He was on a brass bed with a headboard of bent tubes, without a stitch of clothing.

"So you claim to know nothing about this?" DeStadler surmised.

I gave a quick perusal of the photos, and I saw that Randall Lawrence was handcuffed to the corners of the bed frame. There were leg irons on each ankle, opening his legs in a spread eagle position.

"H-how did he die?" I asked.

"Suffocated," Elvis revealed. "With one of the pillows."

I nodded. My mouth felt dry.

"The pipe with your prints was found right there." Elvis pointed to a table in the photo. "Next to a laptop computer."

"I see."

"So you like stories? Being a writer and all?"

"Usually," I replied, not pleased where this was going.

"Here is how we think this could've gone down," Elvis theorized. "You showed up with that gun of yours and told Mr. Lawrence to strip. Then, you locked him up, put the gun away, and suffocated him with the pillow."

"But... but... I don't even *know* him," I stammered. "I have no motive—"

"Well, it is suspicious," DeStadler explained. "I mean you and Ms. Homes go through this big show that you hate each other—"

"In front of a large audience, we were told," Elvis chimed in.

"And yet we find the two of you as thick as thieves having a friendly drink in the hotel bar," DeStadler divulged.

"Yeah, very cozy," Elvis hinted. "And she happens to see you at the ice machine — and vouch for you — almost like she planned to meet you there for an alibi."

"What time did you see her at the ice machine, Mr. Watkins?"

"I don't know," I conceded. "Sometime around 11:00, I guess."

"You guess?" DeStadler questioned.

"I had a pretty woman waiting for me in a hotel room. I wasn't concerned about the hour at that moment."

"Well, we intend to talk to this 'Candy' woman, as well as many other people at the convention, Mr. Watkins."

"Conference," I corrected.

"What?"

"It's not a convention; it's a conference."

"All right then, conference," DeStadler sneered. "If you have anything you want to add to your story, I suggest that now would be the time."

"I-I can't think of anything," I gulped.

"I see," DeStadler snapped. "You'll be at the Hilton until Sunday, and then at your condominium?"

"In case we have any other questions," Detective Elvis cautioned, "and I believe we may have many more."

I nodded wanly. "May I go?"

"Just don't go far, Mr. Watkins," DeStadler said.

12. Shelf Life

Sheryl Homes

I watched as Mark walked out the front of the precinct as I scribbled in my notebook.

"Hey," he announced as he approached. "Are you all right?"

"Yes. I just can't believe it," I confessed, "Randall dead... and those pictures."

"What are you doing?"

"Hmm," I said without looking up. "I'm making notes while it's still fresh in my mind."

"I don't know about you, but I'm starved," he proposed. "I did offer to buy you dinner hours ago."

I glanced up to see concern written on his brow. "Oh, yes. And I could really use another drink." We began to walk as I continued to write in the notebook.

Mark spoke as we walked. "I'm worried. You look pale."

I put the notebook away and sighed. "It wasn't easy."

Mark told me about the pipe and everything he could remember from his interrogation as we headed south on Eighth Avenue. In return, I told him that after I was questioned by the detectives, I gave a statement, which was written up for me to sign.

We went to Victor's Cafe, a Cuban place on 52nd Street. We slipped into the Cuba Lounge and found a secluded table near the bar.

The waitress took our orders for scotch, which Mark was pleased to find that they had a great selection of single-malts. I ordered a Glenkinchie and he settled on a Talisker.

"They kept asking about you," I considered. "How well I knew you, how many times I'd seen you at the conference, any history we've had."

"Since my fingerprints were on that pipe with Randall's, they believe I'm implicated. I think they are convinced I'm either the killer or an accomplice."

"I see," I responded as I sipped scotch and we placed our meal orders. "How did that pipe end up at my place?"

"Your place?" he questioned.

"I'm sorry." I found my hand went to my head in a dismissive gesture. "I meant Randall's... the murder scene... oh crap!" I took another swallow of my drink.

"Are you *sure* you're all right?" Mark fretted.

"It's so weird," I told him, and felt my face flush. "I've written about murder for years, and yet when it happens to someone you know... it's all so..."

"Personal?"

"Yes. I mean — well, I had two mysteries published before the Holmes books."

"*Who Killed Clark Kent?*" Mark clarified. "I liked that one. It had nothing to do with Superman, just a reporter named Clark Kent who ended up murdered."

"You *read* it?" I couldn't hold back the smile that played on my lips.

"Yes, and the follow-up, *Who Killed Bruce Wayne?*"

"So, you were the *one*."

"The one?"

"Those books didn't do very well," I explained, and gave a sigh. "'Disappointing' is what the publisher called it."

"I thought they were pretty clever," Mark mused. "But your writing really took off with the Holmes books."

"Also what my agent said. She told me I'd finally found my voice, and that it was Doctor Watson."

Mark laughed at this. "Sorry, I don't see you as Watson at all, and after reading your books, I think it's Holmes you emulate."

I considered this for a moment. "I guess you're right. To have the kind of mind that sees the slightest detail—"

"Which you did to me this afternoon."

I waved a hand dismissively. "That was easy—"

"Elementary, perhaps?"

I gave a cross between a laugh and a snort, which immediately embarrassed the hell out of me. But I soldiered on, held up the remains of my drink, and saluted. "Elementary, my dear Watkins."

He smiled and we clicked glasses.

As tapas were served, we were able to relax a bit. It was past 11:00 at this point, and it had been a trying day. We made polite small talk, but I couldn't help but pull the conversation back to the murder.

"It was odd, him strung-up like that," I pointed out.

"Was Randall into anything kinky?"

I was sure that this time I turned beet red as memories flooded back to me.

"I'm sorry," Mark attempted, aware that I was uncomfortable. "If you don't want to talk about it…"

I felt myself flush a second time and was annoyed that I was acting like a shy virgin instead of a thirty-four-year-old experienced woman. I lowered my voice. "Randall was into… many things. Unusual, sometimes creative, and sometimes bordering on the perverted."

"I guess you would know," he pondered.

I tried to just shrug it off. "We had 'adventures' during our time together, but he wanted to go further than I was willing."

"Such as?"

I squirmed. "I — don't want to talk about it."

What was it about Mark that made me so reticent? I've regaled girlfriends with some of the antics Randall and I pulled, including a coupling on the steps in the crown of the Statue of Liberty. Why did I want Mark to think I was a demure little thing? Or was it something else? Was it that since he was a more serious man, I wanted to be a more serious lady, who left such adventures behind?

"I understand," Mark said. "But if he was into bondage — considering how he was found — that seems to point to a woman."

I had to agree.

He went on. "As I see it, get him into the room, get him trussed up, and he would be helpless. And with that pipe ending up there… it had to be someone who'd seen me with it."

I thought about my next words carefully. "I might be biased, but I think Candy is a cold enough bitch to pull it off. However…"

"What?"

"What if the murderer wanted the police to *think* it was a sex crime?"

"What do you mean?"

"Upon reflection, the room in the photos is like a stage set," I extolled and pulled out my pad to scribble notes. "Everything put together to draw the attention away from the actual reason for the murder and focus the attention on the sexual angle."

He frowned. "But if that was the case, why not kill Randall using a rope around the neck to suggest sexual asphyxiation?"

"Simple!" I put the stub of the pencil in my mouth like a cigarette. "A rope is rough and might pick up fibers from the murderer's clothing, or show what kinds of gloves he was wearing."

"Gloves?"

"Certainly, the killer must have worn gloves, as the only fingerprints they found were *yours.* The rope could have traces of leather or rubber, which would point to another suspect. By using the pillow and pressing down, the murderer could have worn gloves or not; there's no way to tell."

"Ah," Mark agreed. "Thus suggesting a sexual encounter gone wrong. Well done, Homes!"

"Thank you, Watkins," I giggled. I immediately took another sip of my scotch. Why was I acting like this? First, I want him to think I'm a vestal virgin, now I'm giggling like a fourteen-year-old. I've never made a fool of myself like this with any man before. Why am I starting now?

Mark leaned forward. "If only we could find out who *did* it, then we'd be off the hook."

My head snapped up. "Of course! You're right!"

"What?" He frowned.

"We should find out who the killer is!"

"Us?" Mark responded and glanced around the room. "We're writers."

"Not merely writers," I corrected. "Chroniclers of Sherlock Holmes, the greatest detective that ever lived."

"He didn't live," Mark pointed out. "Conan Doyle made him up."

"You know what I mean. We could solve the case and prove that neither of us had anything to do with it!"

Mark tightened his lips in thought. "Solve the case?"

"Yes," I hissed. "Like Holmes and Watson."

"Sheryl, we know nothing about actually *being* detectives."

By now I was getting into the spirit of the idea. "No problem! We use the techniques that Holmes developed to solve crimes: observation, evidence, deduction—"

"I don't know," Mark worried.

"You have to admit it's intriguing," I decided, and started to pick up my things in preparation to leave. "First thing is to visit the crime scene!"

Mark held up his hands. "Sheryl, we have no authority and no way to get into the crime scene."

I could feel my face break into a wide, wicked grin. "I didn't tell the police, but I still have a set of keys."

13. Mechanical

Mark Watkins

My watch read 12:00 AM as we reached the door of a loft down in the neighborhood south of Houston Street affectionately known as Soho.

We'd paid the bill, taken a cab downtown, then hiked up three sets of stairs in the old factory building that was converted into very expensive lofts.

Here Sheryl reached into a zippered compartment in her handbag, extracted two pairs of rubber gloves, and handed one pair to me.

"Is this necessary?" I wondered.

"Do you want to leave *more* fingerprints?"

I nodded and put on the latex surgical gloves. "You... always carry these?"

"I was a Girl Scout," she asserted.

"How did the police not find them?"

"They didn't ask to search my purse, and I didn't offer."

We faced the large factory-style door. "So this was where you lived when you two were married?"

"Yes," she said as she twirled a key in one of the locks. "It's also where I caught him with Candy Poole."

"Her last name is Poole?"

She undid a different lock and faced me, once she inserted the next key. "You mean to tell me you were about to bang her and you didn't even know her last name?"

I shrugged. "It never came up."

She shook her head and returned to the door. "Honestly, sometimes men are just a penis with legs."

"Look," I said a bit cross, "I don't know about your situation —"

"Damn straight."

"—but I haven't been with a woman in well over two years."

She pulled the door open and gave a low sigh. "You're right, Mark."

"Wait. Did you actually agree with me?"

"No," she said as she stepped into the room and pulled me into the darkness. "I just mean, it must be hard losing your wife."

"Don't pity me," I barked, surprised by the sound of anger in my voice. "I don't need pity."

"I'm not giving any," she challenged. "I just understand that going out and meeting people is tough. And men have, well, certain needs."

"And women don't?"

She shut the door, locked it. "Some of us don't."

"I don't know if I believe you."

She turned on the lights.

The space was tremendous. It ran the entire length of the story and was open with beautiful varnished oak floors. I could see two walled areas in the back that contained bedrooms and bathrooms, but the living room, dining room, and kitchen were open. One space melted into the next. The kitchen had black granite countertops and an island with a range. The dining area had a teak wood table with chairs for six, and the living area boasted contemporary leather furniture and a fireplace.

"Wow," I said quietly.

"It is impressive," Sheryl noted. "Nicer than where I live now, off of Fourth Street. And I was lucky to get that."

She moved into the kitchen and opened the large, stainless steel refrigerator.

"What are you doing?" I whispered.

"Checking the first obvious place."

"Obvious for what?"

"If Randall did bring someone up for fun and games, he would have bought a favorite food or something unusual."

"There's champagne and caviar," I said, and pointed at two bottles on the inside of the door.

"The cheap brands. No, this is what he had on hand most of the time," she said and closed the door. The small notebook at once appeared in her hands like a magic trick.

"For God's sake, what did he do for a living?"

"I told you! He was an investment banker — a very good one," Sheryl answered as she looked down the edge of the countertop. "Made himself a lot of money. Me too, for that matter."

"I thought the breakup was ugly."

"Oh, it was. You see, Randall made a lot of investments in my name, especially when I received the royalties from the books. Since the investments were in my name, I wanted to keep them."

"He wasn't willing to do that?"

"No, he actually gave me a hard time. Told me he'd built them up from practically nothing. I finally had a forensic accountant look over the accounts. He told me that Randall's finances were not exactly what they appeared to be."

"Was he doing anything illegal?"

"I never really knew. With what my accountant found, my lawyer suggested the IRS might want to take a hard look if he didn't give me my little portfolio and a good settlement. That made Randall cave."

She walked toward the bedroom, stopped, and suddenly sat in one of the leather chairs. She leaned forward, and her arms holding the pad and pencil fell limply to her sides as she sucked in deep breaths.

"What's wrong?" I knelt next to her. "Are you all right?"

"I will be," she muttered and sat staring at the wall, her mouth a tight line.

"Sheryl?"

"This is... harder than I thought it would be," she explained and blinked rapidly as she tried to force a smile.

"This was a man you once loved," I sympathized. "You've got to let it out."

"No," she quavered, her voice tense. "I have to accept the fact that he never really loved me."

"I'm sure that isn't true."

"It's true. Four years. Goddamn it! We were married four years, and then I walked in to find that bitch in my bed and on top of him. And after he gave me my settlement, he told me there were many others."

"Sheryl—"

"And now he's dead, and I'm not sure if I'm sad, angry, or pleased the bastard got what he deserved."

"That's very normal—"

"Is it, Mark?" she sniffled and faced me, her eyes bright. "Is that how you feel about your wife?"

I couldn't meet her eyes. "Susie and I were different. We had a very good marriage. I could never be unfaithful to her."

Sheryl sighed again. "And Randall was unfaithful to me from the beginning. But I was so busy working on my books, I didn't see it."

"Sheryl, you can't blame yourself."

She gave me a cold, hard stare. "You blame yourself, Mark."

"I—I—" I stammered. I took a moment to compose myself. "Wouldn't it be best if we looked at the crime scene?"

"You're right." She rose from the chair, her eyes clear. We walked to the bedroom door and Sheryl stopped. "I haven't been in this bedroom since I packed my things and left."

"You can do it," I maintained and moved my hand to the doorknob.

"Hold it," she warned, and I jerked my hand back as she examined the doorway. "Do you notice what's missing?"

"Missing?" I mocked. "How would I know if something was missing?"

"We just entered a crime scene," she encouraged.

My eyes grew wide. "No yellow tape."

"Correct. They didn't seal the outside door, or here at the bedroom." She made another quick scribble in her notebook.

"I wonder why?" I admitted.

"Another mystery, Watkins," Sheryl acknowledged. "Let us go forward with caution."

I was startled by her change in speech. She now sounded more analytical and her voice took on the characteristics of the Victorian Age. If she'd suddenly developed an English accent, I would not have been surprised.

She turned the door handle, and we carefully stepped into the room. She touched a wall switch and the room came alive around us.

I recognized the bed and the brass headboard from the photos. The only thing missing was the naked body of Randall Lawrence.

She studied the room. "They took the handcuffs and the sheets." She withdrew a magnifying glass from her purse.

"Something else you learned with the Girl Scouts?" I suggested.

"Actually, I got this from the Boy Scouts. Always be prepared," she clarified as she traced her way along the brass tubes that formed the headboard. "Ah, here is where the handcuffs were attached."

"Scratches?"

"Very good, Watkins," Sheryl praised. "One end of the metal handcuffs were fastened to the tube and the other around Randall's wrist."

She stood up and went around the bed to examine the other side, then made a few more quick notations.

"But the question is, Homes," I interjected, getting into the spirit of it, "was the victim a willing participant or was he coerced by force into bondage?"

"Excellent, Watkins," Sheryl considered, and I could tell she relished taking on the role of the master detective. "He would struggle once the pillow stopped his breath, which would increase the number of scratches on the brass."

"Detective DeStadler suggested that I imprisoned him at gunpoint," I disclosed. "If the scene was staged, perhaps someone did so."

"Perhaps." Sheryl moved her examination to the foot of the bed and the tubes there. "Examine the room for anything out of place."

"I've never been here before. How would I know if anything were out of place?"

"Hmm, good point, Watkins."

"I think I liked Mark better," I said sullenly. This "Holmes-Watson" thing wasn't as much fun as I thought.

"Come on, play along. It helps me think," Sheryl encouraged as she looked at the table near the bed. "Is this where the detectives said the pipe was found?"

"Next to the laptop," I said and gazed around the room. "But I don't see a laptop."

"It *was* here." Sheryl pointed to the table. "See the dust in a rectangular pattern? This was where he kept it."

"The dust is smeared a bit. I imagine from when the police removed it."

Sheryl knelt on the floor and picked up something.

"What's that?" I said, and she held up a small screw on her finger. "A screw? To what?"

"Good question. It would appear to be a screw from a computer. Considering its placement—"

"It seems odd that the police would take the computer apart here."

She pondered this. "Agreed. It makes much more sense that they would have the Crime Scene Unit examine it in the lab." She made a quick entry on her memo pad.

"Well, Homes, I'm sure that the unit tagged and bagged anything suspicious."

"Perhaps not everything," Sheryl said, as something caught her eye. She crouched down on one knee at the foot of the bed, took the ruffled bed skirt in her hand, and gave it a shake.

There was the sound of something metallic as it struck the floor.

She held up a small metal tube in her gloved hand.

"Is that a bullet casing?" I questioned.

She handed it to me, then pulled at the bed to move it away from the wall.

"Aha! Look at this, Watkins!"

She pointed, and I drew near. There was a small hole in the wall, unseen in the shadow of the headboard.

"A bullet hole?" I muttered.

"Yes, and with the body positioned on the bed the way it was, perhaps no one noticed the hole in the wall."

"Do you think the technicians missed it?" I wondered.

"I'm not sure, but they did miss the casing," she said with a nod. "Now if we only knew the caliber of the bullet."

I held up the casing and examined it in the light.

"You've gone pale, Mark." Sheryl had concern in her voice. "What is it?"

"I am very familiar with this caliber," I whispered. "It's a nine millimeter."

"How do you know that?"

"It's the same caliber as the gun I own."

14. Errata

Sheryl Homes

I t was past two in the morning when we opened the door to Mark's condo.

We ended our examination of the crime scene and hastily grabbed a cab uptown. I decided that Mark should hold onto the bullet casing, as it would be wiser to not leave any evidence that might point to him. After all, we could always give it to DeStadler later.

"There's just one problem," Mark mentioned quietly in the back of the cab so the driver wouldn't hear. "It's called withholding evidence."

"Someone has attempted to implicate us. The last thing we should do is help them."

However, I did run through a mental list of crimes we'd committed by going to Randall's apartment, even though I had the keys.

The cab dropped us off on West End Avenue. We went into the building, Mark going to the sealed outer door and opening it with keys. Once inside, we rode the elevator to the 12th floor.

Once Mark got the three locks on his apartment door open, I followed him into his bedroom. In my defense, I didn't know it was a bedroom until we got in there and I saw the bed.

Whereupon I froze, as numerous thoughts ran through my head. Is he going to make a pass? Do I want him to? Will I be insulted if he doesn't?

I relaxed when he moved to a bedside table and quickly removed a handgun that was still in its holster. He slipped it out and ejected the magazine from the bottom of the pistol grip.

"That's curious," Mark noted.

"What?" I asked.

"I don't keep the gun loaded. I leave the magazine separate in the drawer with the pistol. If someone broke into my apartment, I can load it even in the dark, but I've been trained not to leave it loaded."

"And that's not the way you found it?"

He pulled back the slide, put it to his nose, and inhaled deeply. "This gun has been fired... and recently. The last time I used it was..." He stopped.

"When?" I insisted.

"I have no idea when I last fired it. I cleaned it two — or was it three months ago? Maybe longer."

"But you haven't fired it?" I asked. My notebook re-appeared in my hands as I jotted another sentence.

"Not in a long time," Mark considered and put it back in the holster and returned both to the bedside table, the magazine separate. He then took the shell casing and put it in the same drawer.

"Not a good idea," I pointed out. "If the police come here, you don't want to make it that easy to find."

"What should I do with it?" Mark worried.

I put out my hand. "Leave that to me."

He handed it to me, and then sat on the bed, disheartened. "Well, I wanted to get screwed. Apparently, I have been."

I drew close and put a hand on his shoulder. "This is a very involved case, Watkins."

"Cut the Holmes crap, Sheryl," Mark snapped. "I am out of my depth. A pretty girl drugs me, someone breaks into my apartment, steals my gun, takes a shot at your ex-husband, and then kills him. Whoever did this is way ahead of me. What other clues could he have left that point to me?"

"Candy Poole was the one who drugged you. She has to be in on it. If we can get to her... question her."

"Sheryl, it's two in the morning," Mark complained. "I'm exhausted. I have to sleep."

"You're right, Mark," I agreed.

"That's twice you've told me I'm right."

"That's because it's the second time you have been," I told him with a smile. "We both need to get some rest."

"It would make sense if you stayed here."

I eyed him with suspicion.

"It's not a come-on. I'll take the guest room," he conceded.

I stood dumbfounded. "You have a guest room?"

"More like an oversized walk-in closet, but it does make it a two-bedroom condo."

"And increase the asking price?" I offered.

"Don't I know it," he sighed.

"It's your place, Mark. The guest room is fine for me."

"Okay, the bed *is* comfortable," Mark said. "Let me get some clean sheets... if I have any."

"You seem to be keeping up with the housework." I looked around and peered under his bed as he went to the hall closet and got some sheets. "I don't see any large dust bunnies attempting a coup."

He moved past the "dining room" table, which was actually a table in the part of the living room near the kitchen. He then opened the door to the guest bedroom, which contained a small single bed, and began to put sheets on it.

I watched. It's nice to see a man do domestic tasks with such obvious skill. He didn't have any doubts or confusion, but set to the chore as if it was second nature.

Let me tell you, it was sexy.

Mark talked. "At first, after Susie was gone, the place looked like a bomb hit it. And I couldn't throw anything out — I mean, you know, of hers."

I nodded solemnly. "This was where you lived together."

"It's the only New York apartment we… I ever had. We moved in as renters. When the building went condo, we bought."

"I can see a lot of feminine touches," I said, and picked up a small snow globe from a bookcase. It held a glass rose within it. "There's a sense of history here."

He kept tucking in the cloth and didn't look up. "We were happy."

"I hate to be a bother," I inquired, "but all my clothes are at home or the hotel. Do you have any of her nightgowns?"

He hesitated for a moment. "I… kind of… have all of her clothes in a closet, but I doubt her stuff will fit you. You're a lot taller."

"Anything will do, really."

Mark finished tucking the sheet in, rose, and walked over to the closet. He hesitated for a moment, and then yanked it open.

Mark quickly reached in and extracted a cotton nightgown that looked warm enough but not too hot. As he pulled it off the hanger, tears stung his eyes.

"Mark?" I worried.

"I-I'm okay," he blurted out, and handed me the garment. "Excuse me."

He ran into the bedroom and slammed the door. I held the garment, and then caught a whiff of perfume. It must have been his wife's perfume. Now tears were in my eyes. That must have been so hard, to catch the fragrance of the person you loved and lost. I suddenly felt like an invader who had come in and desecrated something special.

I stepped into the guest bedroom, and fighting back my own tears, quickly undressed and put on the nightgown. I was soon covered and looking quite proper, though the full-length nightgown only went just past my knees.

I softly rapped on Mark's bedroom door.

"Mark," I spoke gently. "I'm sorry, I didn't mean to—"

The door opened and Mark was staring at the floor, the doorknob in his hand. "It's all right. I just—"

He looked at me and his mouth fell open, as if I was the most beautiful thing he had ever seen.

And there it was, that stare of his that made me feel like he was touching, caressing, and loving me all at once. My knees went weak from his intense gaze.

"That was a floor-length nightshirt on Susie," he croaked, overcome with emotion and, could it be, lust?

"You okay?" I babbled, surprised at what I felt. I wanted him to take me in his arms, undress, and make love to me. It was all so immediate and powerful I could barely contain myself.

"Yeah," he said with a stoic look.

I reached up and touched his face gently, and in that moment I wanted to be swept away. I was overcome with desire in a way I'd never known until this moment.

"Get some rest," he implored and pushed the door closed.

I stood there stunned. Didn't he pick up on my signals or my pheromones or something? Then I made a realization and was disgusted with myself. I had wanted Mark to make love in the very bed he and his wife had shared for all those years.

How could I? What was wrong with me?

I trudged wearily back to the guest room, equally aroused and disgusted with myself at the same time. My nipples were erect and rubbing against the fabric of the nightgown, which made matters worse.

I should have said something, asked something, told him of my desires, told him of my needs.

Instead I got into that single bed and lay there still ablaze and without any way to relieve the tension. What if I went to him and begged him to make love to me?

No, he would lose the respect that we both had worked so hard to gain.

I lay there worrying about it, with scenarios running through my head, until I grew so weary that sleep finally came.

15. Escalation Clause

Mark Watkins

*S*usie and I were sitting at our dining room table having breakfast. She wore that white turban she always wore after she lost her hair. Even so, we laughed and made foolish jokes only the two of us would understand.

She looked at me very seriously and said, "I don't want you to be alone, Mark."

"I won't be," I told her jauntily. "Look, you're home and everything will be fine. I am sure you're in remission."

"Sweetheart," Susie said and took my hand. "If the roles were reversed and you were dying—"

I grew angry. "You're not dying, dammit. Don't say that."

"Listen to me," she insisted and put a finger against my lips. "If you were dying, would you want me to be alone after you were gone?"

"You're not going anywhere," I muttered.

All at once, I was awake, in our bed… my bed… and alone.

I smelled bacon.

I sat up and shielded my eyes from the bright light as it poured through the windows. I glanced at my bedside clock and it read 9:30. I threw on a bathrobe and followed my nose out to my small kitchen.

Fully dressed, Sheryl stood at the stove and fried the smoked meat. Next to her was a glass bowl that contain several eggs, mixed and ready to be cooked once the bacon was finished.

"Where did this come from?" I marveled. I didn't have bacon in the house, let alone eggs.

"I went out and bought them," Sheryl teased. "I wanted to surprise you."

"When did you get up?"

"About 7:30."

"But how did you get in and out of the building?"

"I saw you leave your keys on that table on the way in." She gave a nod toward the table near the door. "It gave me a chance to see how hard it was to get in and out of your apartment without being noticed."

I nodded with admiration. "Good idea."

"Also, we aren't leaving here until you change your lock."

"What?" I bleated. "Is that necessary?"

"Completely," Sheryl said. "I examined your keys and there are fresh scratches on the sides of them. I believe someone had them copied."

I stood there, shocked. I finally found my voice. "Which is how someone could have 'borrowed' my gun."

She nodded. "To test my theory, I had the man at that hardware store over on Broadway make a copy of one. The machine holds the key in the very way that corresponds to the scratches."

"Well..." was all I could muster.

"I took the liberty to purchase a new lock. It matches the one you have, so we only need to replace the mechanism itself."

"How did you know what type of lock it was?"

She gave an impatient sigh. "Mark, you've read my books. I did a study of locks for the *Banshee* book. Made myself a bit of an expert."

"Apparently," I admired.

"The new lock is in that bag there." She indicated the brown paper sack on the dining room table. "Get showered. We'll eat and do the job. You have tools, don't you?"

"Yes," I insisted. "Shouldn't we get a locksmith?"

"This is safer. The fewer people who know, the better."

I shook my head in amazement. "Astounding, Homes."

She smirked. "Elementary, Watkins."

I took a shower and cursed myself that I hadn't cleaned the bathroom in a few weeks. Then again, I wasn't expecting a guest, and certainly not a female one. I paid careful attention to my grooming as I shaved, and even put on a little aftershave.

I put my robe back on, slipped into my bedroom, and was dressed in a few short minutes. I sat down to eggs, bacon, toast, and fresh coffee.

"You are an amazing woman, Sheryl," I said.

"Don't get used to it," she replied flatly. "I'm just visiting."

I laughed and we ate.

"What is your plan for the day?" I took a sip of coffee.

"This entire case revolves around the conference," Sheryl pondered. "Randall was deeply involved in the Northeast Mystery Club. Someone there must know something. We only have until Sunday, so we should get down there and find out what we can."

"Finding Candy Poole would be first on my list."

She extracted her notebook and reviewed a few pages. "You said that the last time you saw her was Wednesday night?"

"Yes, in her room, before I blacked out."

"You didn't see her yesterday at all?"

"No, I kept missing her, and then the police—"

"I wonder what she used on you?" Sheryl considered as she thoughtfully nibbled on her toast and glanced at her notes.

"Why?"

"Well, if she used Rohypnol, you should have enough motor control and been suggestible enough that she could have walked you back to your room." She wrote another line in the pad.

"Wouldn't I remember that?"

"No, Rohypnol's major effect is loss of memory. However, it usually takes ten to twenty minutes to take effect. Now, if she used Ketamine, which is an animal sedative, it would explain why it would have worked so quickly and gave you the hangover the next day."

"But then she would have to carry me back to my room," I pointed out.

"Not an easy trick for Candy," she hypothesized. "So, we'll assume you were cooperative." She pulled out her cell phone and quickly input a number.

"Who are you calling?"

She shushed me and began to talk. As she did, she got up from the table and wandered away. I continued eating.

"Okay, Sylvia, thanks," she said before she put her phone and notebook away. "You got anything to hold a urine specimen?"

"I-I have some jelly jars with lids. They're clean," I offered.

"I have a friend who is a hospital technician. She told me that Rohypnol can be tested in the urine for up to seventy-two hours."

"I guess we should check soon."

I quickly located one of the jars leftover from some jelly Susie and I bought at a farmer's market. As I went into the bathroom and provided my sample, I reflected on how almost everything I owned brought me back to a memory with Susie.

Was it any wonder I couldn't get over her? I'd have to sell everything.

I sealed the jar. As I came out of the bathroom, Sheryl handed me the paper bag she'd carried the lock in.

"We'll take it there in this," she said, "and drop it off at the hospital on our way. Now, let's get to that lock."

I pulled my toolbox out from the bedroom closet, and we got to work on the middle lock.

"Shouldn't we replace all of them?" I suggested.

"Only one is needed," Sheryl replied. "Whoever copied your keys won't be able to open the door if they can't unlock all three locks. If we do it right, no one should be able to tell we even switched it."

I looked at the shiny brass plate of the new lock. "I don't know…"

Soon, we had the old lock off the door, and Sheryl put the new mechanism in place. Then I mounted it back and tightened the screws. Sheryl tested it several times to make sure the new key turned easily.

"Do you have any paint?" Sheryl said.

I quickly located a small can of black spray paint. Sheryl drizzled the paint onto a paper plate, then using a Q-Tip, she artfully applied it to the shiny lock plate. In a few minutes, the new part blended in with the door as if it had been there forever.

"That should frustrate our thief, should he return," Sheryl boasted.

I started to put the tools away. "So how did the murderer gain access to Randall's apartment?"

"The most obvious method is that Randall let him in."

"Pointing to someone he knew."

"And again, bringing our favorite person, Candy Poole, to the top of the list," Sheryl snarled.

I nodded. "Let's get to the conference and see if we can find her."

I put the tool box away and grabbed a brown Harris Tweed suit jacket. Sheryl took her coat and purse and we made our way to the door. On the outside, I turned the locks, and then Sheryl said, "Oh! We forgot your specimen."

I unlocked the door.

At that moment, I saw the elevator door open down the hall and two familiar faces stepped out, followed by two members of the NYPD in full uniform.

"Uh-oh," I exclaimed, and Sheryl turned to look.

"Well, and here the two of you are, together again," Detective Elvis declared, his voice carrying down the hall.

"You weren't in your hotel room. But it's very convenient that you are here," DeStadler intoned in a quieter voice.

"Ain't it interestin'," Elvis pointed out, as they drew near. "Ms. Homes is wearin' the same clothes she was wearin' yesterday."

"How can I help you, detectives?" I said. "As you can see, we were just leaving."

Elvis held out a piece of paper. "We got a warrant to search these premises."

"And the only place you are going is downtown," DeStadler said. "Leave the keys in the lock and step away from the door."

DeStadler gave a nod to one of the officers, who took my arm.

"Hey! What do you think you're doing?" I seethed as the officer spun me around and threw handcuffs on me.

"Bag his hands," DeStadler ordered. "If there is any trace, I don't want to lose it."

The officer quickly put two paper bags over my hands and taped them in place.

"Is that necessary?" Sheryl demanded, whereupon the second officer, a female, turned her around and cuffed her as well.

"Afraid it is," DeStadler said. "We located Candy Poole."

"Then she can verify I was with her Wednesday night," I blurted.

"No," Elvis explained, "she can't verify nothin'."

"What do you mean?" I demanded.

"We didn't actually locate Ms. Poole," DeStadler advised. "Only her body."

"What?" Sheryl gasped.

"ME says she's been dead since about 3:00 AM Thursday morning," DeStadler reported. "Shot with a nine millimeter in her hotel room."

"Shot through a pillow," Elvis added, "to cover the noise. Interestin' thing, it was a pillow from Randall Lawrence's apartment."

"We believe it might be the pillow Mr. Lawrence was smothered with," DeStadler gloated.

"Now, who would know to use a pillow to quiet the sound of a pistol?" Elvis considered. "Maybe a guy who writes about murder?"

"Add to that," DeStadler concluded, "it's quite a coincidence that someone's ex-husband and the woman who broke up her marriage died the same night."

Elvis nodded. "With only the two of you to vouch for each other."

"Someone is trying to set us up," I proclaimed.

"We'll see," DeStadler said, then turned to the officers who held us. "Read 'em their rights, book 'em, and keep 'em separated. We'll be down as soon as we toss this place."

"Hello?"

"Jeff, it's Mark."

"Hey, babe, how is the conference going?"

"My speech went great—"

"Good job, babe."

"But I need Hank."

"Hank? The lawyer?" Jeff puzzled.

"I'm in jail, Jeff."

"What?" Jeff bellowed, and I moved the phone away from my ear.

"I need a lawyer, fast. And for Sheryl Homes as well."

"Homes? Why does she need a lawyer?"

"Someone murdered her ex-husband and his girlfriend."

"Okay, I see why she needs one. Why do you?"

"The police believe the girl was killed with my gun," I said.

"Oh!" Jeff answered as it sunk in. "Jesus Christ, babe, where are you?"

I gave him the address.

"We'll be there as soon as we can," Jeff said. "Until then, don't say anything — to anyone."

I finished my one phone call and was moved into a holding cell, where I tried to sit downwind from a wino in the next cell who hadn't bathed in at least a week. My pockets had been emptied and I'd been fingerprinted, photographed, and then a technician swabbed my hands for gunpowder residue.

I tried to think of a way out of this mess.

DeStadler would find my gun. A few ballistic tests and I was sure it would turn out to be the murder weapon. The fact that I had been with Sheryl Homes gave me motive to kill her ex-husband.

It was a perfect setup and somehow, both of us had walked blithely right into it.

Stepped in it might be a better metaphor.

Who could have done this? Who knew I even owned a gun?

I was taking on a fiend as clever as Professor Moriarty, and he'd taken care of any loose threads. Get the girl to drug me and steal my keys; Candy then went to Randall and set him up; then kill Randall; finally, a partner finished off Candy so the truth could never be known.

And me, with absolutely no memory of that night.

I felt doomed.

Soon, DeStadler and Elvis showed up and I was brought into an interview room again.

"We found your gun," DeStadler divulged.

"It was in the drawer of my night stand," I offered. "But I didn't fire it."

"How do you know it was fired?" Elvis wondered.

I considered this for a minute. "When I got to my apartment last night—"

"With Ms. Homes," Elvis leered.

"With Ms. Homes. I thought something was wrong."

"Why?" DeStadler demanded. "Anything out of place?"

"Just a feeling. So, I checked my gun. It was loaded. I never leave the magazine in—"

"It was out when we found it," DeStadler claimed.

"It smelled of recent use," I explained.

"And you didn't immediately call the police?"

"It was two in the morning," I observed.

"But you left here at eleven," DeStadler questioned. "What did you and Ms. Homes do until two in the morning?"

I exhaled heavily. "We had dinner."

"You have the name of the restaurant, maybe a receipt?"

"We weren't there until two," I protested. "Look what is the bottom line here?"

"Well, something for you to chew on, Mr. Watkins," DeStadler said. "Miss Poole was naked when we found her."

"Naked?" I bleated.

"Yes. She may or may not have engaged in sex, but from what you've admitted, and your memory lapse, we have to assume it *is* possible. I just want you to know, if your DNA turns up in, on, or around her, you are facing life without the possibility of parole."

"Life?" I yelped. He thought I was guilty!

"Multiple killings," Elvis pointed out. "That means you ain't ever seein' the outside of a cell again."

"I have nothing further to say until my attorney arrives," I avowed, with the overwhelming feeling that I was a deceased waterfowl.

They put me back into holding, and about two in the afternoon, Jeff arrived with Hank in tow.

Hank Choi was of Asian descent — first generation American — and I had worked with him on contracts with publishers. He arrived in a plain gray suit, and his hair was stuck down with several types of hair product — which may have included glue. He was shorter than me and spoke in a monotone. We were brought into an interview room.

"Can you get me out of here?" I pleaded.

"Mr. Watkins, according to the detectives, they believe your weapon was involved in a crime," Hank said. "They have the right to hold you for seventy-two hours."

"Great!" I whined. "Isn't there anything you can do?"

"I can petition the court to release you on bail, pending charges."

"So you can get me out?"

"Not before Monday," Hank said and adjusted his tie. "But I would suggest you seek a criminal attorney. I'm just a business attorney—"

"I know, but can't you—" I said.

He gave a shrug. "I do contracts."

"He's right, babe," Jeff said. "He's the attorney we use for book deals."

"Oh boy," I said, and put my head in my hands. "I am sooo screwed."

16. Rough Draft

Sheryl Homes

I knocked at the door, and then entered the interrogation room where Mark sat with two other men. I went in with Uncle Louie. Louie is a short, wiry man who chews gum vigorously and wears a two thousand dollar suit and has a bad comb-over, but he's a dear.

We were followed by Detectives DeStadler and Elvis.

"Good," Louie exclaimed, "now we're all together." He shot a finger at the Asian gentleman who was seated across from Mark. "Either of you guys his attorney?"

Mark stood and indicated one of the seated men who had the look of a smoker. "This is my agent, Jeff Moss, and—"

"Hank Choi," Louie interrupted and took the Asian man's hand. "Sorry I didn't recognize you when I walked in. Boy, are you out of *your* league."

"Why, Mr. DeSoto!" Choi seemed flustered. "I've long been an admirer—"

"Yeah, yeah," Louie demurred and turned to Jeff Moss. "You his agent? You got power of attorney?"

"Uh, yes, I do," Jeff assured.

"Great! You got a dollar?"

Mark's agent nodded and pulled out his wallet. He handed Louie a bill and Louie held it aloft for all to see.

"There you go; you are witnesses. His agent gave me a retainer. Mr. Watkins is now my client."

I stood next to Mark, who returned to his seat at the table. He looked up at me and whispered, "What is going on?"

"Just watch," I said and gave him my wicked smile.

"Okay," Louie said, his jaw moving in a rhythm of its own with the gum. "My clients have been cooperative, but they were brought here under duress and now choose to leave—"

"We found a possible murder weapon in your client's condo," DeStadler challenged.

Louie gave a nod. "For which he has a permit! Ain't that right, Mark?"

Mark recognized his cue. "Yes, I even have a carry permit."

"He even has a carry permit," Louie repeated. "I also wish to point out that you gentlemen had a *search* warrant. You did not have an *arrest* warrant."

"We have probable cause to hold them," DeStadler snapped.

Louie held his hands up as if to plead with God. "Great! Another cop who thinks he's a lawyer. It's circumstantial, detective, since you, at this time, cannot prove that Mr. Watkins' gun was indeed the murder weapon, can you?"

"Ballistics is examining it right now," DeStadler fumed.

"I see," Louie snarled. "Well, then unless Mr. Watkins was holding the weapon in his hand while standing over a corpse, my clients are not under arrest until you can produce an *arrest* warrant."

"We'll get one," Elvis assured.

"I have no doubt," Louie sneered. "But until such time as you do, I am demanding release on their own recognizance. Give them back their stuff. We are out of here."

"We already booked them," DeStadler objected, but he could see he was losing.

"Saves you paperwork later, and you are lucky I'm in a good mood and willing to overlook filing an action of false arrest," Louie hissed. "Let's go, folks."

We followed him out to the hall and he led us to the front desk, where he retrieved two manila envelopes with our things.

DeStadler and Elvis glared at us, while Hank and Jeff stood there, amazed, as if watching a magician saw a lady in half while making doves appear at his fingertips.

With DeSoto in the middle, we walked right out of the precinct and out onto 54th Street.

"Thank you, Uncle Louie," I said, and bent to give the short man a peck on the cheek.

"No problemo, sweetie," Louie dismissed. "They'll probably arrest you again, once they've got the paperwork. Say nothin' except 'not guilty' and call me."

He handed Mark a business card. "You might need this. Sherrie knows my number."

"Uh, thanks," Mark marveled.

Uncle Louie was off like a shot, carrying his big briefcase with him.

"Well," Hank Choi said to Mark. "You didn't tell me you knew Louie DeSoto."

"Actually, *I'm* the one who knows him," I offered.

"*Uncle* Louie?" Mark queried.

I shrugged, doing my "innocent girl" act. "He was my father's friend. I've known him since I was little."

"You couldn't get a better criminal attorney," Hank informed me and turned to Mark's agent. "I'll be off. You'll get the bill."

"Right, right," the other man told him. "Thanks, Hank."

Hank gave a wave as he headed for the Eighth Avenue subway.

"I guess you had it all under control," the man asserted, then looked over at me. "By the way, we haven't met, officially. I'm Jeff Moss."

"Mark's agent," I affirmed. "Sorry you had to come down here. I called Uncle Louie as soon as I could. They kept us separate, so I couldn't tell Mark we had nothing to worry about."

"We don't?" Mark stared at me in disbelief.

"Well, not immediately," I reassured.

Jeff reached past Mark and took my hand to shake it. "It's nice to meet you, Ms. Homes. My only regret is that I didn't sign you before you hit it big."

"Well, I haven't really hit it big. I mean, not like Mark."

"You're represented by Gloria Hastings, right?"

"Yes, I am," I told him as I tried to give a winning smile.

"I hear she's planning to retire," Jeff mentioned, looking serious.

"I'm afraid she is. I am currently looking for representation."

"So give me a call," Jeff volunteered, and handed me his card. "Maybe you two could do a collaboration."

Mark blinked and then looked at me.

"That might be fun," I chuckled.

"My best to Marsha," Mark mumbled, as Jeff went to the corner to grab a cab.

I watched Mark as Jeff's cab pulled away.

"Well?" I teased with a glance to Mark.

"What?"

"It *could* be fun."

"A collaboration?" Mark grunted. "I can't believe Jeff would even suggest such a thing."

Mark started to walk in the direction of the hotel, while I stayed planted in one place and felt my anger rise. "Oh, so my books suck so much—"

Mark exhaled in anger and stopped to face me. "Your books don't suck at all! I just have never... done... a collaboration."

"What about all those anthologies you edited—"

"Edited, that's the key word," Mark defended. "I got stories from other people, and in a few I wrote my own stories as part of the anthology. But I didn't write *with* someone else."

"Maybe that's what you need to get you started again." I started to walk, and Mark hurried along to keep up.

"I think we should drop this," Mark suggested testily.

"If that's what you want," I replied purposely using a snotty tone.

"I do."

It's amazing how I can adore this man one moment, and be annoyed by him the next. We trudged on in silence while both of us fumed. I pulled out my notebook once again, and began to review my notes.

After about half a block, Mark spoke up. "So, we *were* going to question Candy Poole—"

"Not anymore," I shot back grimly.

"So, where to now, Homes?"

"Any answers must be at the conference," I told him and glanced at my watch. "We should check on a few things."

I went back to my notes.

"Did the police look through that notebook?" Mark wondered.

"Oh, yes!" I told him. "They made a point to go through my purse this time, right in front of me. Of course, we threw out the gloves after we used them."

Mark frowned. "Didn't your notes about the crime scene make them suspicious?"

I gave a quick "ha" and handed Mark my notebook.

He flipped it open and immediately saw that the pages were filled with pencil scratches of numbers and symbols, with breaks for what might be words, but completely unreadable.

"What is this? Shorthand?"

"Lots of people can read shorthand," I shrugged. "It's my own code."

"Damn!" Mark beamed. "Brilliant once again, Homes."

I gave him a smile. "Protecting my stories, Watkins. I often make notes filled with story ideas. Although I think Allen Alexander is as crazy as a bedbug, it's a way to be sure my stories remain mine."

"Did DeStadler ask you what it was?"

"Oh, yes."

"What did you tell him?"

"Recipes."

He stopped walking. "Everything you'd notated hidden in plain sight."

"Where anyone could see it, but not read it."

"Anyone could see it..." Mark marveled.

"That reminds me, I forgot to mention something I saw before your speech."

I told Mark about my spotting Candy as she spoke to the shadowy male figure backstage.

Mark listened intently and handed me back my notebook. When I finished he said, "So, she had a confederate."

"Of course. If she did go to Randall's place, someone else would have to go get your gun," I surmised. "Plus, she didn't commit suicide. Her confederate shot her."

"You know all the people in the Mystery Club. Who would have a motive to kill Randall or Candy?"

I considered this as we walked. "Randall never liked Allen. I mean, who would? Almost punched him once."

"Randall did?"

"Yes, it was in our first year of marriage, when the bloom was, shall we say, still on the rose. Allen made a vulgar suggestion to me, and Randall almost decked him. Allen stopped bothering me until the divorce. Then, he believed me to be fair game and I became a pursuit, despite shutting him down every chance I could."

"Yeah, he's one classy guy," Mark huffed. "So, there is a history of animosity there."

"Randall was all right with Jon. But then there's Charles—"

"Nederlander? I thought he was Randall's partner."

"He is — was — but any time I saw the two of them together, they were always fighting over something."

"But why would either of them lock Randall up like that? And why kill Candy? I mean, we're talking about a writer, a lawyer, and an insurance salesman. Usually, they don't participate in this kind of violence."

"We need more evidence," I pointed out. "I want to talk to them, see if they know more than they let on about all this."

"I'll keep an eye out for them," Mark acknowledged.

We entered the hotel, and the pair of us took the nearest escalator to the mezzanine level.

"There's something I have to take care of," Mark told me, as we both pulled out our name badges and entered the Marketplace.

"You aren't going anywhere without me," I told him.

"Wouldn't dream of it." He reached out and gave my hand a squeeze.

My heart fluttered. Crap, I had it bad.

We approached the "YE OLDE MYSTERIOUS TOBACCO SHOPPE" booth. I stopped for a moment as we drew near.

"What's wrong?" Mark questioned.

I frowned. "Nothing, just it's odd that the first two words are so close together on that banner."

He shrugged. "Someone miscalculated when they painted it. C'mon."

We walked into the booth and there sat John Stewart.

"You had me worried," Stewart said. "I have a sale for that third pipe."

"Afraid the sale will have to be to me," Mark said, and pulled out his wallet. "The police—"

I shot an elbow in Mark's ribs to make him look at me and gave him a small head shake to say "no."

"What's this about the police?" Stewart grimaced.

"They are… uh… looking for it," Mark attempted. "But I left it in the podium the other night, and when I went there yesterday, it was gone. I think I lost it."

"Now, that's a shame," Stewart said. "Jeez, I feel bad. You using it in your speech helped me sell the other two."

"I can't cheat you, John." Mark offered a credit card.

Stewart took the card and ran it through a small machine near him. It buzzed and crackled as he returned the card to Mark.

"Well, I'm still gonna make sure you get something," John prattled, and he reached behind his table and came out with a beautifully carved wood pipe.

"That's nice," I said.

The pipe had a forty-five degree angle bend but was not as big or impressive as the pipe Mark had at the lecture, but looked like something Mark could use for any future lecture — or smoke if the desire struck him.

My father smoked a pipe. Gave it up years ago, but there was still something so masculine about the idea of Mark with a pipe. Then again, the mood I was in, anything Mark did seemed to excite me.

"You can have this. I get them for a good price," Stewart explained.

"Thank you," Mark responded.

I glanced over his shoulder at the credit card slip. Three hundred and eighty dollars, plus appropriate New York State and city taxes. I swallowed hard as Mark signed the paper.

Mark pocketed the gift pipe, and then we moved down the aisle in the convention room and headed toward the spot where the attendees and participants checked in.

"There's Jon Kane!" Mark announced, and pulled us in the direction of the tall figure.

I watched Kane with an observant eye as we approached. He indeed was tall, and although his suit hid it, he looked fit. Was he strong enough to lift and carry Mark out of Candy's room?

"Jon," I exclaimed as we drew near, and Jon looked over and his eyes grew wide.

"Sheryl? Mark?" he said. "This is… a surprise."

"Why, Jon?" I asked. "Mark and I are participants."

"No, it's just—" Jon said, obviously flustered. He pulled us to the side. "The police were asking about you."

"What about the police?" I insisted. Mark's eyes flicked right and left to see if anyone was close enough to listen.

"I heard about Randall," Jon divulged in low tones, and began to sweat. "And they found poor Candy a few hours ago. And then the police asked me a lot of questions about you and… um… you too, Mark."

"What kind of questions, Jon?" I demanded.

Jon began to squirm. "Look, I really have to focus on the conference right now. It's Friday and the weekend attendees are arriving. I have a lot to do."

"Fine. However, I'm interested in what you said to the police."

"Sheryl, Jesus Christ, everyone knew how you felt about Candy, as well as Randall," Jon said. "I don't think there's any more to tell."

"Perhaps not," I badgered. "By the way, you were the one who booked Mark for the event, right?"

"I booked all the speakers, which were approved by the committee."

"But you knew what room Mark was staying in?"

"Of course. So what?"

"Who else would know?"

"Anyone could've checked the list." Jon frowned. He glanced around one more time and added, "Look, I really have to go."

"Where did you keep this list?" I argued, not letting him go.

"It's behind the welcome booth," Jon conceded. "Usually, I am there, or Candy… maybe Alice. Occasionally Charles."

"How about Allen Alexander?" Mark put in.

I liked the way his mind worked!

Jon glanced at him. "I suppose he could have seen it. Everyone knows he's a member. It wouldn't have been unusual to see him at the booth."

"Were there times the booth was unsupervised?" I demanded, getting Jon's attention again.

"I imagine so. It's unavoidable."

"But a person would have to know what they were looking for?"

"I have to go," Jon insisted and started away.

"See you later, Jon," I said as he walked off.

"Why did you want to know about that?" Mark asked.

"You have your room key?"

Mark pulled it out of his pocket.

I continued to watch Jon as he moved through the crowd. "Notice how it doesn't show your room number."

Mark turned the card over in his hand to reveal the magnetic stripe on one side and the Hilton logo on the other. But there was no information on what room it opened.

"You're right."

"All the keys are like that, in case you lose them," I said, my eyes still observing Jon Kane. "Whoever moved you when you were drugged would have to *know* your room number."

"Well, Candy knew it, so I assume if she worked with an accomplice, she would tell him," Mark put forward.

"And since Candy's dead, it's good to know about any other possibilities."

"Look, I have to get to my room and check my laptop," Mark maintained, and we started for the elevator. "I haven't seen e-mail since Wednesday."

"I could use a change of clothes," I sighed as we got on the elevator and Mark pushed the "12" button.

The door closed, and we both stared straight ahead, and I had an overwhelming desire to kiss him. Where had that come from?

As the elevator rose to the correct floor, Mark asked, "Where do we go from here, Homes?"

"I am not sure," I replied, and I think I had turned pink from my thoughts about kissing. "Whoever did this was very organized. And he had to be after something. More than just to kill Randall. Or why go to these lengths?"

"So far, all we've got are dead ends. We didn't get anything out of going to the crime scene."

"I disagree, Mark," I said as the elevator door opened and we walked into the hall. "I got a lot out of our visit."

"Besides the bullet hole and the shell casing?" Mark pondered aloud.

"How limited you can be, Mark," I sassed, trying to drive the carnal images from my head and focus on business. "There was a lot of information for the *trained* observer."

Mark gave me a look and shoved his key card in the door of 1228. "Sometimes, young lady, you take this 'Sherlock Holmes' thing a little too far."

"Sometimes, 'old man' you don't see the obvious," I teased.

He tried the door, but it didn't open. He inserted the card a second time and a small red LED light blinked.

"What's wrong?" I asked.

"My key doesn't work. The green light is supposed to go on," Mark said and flipped the card around, which also didn't open the door.

"When did you last use it?"

"Well... Wednesday, I guess. I woke up in the room yesterday," he said. "I haven't been back until now. Could they have changed it for a new guest?"

I took the card and looked at it. "Remember how I mentioned that all the cards look alike?"

"Yes."

"What if this is a key for another door?" I suggested.

17. Footnote

Mark Watkins

I stood there dumbfounded.

"Which door would it open?" I wondered as Sheryl turned and walked down the hall.

She strode the few steps to 1230. The doorframe was marked with yellow tape that carried the words "CRIME SCENE" and formed a large "X" to block the door.

"No, no!" I warned as I rushed to stop her.

She inserted the key and the electronic lock blinked with a green light and went "click."

"You are not going in there!" I whispered adamantly.

"Of course not, Mark."

"Thank God!" I exhaled heavily.

"We both have to put on gloves and shoe covers, which I have in my room, then we go in."

She took off in the opposite direction. I gave a startled cry and followed. She quickly pulled out her own room key and opened the door of a room down the hall.

Her room was the same set-up as mine, except that the bed and desk were a mirror reflection. She marched to a hanging bag in the closet and extracted a small, thin box of latex surgical gloves, as well as several white cloth elasticized bags that I assumed were shoe covers.

"Why did you bring those?" I wondered.

"I told you I like to be prepared," she said and threw a pair at me. "Come on, glove up."

"Oh no!" I said, as she began to squeeze her hands into the rubber. "Are you crazy? We've already trespassed one crime scene —"

"Randall's apartment wasn't sealed," Sheryl clarified as she got her right hand sheathed. "So technically, *this* is the first crime scene we're violating."

"Great," I cursed, and with anger grabbed a glove and began to stretch it over my fingers. "I've been honest my entire life. In one day of knowing you, I've become a felon."

"It can only help us to look around, Mark," Sheryl explained, as she pulled out a pair of shoe covers and put them on.

"Unless we get caught," I pointed out, as I sat on the bed and covered my shoes as well, "which will convince DeStadler that we are *guilty!*"

"Come on." Sheryl held the key card aloft.

I sighed, shook my head, and followed her.

We looked both ways down the hall, then she opened the lock with the key and opened the door. The yellow tape came loose from the wood but blocked the upper part of the doorway. We both ducked, one at a time, crept into the room, and silently shut the door.

Sheryl snapped on the light.

"Jesus!" I exclaimed. There was a large brownish-red blotch in the middle of the floor next to the bed. "So much blood."

Sheryl pulled her magnifying glass out of her pocket and walked over to the spot.

"I assume she bled out on the floor after she was shot. But her blood would spatter in a blowback as a mist when she was standing—"

"What if the bullet went right through her?" I offered.

"If so, the spatter at the exit wound would be heavier," Sheryl said, and looked at the floor, then she looked at the wall opposite the stain.

"I don't see a bullet hole here, so I think the bullet didn't penetrate her completely," she mentioned, and then moved to the wall behind me.

She returned to the floor and slowly moved to the wall again.

"Let's see how this plays out," she said. "If the body fell where the stain is — Mark can you move to the left?"

"Here?" I asked, as I shifted my position.

"No, nearer the table."

I moved and looked around. "How can you tell—"

"Absence of blood spatter on the wall. There is a void. This close, the shooter's body would have blocked the spatter." She looked up and down the wall with the lens. "He was taller than you, Mark."

"That's the first good thing I've heard all day," I grimaced.

"Now, raise your arm the way you would hold a gun."

I brought up both hands in a trained shooter's stance.

"Interesting," she said, as she came over to me. She looked at the wall behind me and held her magnifying glass up.

"Hold up just one arm, Mark."

"I would never fire a gun that way."

"I'm sure," Sheryl stated. "And as far as I'm concerned, you are not a suspect."

"Could you tell DeStadler that?" I whined and dropped my left arm, with my right arm pointed in the direction of the red stain.

Sheryl looked at the wall again.

"Mark, can you lower your right arm and raise your left?"

I did, as Sheryl made affirmative grunts.

"Sheryl, if Candy was shot in this room, that begs a very important question."

"You mean why didn't anyone hear it?" Sheryl said, as she looked at the wall behind me with her lens.

"Um… yeah. I know my gun, and it is a lot louder than you'd expect. I can understand how the killer could use it down in Soho —"

"But with a hotel full of people, someone would hear the report," Sheryl considered. "I slept on this floor that night. I heard nothing."

"Elvis said she was shot through a pillow," I offered. "That would deaden the sound—"

"Yes, but not enough. You can lower your arm, Watkins."

I did as she told me.

"A pillow cannot completely deaden the sound of a nine millimeter." She thought it through. "That caliber makes a very loud noise when it explodes. However, if you used a pillow in combination with a—"

"A silencer?" I guessed.

"Excellent, Watkins."

"But how could the shooter know which silencer would fit my handgun? It's over twenty years old. And how did the killer even know I owned a gun?"

Sheryl gave a little chuckle.

"What could you possibly find funny?" I huffed, frustrated.

"I've already discovered how they could have known," Sheryl said. "This morning, I reread the dust jacket of your first book. It was on one of your shelves."

"What about it?" I muttered. "It's just my biography."

"Except it mentioned that you had been a security guard in possession of a carry permit."

I paused for a moment and tried to remember. She was correct, I had mentioned that detail on the back cover bio. The publisher thought it gave the new author some "character."

"Add to that, Watkins, gun permits are public records. A clever person — especially one with Candy's looks — could go to City Hall and find out what type of weapon you own."

I considered the implications of what Sheryl had just said. "Then this was all planned — premeditated. The killer *planned* to use me as a patsy."

"Did you examine the barrel of your pistol to see if a silencer had been fitted into it?"

"Of course not. What would I look for?"

"Scratches on the inside of the barrel — damn!" Sheryl said.

"What is it?"

"I should have thought about that last night and examined your gun. I am afraid I have not been at my best, Mark."

"I think you're fantastic," I marveled.

"Really?" She gave me a broad smile.

"You've deduced a lot more than I could have imagined. Honestly, Sheryl, if we have any chance at all, it will be because of you."

"Sh!" Sheryl said and ran to the door.

"Wha—" But I heard the electronic lock click.

Sheryl hit off the lights and I slid against the wall.

The door opened a crack, and then someone slithered in under the "CRIME SCENE" tape and shut the door.

Sheryl flashed on the lights.

With an "Oh!" of surprise, the figure rose.

There before us, with her white hair, very proper pantsuit, and indignant face was Winsley Cunningham.

18. Makeready Stage

Sheryl Homes

"What on earth are you doing here?" Ms. Cunningham said, her face red.

"I believe we could ask you the same question," I demanded, trying to sound like I was in charge.

"Yes," Mark agreed and stepped away from the wall. "We're here to find out what happened."

"I thought you two were in jail," Winsley retorted with a look of anger.

"Well, we're here now," I jeered. "You'd better tell us what you're doing here."

"How did you get in?" she inquired.

"Someone switched my key for Candy's," Mark told her. "The only other person with a copy of the key would be the murderer."

Winsley turned pale. "Oh my! You don't think I—"

"Winsley, we have nothing to lose by telling the police we were here," I explained. "And we would *love* to let them know you dropped by."

"It was because of my investments," Winsley fumed.

"The ones you have with Randall?" I put forward.

"How did you know about that?" Winsley blurted, aghast.

Mark looked at me with surprise as well.

"I know that you weren't happy with the way Randall ran them," I bluffed, as I tried to remember everything I'd overheard her say to Charles Nederlander.

The older woman threw her shoulders back and stood a little taller, as if to prepare for a fight.

"There's no crime in that!" she argued indignantly. "I am quite convinced that Randall Lawrence was cheating me."

Mark jumped in, "How?"

"Selling and buying shares and funds at a rate much faster than served me," Winsley exclaimed. "I believe he did this often, to increase his fees. I also feel that some of my earnings were not getting to my account!"

"Did you lose any money?" I wondered.

"I'm not sure. According to Randall, I did not. In fact, he claimed substantial gains."

Mark was operating with me now. "Couldn't you check?"

"My online access recently stopped working. I asked Randall to meet me at the conference with all of my financial transactions, so I could bring it to my accountant."

"So you met with Randall?" I concluded.

She eyed me suspiciously. "No, and now we all know why."

"Which brings us around once again to why you are in Ms. Poole's room," I ordered.

"I received a message from Randall on Wednesday," she implored.

"You spoke to him?" Mark asked.

"No, of all things, he left a message on the hotel voice mail."

Mark continued. "What did he want?"

"He told me that he needed to go out of town for a few days, and that he was giving my reports to Candy Poole," Winsley snorted. "He said I could pick them up from her."

"So why come here now?" I insisted.

"And how did you get a key?" Mark added.

We were working together like a well-polished team. Winsley didn't know what hit her.

"I didn't get a chance to see her," Winsley babbled. "I realized that if the police found my reports... well, it might suggest I had something to do with the poor girl's demise."

"I see," I told her.

"So I went to the welcome booth. There is always an extra key for all the staff at the attendee's booth."

"I have to tell you, Ms. Cunningham," Mark expounded, "if there were papers in this room, the police would be sure to take them."

"I thought they might be hidden," Winsley said slyly. "Ms. Poole and Randall were always so clever."

I glanced about the room. "I would say almost everything was collected by the crime scene technicians."

"Well, then," Winsley said with a grimace at the red stain on the floor, "I must be going. I would appreciate it if you did not mention any of this to the police."

"If it suits our needs, we won't." I crossed my arms in defiance.

Winsley's mouth grew tight. She didn't deal well with people not doing as she wanted.

"And if you tell the police you saw us," Mark added, "be assured we will bring up your visit."

"I see," she snarled. "I will not mention it, unless the police do so first."

"Same with us," I shot back as Winsley made her way to the door. She gave a nasty look at us, opened the door, and after she glanced both ways, snuck out.

"Watkins, quick!" I hissed.

"What?"

"Look around the floor, under the furniture. For heaven's sake, keep away from the blood."

"What am I looking for?" Mark worried.

"Didn't you see it?"

"See what?"

I knelt down and peered under the bed. "Ms. Cunningham. Didn't you see what was missing?"

"Missing?" he said, confused. "Did she forget her hat?"

"Aha!" I announced, as I reached behind the dresser. I stood up and held a green piece of jewelry.

Mark gasped as he saw what was in my hand.

A cameo with a silhouette of Sherlock Holmes.

Mark spoke first. "She was wearing that on Wednesday, but not yesterday at the panel."

"Exactly, Watkins. I've seen her wearing this cameo for years, any time I ran into her. How did it get in here?"

"Do you think *that's* what she was looking for?"

"I have no doubt, Watkins," I told him and examined the pin with my magnifying glass. "There's no blood spatter on it."

"What does that mean?" Mark wondered.

"It suggests that although Ms. Cunningham was in this room, she might not have been here when Candy was shot."

"Do you think she was in this room between Wednesday night and Thursday?"

"When you were drugged and Candy was murdered? Possibly."

"So how did the pin end up behind the dresser?"

"Perhaps a struggle," I concluded and ran my gloved finger over the cameo. "We will hold onto this, in case we need it. Let's get out of here."

19. Typesetting

Mark Watkins

A few minutes later, we were back in Sheryl's hotel room. She laid the cameo on her desk, snapped several photos with her phone, and then placed it in a zipper-closing plastic bag, which she also pulled from her luggage.

I'd reached the point where I no longer bothered to ask her why she brought such things.

We took off the gloves and shoe covers, and Sheryl put them in the plastic bag designed to line the room's ice bucket. She then got out her little memo pad and began to write with her strange hieroglyphs.

She then tied up the little bag and stuck it in her purse.

"Why'd you do that?"

"I am a suspect as well," Sheryl said. "I want to dispose of these somewhere else, in case the police search my room."

"Hmm." I was impressed. "But we still have the problem of getting the key to *my* room."

"According to Winsley, we could just go to the welcome booth for a spare, which is an interesting concept."

"How so?"

"If there are copies of all the participants' keys at the booth, anyone could have carried you back to your room."

"But if the killer needed a key to get into my room, he only needed to reach in my pocket for mine. I'm still trying to figure out how I ended up with Candy's key. Do you think this was done to further implicate me?"

"Perhaps. Or both keys were dropped, and the wrong key returned to your pocket."

"My head hurts," I told her, and rubbed my temples with my thumbs.

"Then we must take action," Sheryl suggested. "The next step will be to get you a working key and take a look in your room. Maybe we can find a clue there. Give me a moment."

She reached into the hotel closet and pulled out a gray pantsuit on a hanger.

She gave me the oddest look as if making a decision, then stepped into the bathroom. I sat on the chair to wait, but she was only a few short minutes. She had changed clothes, touched up her hair, and I believe put on a little makeup. She looked fresh and ready to face the mystery.

And not bad at all. To say I was attracted to her was easy, but why did I lack the nerve to act on it? She had stayed at my condo, and when I saw her in Susie's nightgown at the door to my bedroom, I felt an overwhelming desire for her.

And then I froze.

I was never meant to be a Romeo. I'm just a middle-aged guy who hasn't had to attempt a seduction in over twenty years. I don't have the skill set.

Just the longing.

She grabbed her purse with the plastic bag containing our discarded gloves and shoe covers as we headed for the elevator.

As we rode down, I asked, "Should I get the key from the welcome booth or the front desk?"

"The front desk, definitely," Sheryl decided. "Give them the one you're holding."

"Is that wise?"

"It's the best choice," Sheryl said. It was amazing the change that came over her when she moved into the role of the detective. Her decisions became clear and her mode of expression emotionless. "They will erase the encoding and give it back to you."

"I could just throw it out," I said.

"If you return the key as if an honest mistake were made, it would be less suspicious than if we try to dispose of it."

"Are you sure we won't need to get into Candy's room again?"

"I think I have all we need."

The elevator opened to the lobby and we stepped out.

"I'm going to take care of this," Sheryl said and indicated the plastic bag. "Then I want to check on that cameo and a few other things. Meet me in the Marketplace."

I nodded and we parted.

At the front desk, a lovely young lady in a blue uniform smiled as I approached.

"My... uh... key doesn't seem to work," I told her.

"I'm sorry. What is your room number?"

She checked my name and information as I reeled it off for her. Then after checking my identification, she took the same key, ran it through a machine, and gave it back to me.

"It will work now," she assured, and I breathed a sigh of relief.

I took the escalator back to the second floor and started across the lobby toward the Marketplace. Only to hear a shout of "Watkins!" in a voice I knew all too well.

I stopped, and without looking back said, "Not now, Allen."

"Well, well," Allen gloated, approaching me like a hunter about to bag his prey. "Heard you got arrested. Double homicide, no less."

I faced him. "I really don't have time for this—"

"I'm surprised. I mean, I didn't think you had the stones for murder."

I exhaled heavily and started to turn away.

"We know you're a thief and a plagiarist, but murder? And smothering a guy who is all tied up. Kinky stuff, Watkins."

I started walking away. He followed me.

"Not that I blame you. If I had to kill someone to get into Sheryl Homes' panties, I would seriously consider it."

I kept walking.

"But, man, you guys must've been going at it since the divorce. Always wondered why she wasn't into me. Now I know. She was grooming a guy to be willing to kill for her. Tell me, was the screwing she gave worth the screwing you'll get?"

"You're a pig, Allen," I snapped.

"Yeah, but a pig that isn't going to jail." He smirked. "Don't worry. If you take the fall, I'll take good care of Sheryl while you're gone." He drew close to me and said in a low voice, "I would love to find out if she's a *real* redhead."

I turned to him with such an angry glare that Allen backed away a couple steps.

"Ho-ho! Stay calm, Watkins. Don't make me next on your list."

He laughed at his own witticism as I turned away and walked into the Marketplace, trying to control my breathing.

I found Sheryl at the jewelry booth talking to my acquaintance of the other day, Norm Blake. It was interesting to see the two ginger-haired people talking, with their flaming locks being the most visible part as I approached.

Is she a real redhead? flashed through my mind, and I turned red, embarrassed as to where my confrontation with Allen had put my thoughts.

I really did not like that man.

Norm was in the midst of showing a selection of his wares, which he extracted from one of the plastic bins under his table. As Sheryl talked, he slid out a different bin and began to rummage through it.

"Here you go," he said, and pulled out a glass case that was about eighteen inches wide and a foot tall. Inside were cameos pinned to cloth that was part of the display. There were several that showed the unmistakable profile of Sherlock Holmes.

Each cameo had a small oval sticker with a price tag. They each ran about ten to twenty dollars.

As I approached, he gave me a nod in greeting.

"Hey, Norm," I said. "All alone today?"

"No, Cliff just went out for coffee," he explained and returned his attention to Sheryl.

"I like them," Sheryl began. "But I was after a green background."

Sheryl pulled her phone out and showed Norm the photo.

"This is the type I'm talking about," she admitted.

Norm gave a whistle of appreciation and took the phone to look at it closely. "That looks like jade. No wait, green jadeite."

"Really?"

I looked over Sheryl's shoulder and glanced at the photo. She really had gotten a good shot.

"Yeah, you see the depth of the color and the transparency?" Norm said. "To be honest, though, it isn't really a cameo."

"I don't understand," Sheryl questioned.

"I thought a cameo was just a silhouette on stone," I added.

Norm reached into the open bin and took out a display board with the more expensive choices. There were cameo pins of different sizes. He indicated one near the top: it was a pink woman in a dress on a white background.

"You see how the background is a different color? *That's* a true cameo. The art is to have stone — usually agate — with layers of color, and the silhouette is a relief that is a contrasting hue from the background, as it is in a different layer of the stone."

He then pointed at his table where he'd set up several tools. There was a small stone held by a vise that suspended it up so the front of the stone faced out. A large magnifying lens with a light, suspended by a metal arm was aimed to enlarge the surface he worked on. A silhouette was half-carved into the surface, and you could see the background color being revealed as the layers were stripped away. Several tools lay on the table, including a small battery-powered Dremel and something resembling a dentist's drill.

"Like this, see?" He pointed at the piece in the vise. Then he indicated the photo on Sheryl's phone. "That's merely a relief, but the workmanship is very good—"

"Do you have anything like it?" Sheryl said.

Norm gave a derisive snort. "I wish. To be honest, I wouldn't bring something this expensive to an event like this."

"Why not?" Sheryl wondered.

Norm shrugged. "Nobody has the money for a piece like this at a fan-con. I bring the less expensive stuff that people will shell out for."

"So," she said, "how much would this go for?"

Norm looked at the phone again.

"If that setting is gold, which it appears to be — anywhere from two to five, if that's really jade."

"Hundred?" I asked.

"*Thousand*, depending on the artist," Norm said. "But I don't know. It's hard to tell in the photo, but from the color, it might just be Imperial Jade. If it is, you are talking forty grand."

I gave a quick, impressed whistle.

"Well thank you for your help," Sheryl said.

"Here, take this!" He extracted a business card from his pocket. "If you're serious, I might be able to track something like that down for you."

I looked over to see Cliff walking over with two cardboard cups — I assumed coffee. However, he was talking and smiling with none other than Hypno, the woman from John Stewart's booth.

They were both tall, and instead of the dour look she always gave me, she was smiling and possibly laughed at something he said.

She gave a squeeze to Cliff's arm and wandered off, her face becoming hard as she strode away.

"That would be great," Sheryl said to Norm. "I'll call you."

"Thanks, Norm," I said, as Cliff wandered up.

"Hey, great speech the other night," Cliff mentioned, as he handed a cup to Norm.

"You got to catch it?"

"Yeah, man, it was—" he said and stopped as he gazed upon Sheryl. "Um… yeah… you were there, too."

Sheryl took my arm in hers. "Yes, I would never miss a chance to hear Mark speak."

"I… uh… thought you two didn't like each other."

"Where would you get an idea like that?" I said.

As Cliff stared, Sheryl and I wandered off.

"You're tracking down the cameo?" I asked quietly. "I thought we agreed that it was Winsley's."

"Data! Data! Data!" she said as we walked. "I can't make bricks without clay."

I smiled at the Holmes quote. "Well, I wish I'd borrowed the Calabash pipe from him."

"What do you mean?"

"Turns out he had a pipe almost identical to the one I lost, and about two hundred dollars cheaper."

Sheryl stopped walking and faced me.

"You saw this pipe?"

"Saw it? I picked it up and compared them—" I stopped talking as the realization hit me.

"You picked up another pipe?"

"Which would have put my fingerprints—" I started to say.

"On a *second* pipe," Sheryl completed my sentence.

We stared at each other and a smile broke over her face.

"Come on." She grabbed my arm and pulled me down another aisle and around until we could see the jewelry booth of Norm Blake from a different angle.

She put up an arm to stop my forward progression, in a position so we were slightly hidden. She stared at Norm, who was talking to an elfin princess.

I whispered, "Do you think he—"

"I don't know, but it could explain how your fingerprints ended up on a pipe at Randall's."

"But the two pipes were different. I mean, one of them had a red 'X' on the bottom."

"Which one?"

"Mine, I mean, the one I used at the lecture."

The princess nodded to Norm, and as she sashayed away, Norm went back to his work area as Cliff followed her chain-mail covered rear end with his eyes.

Cliff sighed, as Norm picked up a tool.

I wondered, "What are we—"

"Sh."

She watched as Norm started to use the dentist drill carefully on the cameo held in the vise.

She nodded and turned to me. "Okay, we can go."

"What?" I said. "I mean, how come?"

"I saw what I needed to see," Sheryl announced simply.

"What was that?"

"Ah, Mark, you see, but you do not observe."

I smiled. She was quoting Holmes from *A Scandal In Bohemia*.

"Okay." I thought carefully. "I saw Cliff watch the elf lady's ass, and Norm go back to his carving."

"Yes, which he worked on with his *left* hand. He's left-handed."

"What difference does that make?"

Her eyes lit up. "Quick, do you have that pipe Stewart gave you?"

"Yes, but why—"

"Give it to me," Sheryl said. I pulled it from my pocket and handed it to her as we approached the YE OLDE MYSTERIOUS TOBACCO SHOPPE.

John Stewart was getting his booth ready for the Friday night rush, pulling out more things and setting them out to be found quickly. Hypno was there, and they both looked up as we approached.

"I forgot to ask," Sheryl chirped, "can we get some tobacco for this pipe?"

"No need. I'll probably just use it for effect in future lectures," I told her.

"Be a sport, Mark," Sheryl gushed, giving me a look that suggested I should shut up. "We would like some tobacco." She drew closer to Stewart and added, "Something mild."

"What—" I started to say.

"Who is your tall friend?" Sheryl interrupted, with a nod toward the woman.

"That's Hypno," Stewart declared as he went through a box.

The woman gave Sheryl an admiring look from head to toe.

"Hypno, how unusual," Sheryl intoned. She didn't back down, but returned the stare with equal intensity.

"I met her in physical therapy," John explained.

"John has made a lot of progress," Hypno related. "He has a lot more strength than when we met."

"Enough to keep up with you?" Sheryl suggested and seemed to flirt with the Amazon.

"He's one of the few men that ever could," Hypno replied with a wolfish grin.

"Hypno, we should start moving the boxes under the table," Stewart stressed.

She glanced at him, then her eyes grew small and she whispered to Sheryl, "Men. They are always so possessive."

"What do you think would be a good tobacco for this?" Sheryl threw my pipe to the woman.

With fast reflexes, Hypno plucked it out of the air.

"Easy with that," Stewart said. He was not happy about his product flying about.

"It's fine, John." Hypno smirked at him. She turned the pipe over in her hand and shrugged. "Any good tobacco will do."

"Thank you," Sheryl purred, and took the pipe from her gently, then gave her a big smile. "You've been a lot of help."

"Anything you need, keep me in mind," Hypno vowed, not backing down. She then picked up a large plastic bin, hefted it to her left shoulder with no effort, and walked away.

"I tell her to use the dolly, but she don't listen," Stewart complained. He pulled out a pouch, opened the top, which closed like a zipper, and held it out. "Smell"

Sheryl took a deep inhale and made an "ohh!" of approval.

I sniffed at it, and it was very woodsy without being too sweet.

"We'll take it," Sheryl offered, and reached into her purse. "My treat, Mark."

"Okay," I agreed, still with no idea what she was doing.

She drew out a check and began to write. Stewart mentioned a price and Sheryl nodded. It sounded expensive to me, but I went along with it.

"I would suggest," Stewart told me as Sheryl wrote, "that you oil that pipe for a few days."

"Oil it?" I repeated.

"Yeah for the wood," Stewart explained. "Preserves it. Just hit it with some fine furniture oil. Y'know, lemon oil or something. Don't get it in the bowl though."

"For how long?" I said.

"A few days. I wouldn't smoke it until you do."

"Okay."

She handed him the check. "Do you want to see my driver's license?"

"Nah, I know you're with the Mystery Club," Stewart dismissed.

"By the way," Sheryl pondered, and leaned closer to him. "Who bought the other pipes like the one Mark lost?"

"Why?" Stewart said, suspicious.

"Just curious," she shrugged.

"Well, one was a guy walking around in a deerstalker hat," John confirmed, as he pulled out a receipt book and shuffled through the pages.

"I saw him," I noted.

Stewart held up a page in the book and said, "The other was Charles Nederlander."

20. Fore-Edge

Sheryl Homes

"Charles bought the last pipe?" I said in my best bubbly voice. "Really?"

"He told me it would be a good addition to his collection," John responded. "Didn't buy any tobacco, though."

"If Mark needs to order more, do you have a business card?"

John reached into the plastic bin and brought out a card.

I took it with a smile. "Thanks so much."

"No problem," John admitted, and went back to putting out items for sale. "Visit us anytime. We're out in New Jersey."

"I see." I glanced at the card. "In Somerville. How far is that?"

"'Bout an hour."

"Thanks," Mark said, and gave a wave as we strolled away.

I could feel him watching me. I didn't want to meet his eyes and start the randy roller coaster going again. Jeez, I had him in my hotel room, and what did I do? I wimped out and changed in the bathroom. If I had started to undress in front of him, that might have gotten a better reaction.

Then again, I all but offered myself to him at his bedroom door, and that didn't get a rise out of him. I guess when it finally became time to take this to the next level, I would have to be the one to do it.

I was at the point where I was ready to club him and drag him off, if that would work.

I drove my lusty thoughts away and tried to focus on the case.

"You okay?" he asked.

I started, embarrassed that once again I had fallen into wanton meanderings. "Yes, sure, sorry."

"Where are we going?"

I tightened my mouth to a firm line. "To find Charles Nederlander."

We walked into the lobby. The welcome booths were getting quite busy at this point. People were stuck in lines, carrying suitcases, computer bags, and backpacks.

A few people milled around in costume, but I was sure the number would increase as the evening unfolded. We wended our way past the Benedict Cumberbatch lookalikes, guys in deerstalker hats, and even one fellow dressed like Peter Falk in *Columbo*.

Mark hurried to keep up, as I have quite a long stride. We moved past the elevator banks and down a long hallway to the other side of the building where the meeting rooms were filling with people for the lectures and panels of the day.

Ahead of us down the hall, I could see Charles Nederlander.

He stood in the doorway of a meeting room, and I heard the voice of a lecturer who sounded like Winsley Cunningham.

As we approached, he blanched and began to close the door, so people in the meeting wouldn't hear us.

"Sheryl," he said quietly but enthusiastically. "So glad to see that the police are not holding you. What a terrible situation—"

"Can it, Charles," I told him.

Charles backed up and looked at me with a deer-in-the-headlight stare.

I drew close and stabbed his chest with my index finger. "Why did you buy a pipe from the YE OLDE MYSTERIOUS TOBACCO booth?"

"Sheryl, I collect a few odds and ends—"

"But why the same one as Mark?"

He hesitated to collect his thoughts. "Well, he used it at his lecture, and I thought it was quite a fine specimen. Really, Sheryl, I don't know what I've done to make you exhibit this kind of behavior—"

"There are a few other things that don't add up," I went on. "Candy was shot—"

This made his color fade a little more. "Yes, a tragedy and right here at the hotel—"

"The police think Mark did it."

Nederlander glanced over at Mark. "Really? Mr. Watkins, I am so sorry to hear—"

"The police are wrong," I interrupted.

His eyes darted back to me. "Of course, they're wrong. Mr. Watkins would never—"

"No, they are wrong because the killer was over five feet eleven inches tall and left-handed."

Charles flushed. "Well, that's all very—I mean, how do *you* know that?"

"You're left-handed, Charles, and you are about six feet tall," I asserted. "And my guess is that you are the right build—"

"This is preposterous!" Charles fumed. "How could you possibly suggest this?"

"Blood spatter, Charles," I goaded. "It leaves the body as a fine mist, but in close quarters it would spray the shooter. If the shooter was near a wall, as in this case, it would leave a rough outline in the victim's blood."

"You couldn't know—" Then he looked at both of us in horror. "Oh my God, you went *into* Candy's room."

"I think the police will be interested in my conclusions, and they have the technology to prove my assumption."

"Fine!" he bellowed. "Everyone knows you hated Candy and Randall. I have no motive—"

"What if they look at your *finances*, Charles?"

"What?" He was shaken by this. "My finances? What does that have to do with this?"

"I believe everything. Ms. Cunningham was pressuring you and Randall to supply her with a full accounting. In my divorce, we found some inaccuracies in Randall's records."

"I am not aware of any inaccuracies—"

"Even if there are, you don't have to worry now. You can just blame any problems on your deceased partner."

Charles glared at me. "I am sure evidence will be found that will point to the killer, whoever it is!"

"Know something the rest of us don't, Charles?" I demanded.

"I don't have to take this from you!" Charles chided and turned away.

"Just be sure you can show that pipe to the police if they ask, Charles."

We walked away as I pulled out my notebook and angrily scrawled notes. We arrived back at the elevator, as I continued to jot my ideas down.

Mark interrupted. "You know that the killer was over six feet tall and left-handed because of the blood spatter?"

"Yes." I wrote while we walked. "That's why I had you stand in different positions and hold up your arms. I was looking at the wall behind you. I think if we can bring that information to Detective DeStadler, it could put them in the correct direction."

Mark stopped walking.

"What is it, what's wrong?" I asked, and looked up from my pad.

"That's what you were checking at the jewelry booth! Norm was left-handed," Mark marveled.

"Of course. That was also why we stopped at the tobacco booth, and I threw that Hypno person the pipe. She caught it with her left hand."

"Wow," was all Mark could manage.

"Well, with only about ten percent of the population being left-handed, it is a remarkable coincidence that so many of them are here… and connected to Candy's murder."

I looked around at the halls that were rapidly filling up.

"This isn't the place to discuss this," I suggested and took Mark's arm to direct him to the elevator bank.

We got into an elevator and Mark pushed the "12" button.

"That means I didn't kill her," Mark disclosed.

"Of course not."

"I wasn't absolutely sure until now."

"Mark, you couldn't do something like that."

"Sheryl, I can't remember a *thing* from that night. It's possible I could've killed her and then blanked it all out."

"You were drugged, Mark."

"So, someone set me up to be the fall guy."

"It might be more than that."

"Then what?"

I gave him a sly smile. "I don't have all the facts yet."

"Will it be enough to clear me… uh… us?"

The elevator door opened and we stepped out. "The problem is," I went on as we walked, "that we are not aware of any other clues that the murderer may have created to misguide the—"

I stopped as we both looked at the door to Mark's room, number 1228.

It was open.

I put a finger to my lips and we moved to the wall and slowly made our way quietly to the door and peeked in.

A uniformed officer spotted us. "Here they are, sir," he bellowed, and in one quick movement, he grabbed Mark by the collar and me by the arm.

"Well, look who we have here," a familiar voice rang out.

"Detective DeStadler," Mark greeted and attempted to remain glib, despite the officer holding him so near his windpipe. "Been so long, I thought you didn't like us anymore."

"No, you are two of my favorite people. Especially since I've got the nail for your coffin, right, Bobby?"

"Um — yes, sir," a thin young man answered. He looked about sixteen and had a protruding Adam's apple. Mark and I were brought into the room, where the young man was standing in front of Mark's laptop, which was open and running.

"Hey!" Mark protested. "What are you doing to my computer?"

"We have a warrant to go through your hotel room, as well as your personal effects," DeStadler reported, and showed a paper. "Actually, all we had to do was ask the hotel to let us in, but since you are now represented by Louie DeSoto, I wanted to make sure that nothing gets thrown out of court."

"But my laptop…" Mark attempted.

"Bobby here is with the Computer Crime Unit," DeStadler explained and gave a nod to the young man. "Seems he found something interesting."

"Look, if you came across my new book idea, it really isn't very good," Mark observed as DeStadler took his arm and pulled him toward the computer.

"You have a right to remain silent, do it!" DeStadler warned. "Bring it up, Bobby."

Bobby opened the computer's e-mail program, then opened a folder of messages. A window appeared on the screen. Both Mark and I peeked over the policeman's shoulder and saw the message. It read:

S-

The task is done, just the way you asked.

M

"What is that?" Mark demanded.

"Look at the recipient," DeStadler chuckled, and I could tell he enjoyed this.

On the address line was shomes@sherylhomes.com.

My email address.

"Also look when it was sent," De Staler exulted, quite pleased with himself.

The message was dated on Thursday morning at 03:45 AM.

"I—I—" Mark said profoundly.

"This is bullshit," I barked, furious.

"Oh, I don't know, Ms. Homes," DeStadler said. "That *is* your e-mail address, isn't it?"

"Yes, it is, detective," I fumed. "I think the fact that this was sent from here makes it obviously planted, even to you."

"Looks to me like it proves a connection, and that the two of you planned these murders," DeStadler accused. "Cuff him, officer."

Mark was whirled around and cuffs once again were slapped on his wrists.

"Really, Detective DeStadler," I complained. "I was staying in the hotel and didn't bring a laptop or tablet. I wouldn't return home to my computer until Monday. Why would Mark send me a traceable e-mail when he could just walk down the hall and tell me, without leaving a record?"

DeStadler paused for a moment. Apparently, this idea had not occurred to him. But he blustered through it. "You could have read it on your phone. Besides, Bobby hasn't had a chance to dig very deep. I'm sure there are a lot more messages between the two of you that were erased."

At this point, I'd had it. I got into his face. "Wouldn't a more logical theory be that whoever drugged Mark and moved him to this room dashed off a quick e-mail to incriminate us?"

DeStadler took a step back and glanced at Bobby.

Bobby shrugged. "The computer isn't password protected. Anyone could have turned it on and sent the e-mail."

"Bring that," he spat at Bobby and pointed at the laptop. "And bring him," he said to an officer who pushed Mark forward.

"You can't!" I yelled.

"Oh yes, I can," DeStadler roared. "I brought an arrest warrant for Mr. Watkins, and Detective Elvis will be executing a search warrant at *your* residence."

"My place?" I said. I had to admit, this threw me.

"You have a choice," DeStadler jeered. "You can give me your keys, or we can break down the door."

I reached into my pocketbook, extracted the keys, and handed them over to the detective. "Where will I stay, while you violate my property?"

He shrugged. "You can stay here at the hotel, or if you prefer, I can arrange for you to spend the night in a holding cell."

I was whipped. No point dragging it out. "I'll stay here."

"Don't leave the hotel," DeStadler ordered.

"I won't," I replied, wanting to kick the bastard in the crotch. I looked at Mark. "I'll call Uncle Louie."

DeStadler gave an explosive laugh. "Even he won't get your accomplice out of a cell before morning. Okay, officer, take him out."

I ran up to Mark and grabbed him in a ferocious bear hug. "You take care, Mark." I pressed my lips to his.

"Enough of that," DeStadler said, and the officer pulled us apart.

As we parted, I saw a look of amazement on Mark's face. It was as if the intensity of our kiss surprised him. I had to admit, I was breathing heavily myself, overwhelmed by the heat of it.

Mark was led out of the room, a smile on his face. I had been unexpectedly thrown into a heady trance, but I still managed to swipe his house keys from his jacket pocket and palm them so the police didn't see.

21. Narrative

Mark Watkins

DeStadler might not have been right about my guilt, but he was right about one thing: I spent the night in jail.

Of course, DeStadler questioned me in an interrogation room, and I took that opportunity to suggest he check the blood spatter on the wall to gauge the height of the killer.

"How did you know there was blood spatter?" he demanded.

"You said Ms. Poole was shot point blank," I chided. "It's a small room and it's a logical deduction, especially if she was shot with a nine millimeter, which you also suggested."

"You and Ms. Homes are full of theories," he chided. "Let me make it clear to you. You are not a detective. You are a suspect."

"I'm just trying to clear my name," I related.

"Or hide evidence and send us in the wrong direction. Well soon, I'm gonna have ballistics to prove Poole was murdered with your gun."

I decided it would be wise to not speak any further without my attorney present.

DeStadler grumbled and had me escorted to one of the holding cells.

I sat and made myself as comfortable as one can in a cell. I didn't know what time it was, as my watch, wallet, and phone, as well as my gift pipe had been confiscated. I decided I was lucky they didn't take my shoelaces and belt as well.

I may have dozed for a few minutes when I felt myself being shaken.

"Wha—" I opened my eyes to see a police officer there.

"Your lawyer is here." I rose and he escorted me to another interrogation room.

At the table sat Louie DeSoto. He nodded to the officer, who took the cuffs off me and left the room.

"Hey, Mark, how ya doin'?"

"As fine as can be expected," I conceded. "I guess you heard?"

"Yeah, Sherrie called me, brought me up to speed."

"What happens now?" I inquired.

"They're moving you to Central Booking and you'll spend the night at Rikers Island."

"Great," I groaned. "What time is it?"

"About 6:30. Sherrie told me about the email. That doesn't prove a thing. However, if ballistics can prove that your gun is the one that killed Ms. Poole, it is *not* going to help."

"I'm sure of that." I shook my head. "Whoever set this up did it very well."

"Sheryl said not to worry."

"Really, is she planning a prison break?"

"Actually, she told me to tell you that she thinks she's on the right track."

"I find that hard to believe," I protested. "This track keeps taking twists that no one could see coming."

"Well, if anyone could, I'd put my money on her," Louie affirmed. "So, when you get to Central Booking, at some point they'll stick you in front of a judge. Plead 'Not Guilty' and say nothing else. Got that?"

"I got it."

"They will schedule a bail hearing for tomorrow morning. Me and Sherrie will both be there, okay?"

"So, I'm spending the night at Rikers?"

"Hey, it could be worse."

"I cannot imagine how."

"I'll see you in the morning."

Louie was up and was buzzed through the door. I was returned to my cell where I spent the next hour or so.

I was finally pulled out of my nice holding cell, put in a police car, and driven downtown to Central Booking at 100 Centre Street in downtown Manhattan.

I was seen by an Emergency Medical Technician to make sure I was "medically fit." He checked my blood pressure and put a stethoscope to my chest. I got a passing grade.

Then after going from location to location and having paperwork filled out about me, I was taken to a shabby room and interviewed by someone from the prosecutor's office who seemed overly concerned that I was a flight risk.

I said as little as possible and signed papers where I was told.

Then I was fed a cheese sandwich, went to court to see a judge, and entered my plea of "Not Guilty." The judge set my bail hearing for the next morning, as Louie had predicted.

After that, I was loaded onto a bus with several other hardened criminals and driven to Rikers Island, where I was sent to the Eric M. Taylor Center. That facility usually houses adolescents, but also seems to house people who are considered "non-violent," or in my case "easy prey."

I was stripped naked to see if I carried contraband. They were very thorough in my inspection. On the humorous side, it was the most physical contact with another person I'd had in two years.

I was then given a fashionable orange jumpsuit, led to my cell, which fortunately only had two bunks. The halls possessed the overwhelming smell of urine, sweat, bleach, and stale food in a combination that was an impressive and overpowering fragrance.

In the cell, the toilet was in plain sight, as I knew it would be. Some of the novels I did before the Holmes books had prison scenes, and I made a point of doing my research.

Still, it was disconcerting to lose all of my privacy.

My bunkmate was in the cell, a thin little man with glasses, who seemed relieved that I was not a large, burly fellow with multiple tattoos and scars.

He tried to strike up a conversation and explained he was there for embezzlement, but that it was all a misunderstanding.

He asked what I was in for.

"Double homicide," I told him.

He ceased trying to make small talk with me after that.

At dinner we were escorted to the cafeteria, which was reminiscent of high school with the same type of bench tables with the seats being one unit that all folded up when the meal was done.

Of course, the food was terrible and you had only about five minutes to eat it.

I kept my head down, and I was mostly ignored at dinner. It probably helped that most of the prisoners were adolescents. My bunkmate and I were escorted back to our cell to sleep, which was difficult with the lights on, the unending noise, and the loud snoring of my skinny embezzler roommate.

In the morning, tired, untoward, and groggy, I was allowed to change into the clothes I'd arrived in and driven back by bus to 100 Centre Street for my court appearance.

I was put on a line and we entered what I later found out was called "The Tombs." It was a series of holding cells in the building next to the courthouse. We each passed a small desk and a man checked our names on a list. When he located mine, he had an officer escort me immediately to an elevator.

I cannot tell you how happy I was to walk into the courtroom and see Louie DeSoto there. I also looked up to see Sheryl in the first row of the gallery. She looked so amazing, I literally lost my breath for a moment. Her eyes flashed when she caught sight of me, and I wanted to take her in my arms with every fiber of my being.

"Hey, Mark, sleep well?" Louie asked quietly, his jaw moving as he bit into a fresh piece of gum.

"More than I expected, I guess," I remarked.

"ALL RISE," the bailiff yelled.

We stood as the judge, a heavy man with a thick mustache in a robe that barely covered his girth, climbed slowly up on the bench. He sat and began to go through papers.

"You may be seated," he told the crowd, and we returned to our seats.

"The people of the state of New York versus Mark Watkins," the bridge officer said, then turned to Louie. "You waive the reading?"

"Yeah, yeah," Louie said. I shot him a glance, not knowing what any of this meant, and he held up a hand, as if to say he had it covered.

The bridge officer gave the judge a folder, and the judge carefully went through it.

The woman at the other table in a cheap but neat pantsuit, who I assumed was the prosecutor, waited until the judge finished perusing the documents, then stood and spoke. "Your Honor, we want to make notice that this case is One-Ninety-Fifty, and we are making a Seven-Ten-Thirty-A with it."

Again I looked at Louie, but he kept his small beady eyes on the judge, who made a few pencil notes on the folder.

"Bail?" the judge said.

"Your Honor," the prosecutor announced, "this is a double homicide. We recommend the defendant be remanded."

Louie stood up and raised his hand as he spoke. "Louis DeSoto representing Mark Watkins, Your Honor."

"Yes, Mr. DeSoto," the judge sighed wearily. He seemed quite familiar with Louie.

"My client is a respected member of the community, who owns a condominium where he has lived for over twenty years—"

"And is the suspect in a murder-for-hire plot," the prosecutor said.

"At this time, the investigators have no proof that it was my client's pistol that was used in said homicide. I would also like to point out that my client only owns a handgun because of his close connection to law enforcement."

"The defendant was a security guard, years ago," the prosecutor complained.

The judge frowned. "Has this case been presented to the grand jury?"

"The murders occurred Thursday, Your Honor," the prosecutor admitted.

"And it's Saturday. Who says we don't make quick arrests in New York?" the judge noted. "Until the charges come from the grand jury, I will release Mr. Watkins on $100,000 bond. I will also ask that his passport be surrendered."

He pounded his gavel, and Louie slapped me on the back and walked with me out of the courtroom.

"That was a lucky break," Louie said. "I got you in the morning calendar because I knew they wouldn't have enough evidence yet."

"Yeah, but I don't have $100,000," I stated.

"It's a bond. You'd only need $10,000."

"Oh!"

"Don't worry, I think we've got you covered," Louie said, and then his face grew serious. "By the way, did you say something to the police, anytime they questioned you?"

"Nothing important that I can think of," I said.

"Well, the prosecutor made a Seven-Ten-Thirty-A notice. Which means what you told them is going to be used it court. Did you confess to something?"

"N-nothing comes to mind."

"Well, think about it," Louie said, his jaw moving quickly on his gum. "I need you to get me your passport by Monday, okay?"

I nodded.

We were soon in an office, filled out the necessary paperwork, and I was released.

I walked out puzzled, since I hadn't made any financial arrangements. Sheryl walked up holding a manila envelope and gave me a hug.

She took a step back and crinkled her nose. "My, that is quite a smell you have on you."

"Yeah," I snickered, "there is nothing like the stink of prison." I turned to Louie. "How did my bail get covered?"

Louie glanced sidelong to Sheryl. "Ask her. In the meantime, I got other clients. She's got your stuff. We'll talk."

And with a wave, he was gone.

Sheryl handed me the envelope and I extracted my wallet, watch, phone, and even the pipe I'd been given yesterday.

"Your house keys are there too," she said quietly. "I threw them in there."

"What happened to the bag of tobacco?" I wondered.

"That was in my purse, remember?" Sheryl said. "I left it at your place."

"Good plan," I said with a nod, and moved the items to my sports coat pockets. The pipe went in my outer right one.

"You look terrible."

I paused and looked over this beautiful woman in front of me. "And you look like a dream."

She smiled, and her eyes lowered to slits as if my statement had sent a shiver down her spine. "My place isn't far from here. How about you come have a shower and some breakfast?"

"I cannot agree fast enough," I complied.

We walked down the long court staircase to the street to catch a cab, and I asked, "How *did* my bail get paid?"

"I covered it," she explained, her head down. "Uncle Louie knows a bail bondsman. We set it all up this morning."

I stopped. "You did?"

"Mark, you got pulled into this because of me. I felt I owed you, and I don't think you're going to skip town." Her eyes twinkled as she looked at me. "Besides, I believe I know who did it!"

22. Backlist

Sheryl Homes

M ark stopped and stared at me as I flagged down a cab. "Who?"

"Not here," I confided as we got in the cab.

The yellow taxi was driven by a man whose body odor easily overpowered even Mark's prison smell, and after I gave him the address, he drove north toward Greenwich Village.

"So when you took my keys…"

"Yes?"

"Was all that just an act?"

I flushed so red, I was surprised I didn't light up like an LED. I couldn't meet his eyes, so I just stared at the floor of the cab, trying to control myself.

I cleared my throat. "Maybe not all of it…"

Mark smiled, and it was glorious to behold. "Good!"   H e glanced at the cab driver and spoke quietly. "Because that kiss was something."

I kept my eyes on the floor, flushing even more if it was possible. "I agree."

We rode on in silence. I felt that we both wanted to say more, but we were just too tongue-tied. I spoke first. "You're very quiet."

Mark jumped. I decided he had been thinking about this admission as well. "Sorry, lost in thought. I guess I seriously need a cup of coffee."

We got out of the cab near Broadway and West 4th Street, and Mark followed me to the six-story brownstone my apartment is in. I like the building because it's old, but recently renovated, with large cement steps and a wooden arched front door. I pulled out my keys, and we went up one flight of stairs inside the building.

My apartment is the entire second floor and similar to Randall's open floor plan, though much more modest. Mark was impressed as we walked into the kitchen, which opened to the dining and living area. The kitchen did have new fixtures and the living room contained good, solid furniture.

Mark gave a whistle. "I think your books are doing better than mine."

"I got money in the divorce."

"Apparently more than I imagined."

Mark took off his jacket as I led him to the master bathroom, which contained a large bathtub, as well as a shower, and a dual sink counter.

"Your tub is larger than my entire bathroom," he chuckled.

"I put out a robe," I told him, "and I picked up underwear, socks, and a fresh shirt while I was at your apartment last night."

"Is that why you stole my keys?"

"No, picking up your stuff was just a side benefit. At least, for you. I stole your keys to catch the killer."

"So who is it?"

I couldn't fight the smile on my face. "Get cleaned up and I might just tell you."

"Tease," he accused with a smile.

"Nothing but," I told him as I exited the bathroom and shut the door. I stayed on the other side of the door as I listened for the shower to turn on. When it started, I leaned against the door and shut my eyes, as the image of Mark naked ran through my head.

I shook myself and walked past my full-length mirror and caught my reflection. Yes, I was red with embarrassment once again. I needed to get a handle on that. But I also saw something else in my own eyes.

I had spent the time since the divorce avoiding the idea of dating, and I had simply shut down sexually. But I saw myself and I looked vibrant, alive. Wanting Mark and reacting to his desire for me had made my eyes brighter, and I was surprised by the change.

I heard the shower finish, and I went to my desktop computer and tried to focus.

Mark came out in nothing but a bathrobe. He was clean, his full head of hair wet, and I had to admit, even the stubble on his chin looked damn sexy. I focused on my screen, not daring to look at him.

"My clothes?" he asked and gave me a smile. "Unless you prefer me like this."

He had given me an opening. I wanted to go all sultry and say, "That's perfect. Why don't we both get comfortable," or at least knock out a double entendre or even stand up and yank open his robe. Instead, I squeaked, "In the bedroom, you'll find the clothes I brought."

He gave a nod and walked where I pointed. When he closed the door, I fell into my chair and slapped my forehead with the palm of my hand. What the hell happened to me? I used to know how to entice a man! Now, I possessed all the seductive charm of a vacuum cleaner.

Mark dressed quickly and came out in his underwear to get his pants, and I nearly lost it, flushing beet-red again, and then cursing myself for doing it.

I pretended to keep working on the computer until Mark was completely dressed. Then when he came out, I jumped up to make him coffee so I had something to do and hopefully not make a fool of myself.

"You wanted coffee, right?" I told him and stood in the kitchen where the large island acted as a table. "Are you hungry?"

Mark moved to the table, his eyes still burned into me. "Ravenous."

"I made soup. I'll get you some while I bring you up to date."

"Up to date?"

I turned to heat the pot on the stove and began to brew coffee in my little one-cup coffeemaker. "About our killer."

As the coffee machine gurgled away, I pulled a white bowl from a frosted glass-front cabinet and ladled soup into it.

Mark sat and watched me. "I thought you didn't cook."

"This is a special occasion," I chirped.

I turned to face him and our eyes met, and I almost dropped the soup. I carefully put it down in front of him, feeling all warm inside.

He took the spoon and ate, and I soon put the mug of coffee next to the bowl.

Twenty minutes and a second helping later, Mark pushed the bowl away and said, "So, I'm ready to hear what you found out."

"Good," I said, and got my head to business. "Well, you know that I got your keys last night—"

"Nicely done," Mark smiled, I hoped, from the memory of that kiss.

"That was part of my plan. I used your keys and spent the night at your place."

His mouth fell open. "Despite DeStadler telling you to stay at the hotel?"

"I didn't bother them while they searched here, did I?" I protested. "I hate the idea that they were going through my stuff. They confiscated most of my lab."

"Your lab?"

I gave him my wicked smile. "I found it helped when I wrote the Holmes books if I had my own little lab, just in a corner over there. Simple things: a microscope, a chemistry set, fingerprint powder, scanner. They took everything." I sighed. "I'm just glad they left my computer. However, I am sure they cloned the hard drive, so they could look at my emails and such."

"Wish they'd done that with my laptop, that way I'd still have it. So you camped out in my apartment?"

"I was certain our killer would return," I pointed out.

"How so?"

"He made copies of your keys. Why make them if you don't want to get in? I also assumed he knew you were arrested."

Mark nodded in agreement. "You deduced that if he was going to plant more false evidence, it would be whilst I was in jail."

"Whilst?" I chuckled. "Yes. But he wouldn't know I was there or that we'd changed the lock."

"I'm certainly glad we did—"

"So, I slept on the couch for a while. At about midnight, I heard someone put a key in your door. I roused myself and crawled over to listen."

"What happened?"

"He had no trouble opening the two old locks. His key fit the new one, but he couldn't open it. While he struggled, I looked through the fisheye lens in the door."

Mark stood up. "Who was it?"

"The hall was pretty dark, and that fisheye distorts things a bit, but I did get a good look."

Mark leaned toward me. "And it was?"

"Jon Kane."

23. Foolscap

Mark Watkins

I sat still as death for a moment and tried to get my brain around this new information. "Jon Kane?"

"It makes sense, Mark," Sheryl offered.

I considered this. "He's the one who hired me for the conference."

She ticked off each point on her fingers. "He had access to the spare room keys. He had a business relationship with Randall, and he was in charge of the conference."

"With Candy working under him."

Sheryl raised an eyebrow. "So, he could convince her to drug you."

"I don't get it. He eliminates Randall and then Candy. Why?"

"I think it all goes back to Randall's money, and the fact that Ms. Cunningham was demanding an accounting. Last night, I spoke to the forensic accountant that worked on my divorce. In the past, he'd told me there were discrepancies with Randall's income versus his wages."

"How did he find that out?" I pressed.

"Randall's income compared to his lifestyle. The accountant felt that Randall had an income stream that could not have legally come from his clients."

"So, you believe Randall created some kind of 'slush' fund illegally?"

She nodded. "In retrospect, I don't think it *is* one fund. That doesn't sound like Randall. I think he would have had a series of hidden accounts."

"Why do you believe that?"

"Several accounts would be smaller, less likely to attract too much attention."

"I see. But we have no way to track anything like that down. It's not like we're detectives—"

"I asked the accountant to take another look. He has access to information you and I wouldn't. The only reason I stopped pursuing this during the divorce was Randall gave me the settlement I wanted."

"So you think your guy can locate this money?"

"I don't know. But, if what Ms. Cunningham told us is true, someone *did* track those accounts down."

"I'm not following you."

"She was looking for 'reports' she said Candy had. Yet, Candy ends up dead before Winsley can get them."

"You think Candy found those hidden accounts?"

"Or worked with someone who brought her in on the deal. Perhaps the idea of a lot of money made her greedy."

"But, if this is true, why kill Randall?"

"Simple, Watkins," Sheryl observed and slipped into her analytical "Sherlock" persona. "We can deduce that by looking at the evidence left on the scene." She reached into her purse and pulled out a tiny screw. "Remember this?"

"Is that the screw you found in Randall's bedroom?" I asked.

"Yes," Sheryl said. "Bright and early this morning I took it to a shop where they repair computers. As it turns out, it is a most unusual screw. You'll notice it's very short and flat."

I took the screw and turned it over in my hand.

"It is specifically made to hold a laptop hard drive in a small metal bracket that keeps it secure," Sheryl said.

I met her eyes. "The police took the hard drive out?"

"I don't think it was the police."

"You believe the killer took it?"

"Correct."

"I still don't get—"

"Randall had an office computer, but brought his laptop everywhere. Both machines possessed double and triple-level security. He did everything online for *all* his finances — stocks, bonds, and most important: transfers."

I snapped my fingers as I saw her line of reasoning. "So you think the killer was out to steal the information — account numbers and the like."

"Good, Watkins, but you are still not seeing the whole picture. Let's say a clever person finds Randall's accounts. How could they access them?"

I thought for a minute. "I assume they would need the necessary passwords."

"Which only Randall knew."

"So, they would have to go online to the accounts and have Randall give them the codes," I said.

"Now you see."

"I'm not sure," I mused. "Do you think Candy got to Randall through the offer of a kinky evening and tricked him into letting her cuff him up? Then her accomplice came in and threatened Randall to give up his passcodes while he was helpless?"

"Exactly!" Sheryl announced with a broad smile. "Once the accounts were accessed, they could use the laptop to transfer the funds to anywhere in the world."

"So, you think they used my gun and fired a shot in the wall to persuade him," I speculated.

"To show they meant business. They also could have used the pillow to scare him, not suffocating him, but threatening to—"

"Until the final *coup de grace*. So, it wasn't revenge or a sex crime. It was flat-out robbery," I deduced.

"Exactly!"

"But why kill him?"

"Because he was the only one who knew about the accounts and the only one with the skills to get his money back."

"Which made the robbery untraceable," I considered with my mouth agape. "The perfect crime."

"Except for one thing. The hard drive of the laptop would have a record of the transfer."

I exhaled heavily. "So, why didn't the killers just take the laptop with them?"

"Too risky. There might be a way to trace it. Much safer to remove the hard drive with the data."

"Pretty cold-blooded, to smother him and then take apart the computer with him lying there. You really think Jon Kane could do that? And that Candy would help?"

"If there was a big enough prize, I think Candy would've enjoyed getting him trussed up and getting the information," she hypothesized and stood up. "But I am not sure she would want to smother him."

"If Randall cheated on her, like he did you, that could have motivated her," I decided.

Her face shifted. All at once, the stern persona seemed to melt away before my eyes. She fell into her chair suddenly.

"What is it?" I worried.

She stared at me with a wild look in her eyes. "Mark, what's wrong with me?"

I got down on my knees in front of her and took her hands in mine. "You? Why nothing! What are you talking about?"

"How could I marry such a man?" Sheryl lamented and wouldn't meet my eyes. "And not see how he was? I'm a failure."

I held her hands up in front of her. "You are not!"

"Look at me," she said and raised her head to face me. "I want to cry and scream, but I can't. My emotions just blank out."

"You've been through a very tough few days…"

"If I'm a great observer, like Holmes, why didn't I see that he was unfaithful? Or that he never loved me?"

"Holmes said in *Hound Of The Baskervilles:* 'Evil indeed is the man who has not one woman to mourn him.'"

"Actually, it was Victor Hatherly who said that—"

"The point is, I'd like to believe that we always give those we love the benefit of the doubt."

Sheryl thought about it for a moment. "Randall could be so charming. But it was more like we were roommates. We had no joint accounts, no combined finances—"

"Maybe that's a good thing. If you had shared accounts, the killer might be after you," I cajoled. "Which begs the question: how did the killer find out about these secret accounts?"

Sheryl frowned. "I see your point."

I released her hand and let it relax into her lap. "You were his wife and you didn't know. I doubt he'd have told Candy, who was basically the 'Flavor of the Month.'"

Sheryl stood still for a moment and stared at a spot on the wall just above my head.

"You're right." She quickly pulled out her pad. "While not being brilliant yourself, Watson, you inspire brilliance in others."

"Now *that's* a Holmes quote," I said. "The second part is: 'It may be that you are not yourself luminous, but you are a conductor of light. Some people without possessing genius have a remarkable power of stimulating it.'"

"Good show, Watkins," she effused. "And you are inspiring me, much like Watson did Holmes."

"How?"

"You have hit the point of the matter. We must conclude that it was the killer who knew of Randall's accounts and brought Candy in with the promise of a large payout."

I stood. "So, who would have the ability to find accounts that Randall guarded so zealously?"

"It is possible that one or both of his partners could have stumbled across bookkeeping inaccuracies," she said. "As well as have access to the computer Randall used at work."

"That does point to Jon Kane again. Why do you suppose he was trying to break into my apartment last night?"

"Logically, it can only be one of two conclusions. He either went there to *leave* something—"

"Incriminating evidence, like the killer has done to us so far —"

"Yes, or to *find* something."

We sat and pondered, as Sheryl scribbled away. Suddenly, I wished I smoked to have something to do with my hands. I reached into my pocket and pulled out the smaller pipe John Stewart had given me. I turned it over in my hand as I thought about our conclusions. I don't know why he recommended I oil it. The finish on it appeared quite fine and the wood glowed in the morning light from the windows. "But what would he have been looking for? If he'd already transferred the money—"

At that moment, as if on cue, my cell phone rang.

"Probably the police," I said with a sigh. "Calling to let me know I'm about to be arrested again."

"Mark, try to keep a positive outlook."

"Very well. I'm positive I'm going back to jail." I activated the phone. "Hello?"

"Mr. Watson?" came a male voice I couldn't place.

"Wat-KINS, yes," I said.

"Sorry. It's Joe, the sound man from the conference."

"Oh yes!" I cheered up. "What can I do for you, Joe?"

"We finished up the speeches in the main ballroom and have been loading things out. On my last walk-through, I found that pipe you were looking for."

My mouth went dry. "The... pipe?" I repeated and for some reason held up the smaller pipe in my hand.

"Yes, it must've fallen off the shelf and was down in the bottom of the podium behind some wires. I was removing the wires or I would never have seen it. I am about to go. You want me to leave it at the front desk?"

"Are you sure it's my pipe?" I said and stood.

"Looks like it. Who else would have left a pipe here on the podium?"

I covered the mouthpiece. "He found my pipe!"

Sheryl gazed at me in surprise, but then a look came over her face — almost idyllic, as if she'd learned a great secret.

"I guess you could leave it at the front desk," I said.

"No, Mark," Sheryl insisted vehemently and drew close. "We must pick it up at once, and he must tell no one."

I spoke into the phone. "I'll come right down and pick it up. Can you give me ten minutes?"

"I'm only here for a half day."

"I'll hurry. And do me a favor. Don't tell anyone you found that pipe."

"Sure. See you soon."

I hung up the phone and looked at Sheryl. She was writing up a storm in that little notebook.

"I don't get it," I wondered. "The police said they found a pipe with my fingerprints at Randall's apartment. I always thought it was—"

"If this is the pipe you had at the speech, the one in police custody must be Norm Blake's," Sheryl decided, as she hid her notebook and grabbed a light jacket. "It's the only other pipe that had your fingerprints on it. Another part of the puzzle."

It was indeed a puzzle. For the life of me, I could not make any sense of the pieces.

24. Gray Literature

Sheryl Homes

We grabbed a cab uptown to the Hilton and got there in less than ten minutes.

The hotel was insanely busy now that the conference had moved into "weekend" mode. There were a lot more people — with so many in costume it looked more like Comic-Con.

We wormed our way past the different characters and took the elevator to the ballroom level, and I led Mark through the hallways, past conference rooms where lecturers droned on and on about their different topics.

Soon, we slipped in a side door of the Mercury Ballroom.

The ballroom had undergone a change. With the celebrity speaker finished the previous night, the crew had begun to break the room down. The platform stage was gone, as were the screen, curtains, and folding chairs that created the illusion of a theater.

The lights were subdued, but I could see the huge empty room. The only thing left from Mark's speech was the large podium.

I drew close, as the semidarkness made the room seem threatening. "Are you sure we should've come here?"

"I… think so," Mark attempted.

"You made it!" a voice said, as Mark and I both jumped.

I took a deep breath to calm my racing heart. We turned and faced a shadowy figure as he approached.

"Joe, thanks for calling," Mark told him with relief.

"No problem," Joe stated, "it was a good idea that you gave me your cell number." He went to the podium and held out the elaborate pipe.

Mark took it from him carefully.

"Why all the secrecy?" he wondered.

I answered for Mark. "No reason. It's just so busy now. Mark, we really should go."

"Hey!" Joe said. "You were the lady that asked all those questions. I got the impression you two didn't like each other."

"How did you ever get an idea like that?" Mark said with an attempt at a casual laugh.

I hoped Mark's laugh didn't sound as fake in Joe's ear as it did in mine.

I decided I should help. I moved close and took Mark's hand. "I just like to challenge him."

Joe gave a confused wave and headed out another door.

We were alone in the dark theater and Mark turned to me, our hands still connected. I bent slightly and our lips met.

Electricity shot through me from my toes to my scalp, and I felt as if I melted into a puddle of want.

He pulled back, and we looked at each other with bedroom eyes.

"Had to make sure that first kiss wasn't a fluke," Mark croaked.

"Of course," I sighed.

Still holding hands, Mark led me into the well-lit hallway and both of us leaned against the wall and breathed hard, trying to gain some equilibrium.

I fought to get my mind off my desire and back on the case. "Is that the pipe you got from the tobacco booth the first day?"

Mark turned it over in his hand. "Look! It has the small red 'X' on the bottom."

I frowned. "Is that significant?"

"The pipe I was given had this mark. When the police showed me the pipe with my fingerprints, I didn't think to look for it."

My mind was getting clearer now, though that was one hell of a kiss. "So, you're sure *this* is the one you were given?"

"Yes," he confirmed, "which begs the question, whose pipe do the police have?"

"Fancy seein' you guys here," a big voice growled.

We both turned to see the huge shape of John Stewart. He wore his odd broken smile and his eyes were fixated on the pipe in Mark's hand. He slipped his cell phone into his pocket as he approached us.

"Hey! You found it," he blurted, and bent a bit to look closely at the pipe with his good eye.

"John!" Mark said. "What are you doing here?"

"Came up to hear a lecture." He gave us his twisted grin. "I got Hypno watchin' the booth. Gotta have some fun while I'm here, you know."

"Of course," I exclaimed, and exchanged a glance with Mark. My suspicions were aroused that his arrival was so timely.

"Well, since you found that one," John remarked. "I could take it back and give you a refund."

There was a dead silence as we all stared at the pipe.

Then John added, "I mean, if you want. I'll still be able to sell it."

He reached out for it, but Mark pulled it back.

"Actually, I want to hold on to it," Mark proclaimed, "I know some people who will be very surprised to see this."

"Mark, isn't it time for that thing?" I attempted to sound chatty.

"What?" Mark responded. Honestly, I thought he was better at picking up cues.

"That thing we have to do, it's time," I pointed out with a glance to my watch. "Nice seeing you, Mr. Stewart."

"Call me John, everybody does."

I took Mark's arm and led him down the hallway.

"I have to ask," I murmured as we walked. "Who knew you had the pipe, and who would be able to replace it at the crime scene?"

"Anyone who saw me use it on the stage," Mark pointed out. "But should we show this to DeStadler? The precinct is only a few blocks away—"

"Not yet. He will confiscate it, and we still don't have all the facts," I protested.

"Then what do we do now, Homes?"

I turned to face him. The idea of going upstairs to one of our rooms and ripping each other's clothes off was my strongest urge. It had been two years for Mark and over a year and a half for me. But I tried to think with my brain and not my loins.

"Our first matter of business is to find if there is something special about this pipe. Let's go to my place. I have a microscope and other equipment."

"Didn't you say the police took your paraphernalia?"

I dropped my head. "That's right!"

"Any other ideas?"

The image of Mark in the bathrobe and the empty hotel room resurfaced, but I pushed it down. "Actually, I have one. Follow me."

We worked our way through the crowd and headed toward the escalator. Out of the corner of my eye, I saw a tallish man walk past us and realized it was Cliff from Norm Blake's jewelry booth.

He seemed in a hurry and rushed by without an acknowledgment. Perhaps he hadn't seen us.

I realized Mark probably shouldn't carry the suspicious pipe out in the open. We had walked by crowds of people with it right in his hand in plain sight.

"Mark," I whispered. "Put the pipe in your jacket pocket!"

He gave me a surprised look, then did so.

Once we were out on the street, I was off like a shot, headed west, with Mark running to keep up.

I pulled out my cell phone and texted as Mark huffed and puffed behind me. This was one way to work off excess physical desire.

I finished and looked over at Mark and immediately slowed my step. "Are you all right? You're flushed."

"It's nothing," he muttered and avoided my eyes. Had our kiss pushed him past the self-control ledge as well?

It took about twenty minutes, but we walked over to Tenth Avenue and 58th street and went in the front entrance of Saint Luke's-Roosevelt Hospital Center.

The lobby was several stories high and all glass. Several security officers eyed us as a twenty-something girl approached me.

"Hey, Sylvia," I greeted my friend.

"Hey, Sheryl. You two have to sign in," she explained.

She escorted us to a massive front desk where a woman in a very official uniform looked over our identification and took our photos with a web camera. She quickly gave us a pair of paper name badges, and we followed Sylvia to a bank of elevators.

"Sorry to call in so many favors in one day," I began, as we got into the elevator and went down.

"That's fine," Sylvia told us. "You picked a light day, especially for a Saturday. I think I can handle everything. Besides, your test is almost done."

"Test?" Mark wondered.

I gave him a smile. "Yes, remember that sample in the jelly jar? I brought it to Sylvia this morning."

Mark looked at me seriously. "Do you ever sleep?"

I wanted to say, "No, I met this guy, and he has me so turned-on that I can only grab two or three hours before I have a wet dream and start thinking about him again." But I resisted the urge. What I did say was, "I had to be at the hotel when Detective Elvis returned my keys, didn't I? Plus, I had to meet with the bail bondsman—"

"So the answer is no," Mark said.

God, sometimes he's dense. Was he experiencing *any* of the feelings I was going through?

The door opened and we stepped into a well-lit hallway. Since the lobby was street-level, we were underground. Sylvia took us through a labyrinth of hallways to a good-sized lab. It was filled with machines that I couldn't name if I had to, let alone discern what they did.

We walked through the lab and Sylvia looked at a machine with a digital readout. Satisfied, she turned and gave Mark a quick once-over. "Not bad."

Mark frowned and looked questioningly at me.

I turned beet-red, yet again. I realized I may have told Sylvia far more about how I felt than I should have. "This is Mark, Sylvia. He's the one I asked you to test."

"I figured," Sylvia divulged. "You said it was urgent. What else do you need?"

"Gloves, a tray, tweezers, forceps, a magnifying glass, maybe a Spectrometer."

"I'll set you up over here," Sylvia expounded, and led us to a workstation with two chairs. "I'll get what you need, but I'll run the Spectrometer if you need it."

"That's fine, thanks," I told Sylvia. When she walked away, I looked at Mark and mentioned, "That's impressive."

"What?"

"You passed the Sylvia test."

Mark looked even more confused. "She said I was 'not bad.' That's a passing grade?"

"You should've heard what she called Randall on their first meeting."

"How do you know her?" Mark wondered.

"I met her at a writing class I taught at the New School years ago. She's a gifted technician, but she wasn't good at putting her results into the written word. I helped her express herself and edited a few of her papers. We've been friends ever since."

Sylvia brought a tray that contained the tools wrapped in plastic and a box of latex gloves.

"This will do nicely," I responded. "Do you have a camera, in case we need to document?"

"Just use your phone."

"That works," I agreed, and Sylvia gave a nod and was off again.

"How old is she?" Mark asked.

I thought about it. "Twenty-seven — no, eight. Why, do you like them young?"

Mark's back stiffened. "Actually, I've never been with anyone much younger than myself." He gazed deep into my eyes, and I got that feeling of being caressed again. "How old are you?"

"You first." I gave a nervous laugh.

"Okay," Mark replied timidly. "I'm fifty-two."

I had thought he was younger. "You look good."

"How nice. I've reached the you-look-good-for-your-age phase of my life," Mark joked, as I took the tools out of the tray and put the pipe in it. He went on. "Okay, so I fessed up. How about you?"

"Thirty-four," I admitted in a low undertone. I slipped gloves on, pulled out my phone, and began to snap photos of the pipe, not looking at Mark.

Eighteen years my senior. He was eighteen when I was born. The idea didn't compute with the lusty thoughts I'd been having for him the last few days.

Why was it important? After all, at this point we were nothing more than friends, and according to the police, co-conspirators.

But the way he made me feel! And those kisses. Just the *kisses* had been mind-blowing. Was he an exceptional kisser, or had it just been so long for me I couldn't tell anymore?

I focused on the pipe, turned it over, and photographed the red mark. Then I took snaps of it on one side, then flipped it to the other side.

"How's it going?" Sylvia said as she walked over.

"Good, I guess," Mark told her as he watched me.

Sylvia pointed at a large machine on the other side of the room. "I'll be over there if you need me."

"I can't thank you enough, Sylvia," I told her.

"Glad to help. I assume you'll explain the entire story once you have the answer to your problem?"

"You'll be the first to know." I tore open a plastic bag and extracted the forceps. It had two circles of metal, which I held with my thumb and middle finger, and a bent nose like a pair of needle-nosed pliers.

Clamped to our workbench was a large, circular magnifier lamp on an adjustable arm. I moved it into position over the tray and turned on the light. It flickered twice, and then shone a cold, fluorescent light upon the contents of the tray.

I picked up the pipe and examined it through the magnifying lens. "This is a lot better than the glass I carry in my purse."

"See anything?" Mark asked.

I pulled the shank loose from the stem and looked into both holes carefully.

"What are you looking for?" Mark asked as he tried to look over my shoulder. His hot breath fell on the back of my neck, and suddenly I had goose bumps.

"Don't know. See here, what's this?" I peered into the bowl of the pipe. I took the forceps, reached into the narrow bowl, and carefully extracted a small metal rectangle.

"What is that?" Mark wondered.

"I'm not sure," I said, and turned it over in my gloved hand.

"It looks familiar," Mark pointed out.

"It does, doesn't it?" I looked in the bowl of the pipe and could see a small piece of clear tape inside, which I surmised held the metal in place. It was a clever way to hide something, as you couldn't see it in the deep bowl from a cursory glance.

I straightened up and walked over to Sylvia.

I consulted my friend. Once she agreed with my hypothesis, I went back to Mark.

"Any luck?" he asked.

I turned one end of the small piece of metal toward his face. "Look familiar now?"

He shook his head and stared at the small rectangle. "Wait. Is that a USB plug?"

I smiled. "It's a flash drive with a USB connector. Usually, they are built into a case or holder, but this is just the inner workings."

Mark stared at it again. "A flash drive? What's on it?"

I spoke quietly. "No idea. But here is a suggestion. What if Jon Kane was looking for this when he came to your place last night?"

Mark's expression grew dark. "We don't know that's why he was there. He may have been after you."

"How would he know I was there?"

"He could've followed you. Maybe he waited until he thought you were asleep."

"If he wanted to kill me, Mark, he could have done so Wednesday night by getting the spare room key from the booth. No, I am sure my deduction is correct. There is something of interest on this flash drive." I turned to Sylvia, who at that moment was bringing a laptop over.

Sylvia took the plug and inserted it into the computer's USB port.

An icon appeared on the screen with the word "INFO" under it.

Sylvia double-clicked on the icon, which opened a file folder. When she clicked on it, a document opened up. The page was filled with gibberish — letters and numbers that made no sense.

"What are we seeing here?" Mark wondered.

"It's encoded," Sylvia decided as she closed the file.

"Anything we can do?" I felt disappointed.

Sylvia looked at the file folder on the screen.

"I could run some decoding software I came up with. Let me copy the file. I don't want to risk damaging the original."

She made a quick backup of the file, then removed the USB drive from the computer and returned it to me.

"Now, what do we do with it?" Mark countered.

"Maybe put it back in the pipe?" Sylvia suggested, and I nodded in agreement, as a laser printer began to hum a few feet away from us. Sylvia turned to watch the papers printing.

"We could give it to DeStadler now that we've copied it," Sheryl pointed out.

"You think it might convince him that the pipe at the murder scene was planted?" Mark hoped.

"It couldn't hurt," I told him. "And the police have their own code breakers who might be able to find out what is on that flash drive faster than we can."

"I resent that," Sylvia complained as she collected the pages from the laser printer. "I have a little algorithm of my own built into a program that should make short work of it."

She handed the papers to me and pointed at a page, as Mark peeked over my shoulder, which wasn't easy since I had several inches on him.

"You were right, traces of Flunitrazepam in combination with a bit of GHB," Sylvia said.

I exhaled heavily. "Damn! Mark, you were lucky they didn't give you a higher dose."

"Oh yeah, combining those two could've suppressed your breathing." Sylvia grimaced. "Do you have a heart condition?"

Mark shook his head. "No, my heart's fine. So's my blood pressure."

"Good thing," Sylvia muttered.

"Could that have been part of the plan?" I deduced. "I mean, if Mark died, then all the loose ends would be tied up."

"And all the evidence pointing directly at you as the mastermind," Mark concurred.

"What do you mean?" I felt my eyebrows rise.

"Think about it," Mark went on. "The incriminating email supposedly from me? Randall and Candy were dead by that time. If I died as well—"

I found that my hand went to my mouth as the realization sunk in. After a moment, I found my voice. "I didn't like her, but I find it hard to believe Candy would give you a fatal drug overdose."

"It *does* tie it up in one pretty little bow for the police," Mark stressed.

"Not quite," Sylvia interrupted. "They would run a tox screen in the post-mortem. This drug combination would have definitely raised red flags."

"You're right, Sylvia," I agreed. "I think they needed you alive."

"Okay, I've got the backup of the file from that flash drive," Sylvia surmised. "I am going to run my program, and I have to actually get back to my job."

"Of course." I slipped the pipe into a plastic bag and handed it to Mark. "Sylvia, you'll call me if you get something?"

"First thing," Sylvia assured and pointed at the papers in Mark's hand. "If you are going to the police, you really want to bring those with you."

Sylvia looked from Mark to me and back again. "I just have one question. Why would anyone want to frame you two?"

I smiled. "Elementary."

Mark smiled as well. "To get away with murder, of course."

25. Plot Twist

Mark Watkins

We came out of the underground lab, peeled off and returned our badges, and walked out the front of the hospital.

Sheryl folded the pages of my toxicology report and put them into her handbag, while I carried the evidence-ridden pipe in a shiny new plastic bag.

"This could change everything," I told her. "Maybe get DeStadler on our side."

"I don't know," Sheryl said. "He seems like a hard nut to crack. But this is *evidence!*"

"He seems to only like evidence when it points to you or me. Especially if it points at me."

We turned down 58th Street and walked the long block between Tenth and Ninth Avenues.

"You can hardly blame him," Sheryl went on. "About twenty percent of all murders are committed by a spouse or family member."

"That high?" I said as we walked along.

"Yes. So naturally that makes me a prime suspect. And with our relationship—"

"We have a relationship?"

Sheryl flushed and looked away. "You know what I mean."

I stopped walking and turned to her. Even though she was three inches taller than me, I took her hands and looked up into her emerald-green eyes. "Not really. What do you think it means?"

Sheryl glanced around uncomfortably. "Mark, this isn't the time or the place."

"There hasn't been a good time or place since I met you. I mean, the other night when I saw you in Susie's nightgown. My God, you were so beautiful."

"A smart man might've made a move," she grumbled.

"I didn't know if it would be welcomed."

Her eyes met mine. "I have to admit I have concerns…"

"It's the age difference, isn't it?"

"I don't know. Possibly. Or my own doubts. Honestly, Mark, you bring up feelings I haven't had in years. Some of them I've never had before."

"Really?" I couldn't help but smile.

A flash of anger traveled through her eyes. "You think it's funny?"

"Not in the least," I told her, and she calmed down. "I've experienced emotions I thought I wouldn't ever feel again. I mean, after Susie died."

"That's good, isn't it?" She sounded unsure.

"Very good. The question is, what are we going to do about it?"

"Well, not to be under suspicion of murder would be a good start," she effused, and still holding one of my hands, we began to walk again. "But once DeStadler sees the pipe, and the flash drive in it—"

"Still doesn't explain how my fingerprints got on the pipe at Randall's."

"Technically, all anyone had to do was place a similar pipe in your hand, even when you were unconscious, to get your prints on it."

"So, you're suggesting this might not help us at all," I sighed.

"Perhaps this will motivate him to look at other people. Maybe he'll even check up on Norm Blake," Sheryl mused. "Y'know, I did see his assistant, Cliff, as we headed down the escalator."

I turned and faced her. "Really? What do you suppose he was doing near the ballroom?"

Sheryl shrugged. "In that crowd, I only noticed him because of his height."

"It was also weird running into John Stewart in the ballroom," I added as we started to walk again.

"It was almost as if he knew we would be there," Sheryl said.

We turned the corner at Ninth Avenue and started to head downtown. It was now early afternoon, and the day had grown warm. It was a lovely spring day in New York with temperatures warm enough so you didn't feel cold, but cool enough that a sports coat didn't make you sweat.

There was a lot of foot traffic, and the sidewalk was busy but not too crowded. Every type of person rushed about at a pace only New Yorkers can maintain.

A small restaurant across the street had just opened, and the staff was putting tables and chairs outside so that diners could enjoy their meal *al fresco*.

Despite the people who walked past us, I suddenly heard footsteps. I caught a glimpse of a figure in black out of the corner of my eye.

Before my reflexes could act, a tall person in a large black coat moved between Sheryl and me. Whoever it was pushed us apart with enough force to knock both of us down.

Everything seemed to move in slow motion, as the figure snatched the plastic bag with the pipe out of my hand when I fell.

I glanced up, only to see a black ski mask and sunglasses, which completely covered the face of our assailant.

As my knees painfully struck the pavement, time resumed its regular speed, and I looked up to see our attacker as he took off. It was a tall fellow in black pants with a large black pea coat, which was unbuttoned and flared open as he ran.

I must have been muddled, as the only thing going through my brain was how odd it was to wear a ski mask on such a warm day.

People stopped to watch the assailant run off but did nothing to stop him.

Typical New Yorkers.

Sheryl, however, was only knocked off balance. She straightened up and threw her purse to me.

"Take this," she said as she took off in hot pursuit of the black-clad perpetrator.

"No," I croaked, and raised my hand to reach out and stop her, but I was too slow.

She was gone like a shot after him.

I fought to get up with pain in my legs, and with her purse in my hands, I began to follow the pair of them.

They were more than a full block ahead of me. I saw the dark shape weave in and out through the crowd as he ran. Sheryl tried to gain ground, but our foe moved quickly to get farther away.

I pushed myself into a full run, but Sheryl was faster than me, and our thief was faster than us both.

As I reached 56th Street, I had no choice but to stop. I grabbed a nearby light post to hold myself up. I stood there and panted hard, the air painful in my lungs as my heart felt as if it wanted to burst from my chest. I looked up and saw that the pedestrian crossing sign blinked "Don't Walk."

I had to agree.

I looked down at my pants. Both the knees were dirty, and the left knee had a tear in it. I saw a small trickle of blood and decided that any career I might plan as a marathon runner would have to be put on hold.

I stood there for about five minutes with the purse in my hand as I tried to catch my breath, until I saw Sheryl stride back through the pedestrians toward me.

She also panted, but at least she was still upright and able to move forward.

She reached me, and I offered her back her purse.

"Thanks," she puffed, and held onto the pole with her free hand. "Fast."

"Yeah," I panted back. "You... you're pretty... fast... too."

"Odd," she said.

"Hmm?" I managed.

"I thought... he was... a purse-snatcher, but... didn't try to... get... my purse."

I nodded. "Only the pipe."

"How could anyone... know... it had anything... to do with a murder?"

"I can't... imagine."

She looked me in the eye, and then looked back in the direction our mugger went.

"Damn," she muttered.

26. Multiple Submissions

Sheryl Homes

An hour later, DeStadler paced the room like a wild animal and stared at the photos on my phone. "At least this time you walked in here, instead of me tracking you down."

He glowered at the pair of us.

"I don't see what you are upset about, detective," I attempted, and tried to stare daggers right back at him. "We found important evidence and made an effort to bring it to you. That should count for something."

"It's not our fault it was stolen," Mark pointed out.

"And we did bring you the pictures," I defended.

"Yeah, very convenient," DeStadler griped. "You find something that might clear you, and it is mysteriously stolen in broad daylight by a mugger you cannot describe as anything more than 'tall.'"

DeStadler's face was as red as a lobster just out of the pot.

"Detective," Mark explained, "I didn't notice if the pipe you found at the crime scene had the red 'X' on the bottom."

"You mentioned that, and I can see the 'X' on this one in the photo," DeStadler scoffed and put my phone on the table in front of me. "A point that you bring to us *after* the fact. If you had mentioned this 'X' mark when we first brought you in or when you first saw the pipe we had in evidence, I might've bought it. For all I know, you purchased this pipe and put the 'X' on it yourself."

"Why would I do that?" Mark challenged.

"To create doubt. You have to admit, even the receipt you showed me is dated *after* we brought you in the first time."

"I have explained that I thought it was lost," Mark argued. "And that I was paying for it."

"Yeah, yeah," DeStadler grumbled. "And we *still* have no explanation why your fingerprints were found on the pipe at the crime scene."

I interrupted. "There was a second pipe Mark touched at another booth."

DeStadler stared at both of us. "You mentioned that when you got here today, and I had someone check up on this Norm Blake. He is just a guy who sells jewelry — no criminal record. Not even an unpaid parking ticket. We don't have any logical reason to get a warrant for his stuff."

Mark held up the lab printout and complained, "We also brought proof that I'd been drugged."

"A lab test that you cannot even show was a sample taken from you? Look, we have actual evidence. The gun—"

"Circumstantial at best!" I announced and folded my arms in defiance.

"Yes, and what you told me about Jon Kane showing up at Mr. Watkins' apartment last night is circumstantial as well," DeStadler growled, and focused his attention on me. "By the way, I distinctly recall telling you not to leave the hotel, and yet somehow you ended up in Watkin's apartment."

I was frustrated at this point. "I think that Jon Kane was trying to find that pipe!"

"Ah, yes. This mysterious pipe with a magical hidden flash drive," DeStadler said. "Look, we took a statement from Mr. Kane. On the night of the murder, he was seen at a bar at the hotel until 1:00 AM. Then he went to his room."

"Can he prove that?" I snapped.

"We checked the surveillance video at the hotel. According to the time stamp, Mr. Kane got into the elevator at 1:15 and went to the 12th floor. There is no way he could get downtown in time to kill Mr. Lawrence."

Mark rose up in his chair. "There are cameras at the hotel? This can prove I was carried to my room—"

"Way ahead of you, Ace," DeStadler interrupted. "The camera on the 12th floor went out a few days before the conference, and they're still waiting for parts to fix it."

Mark sat back down and shook his head. "I can't seem to catch a break."

I, however, was undaunted. "Did the elevator cameras tell you when Ms. Poole left the 12th floor?"

DeStadler nodded. "According to the time stamp, Ms. Poole took the elevator to the lobby at about 11:30, and she returned about 1:30 AM." He faced me. "That's why we're having trouble with your story, Mr. Watkins. If you *were* drugged, it suggests that she left you alone in her room for two hours. Why would anyone drug someone and then leave them in their room?"

I began to see why it had been difficult to convince DeStadler of Mark's innocence, but I still wanted to press the matter. "It doesn't explain why Jon Kane was at Mark's apartment last night, or the fact that he had duplicate keys."

DeStadler folded his arms. "So why couldn't he get in?"

"I changed one of the locks," Mark disclosed.

DeStadler frowned. "Why?"

Mark went on. "Well, since I believe someone broke into my apartment and stole my gun and then returned it to make me look guilty, I decided it might be a good idea."

"Detective," I pestered, "the least you can do is try to find out if Jon Kane has copies of Mark's keys."

"Don't tell me my job," DeStadler sputtered and stood to walk over to the mirror on the wall we faced.

He knocked on the glass twice and said, "Elvis, go pick up Jon Kane and get a warrant for his apartment."

"Also," Mark claimed, "we can get you the data on the flash drive we found—"

"Oh yeah, the one in the pipe," DeStadler jeered.

"That's right!" I agreed.

"Well, that's gone with the pipe, isn't it?"

Mark and I exchanged a look.

DeStadler glared at us. "If either of you are holding back evidence—"

"We may have…" I admitted, "made a copy."

"What?" DeStadler barked. "Why didn't you tell me that right away?"

"We were trying to find out what the files on it were," Mark explained. "It's encoded."

"A friend of mine is working on breaking the code," I conceded.

"You get that to me," DeStadler asserted and pulled out his business card, which he gave to me. "This has my email address. Get your friend to send them, now!"

I nodded and picked up my phone to text Sylvia.

"We have the best computer guys in the city. I don't want some amateur corrupting files that might have to do with a murder."

"Yes, sir," I said as I finished the text with DeStadler's email and a request to send him the files.

DeStadler walked over, pulled Mark to his feet, and pulled out his handcuffs. "You need to come with me."

Mark put his hands behind his back.

I panicked. "I thought he was released on bail?"

"He was," DeStadler stormed, as he clicked the cuffs tight around Mark's wrists.

I rose from my seat. "You can't just—"

"Sit down!" DeStadler shouted. "And get me those files! You are going nowhere until I have those files!"

I am sure the look on my face could've scared children, but I slowly sat down, picturing several horrible deaths for the detective.

"I'll be back for you," DeStadler said as he led Mark out the door.

As the door slammed behind them, I glared up at the mirror and stuck my tongue out at whoever was watching.

I would have to call Uncle Louie and have him ride in on his lawyer white horse. How dare they arrest Mark again, after we came here to give them information they should have found? I wanted to kick something.

And Mark would be in jail again, so another night where I would be tossing and turning like a cat in heat. You think a girl would be able to get laid when she wants to.

But that had been the problem for the last year and a half. I didn't want to. I worked on my books, I had drinks with friends, I went to the occasional dinner party, and I didn't want to have sex with anyone. I had decided I was just an ice goddess, and the sensual woman I had been was part of my younger life.

Then I met Mark and it all came flooding back.

Flood? More like a tidal wave.

What was stranger was the realization that I probably never had felt anything like this with any man. Randall had been a good lover, back when he cared. Adventurous, no doubt, but it was fun and silly and I enjoyed myself.

But he never got my emotions going the way Mark did.

Then, a terrible thought hit me. What if, in bed, Mark and I are not compatible? What the hell would I do then?

Just as that devastating thought wrapped its tentacles into my brain, Mark opened the door and walked into the interrogation room.

I jumped. He wasn't handcuffed and had opened the door on his own. He held it open and reached out a hand for me.

I walked to him as if in a daze.

"Oh my God," I said in hushed tones, "you didn't kill him, did you?"

Mark chuckled from the earnestness of my tone. "He's giving us a break."

"He is?" I marveled. "Why?"

"He is beginning to believe we may have been set up," Mark noted. "But he insists that we both go to my condo and stay out of his way."

"Ah! That sounds more like DeStadler," I responded. "We may have to stop at a store. I'm running out of underwear."

Mark chuckled, a deep throaty one that made me smile. "Always practical. I think we should count our blessings and get out of here."

"I second the motion."

We gingerly made our way out of the police station, and as we stepped onto the pavement, Mark took a deep gulp of air.

"What was that for?" I inquired.

Mark looked very serious. "I just had the realization that if we don't figure this out, I might not be able to breathe air as a free man for very much longer."

27. Trim

Mark Watkins

The trip uptown via cab was uneventful, though we did get out on Broadway instead of West End Avenue so that Sheryl could buy a few necessities, which included new ladies underwear.

As we made our way to the counter, Sheryl asked, "Is it okay if I wash out my bra in your sink?"

It was actually a harmless question, but once again I turned beet-red.

"Uh — sure," was my pithy reply.

She smiled broadly. "You are so cute — the way everything embarrasses you."

"You're one to talk," I challenged. "You've blushed at half the things I've said."

She turned away and set her jaw. "I guess we have something in common!"

We grabbed some sandwiches at a nearby deli, as well as a bottle of wine, and made our way to the condo.

As we rode up in the elevator laden with packages, Sheryl's phone went off with some exotic ringtone.

She maneuvered a few bags and extracted it.

"Hello," she said and began to nod. "Really? Can you email it to me? That's great. I owe you big time."

She shut off the phone just as the elevator arrived on my floor and the door opened.

"That was Sylvia," she began as I brought out my keys and unlocked the door. "She's finished decoding those files."

"That was fast," I said as we walked in and began to put things down. "Does she have any idea what they are?"

"She told me it's some kind of spreadsheet."

I went to the kitchen and located a corkscrew for the wine as Sheryl took food out of her bags. Then she walked into my bedroom and came out with her suitcase.

"Where did you get that?" I chuckled.

"Last night I came directly from the hotel," Sheryl explained. "So I brought it with me. At least this way I have some clothing choices, as well as my toothbrush."

"That reminds me," I said, and with the bottle of wine in my hand, I went into the bedroom and quickly returned with my passport.

"I have to give this to Uncle — I mean, Mr. DeSoto."

I placed it on the table in plain sight so I would remember it.

"I'll make sure he gets it if you don't," Sheryl offered.

"By the way, what did you do with that shell casing? DeStadler didn't mention it, so I am under the impression it wasn't found."

"Oh, that! Did you ever read *The Purloined Letter*?"

"Edgar Allan Poe, sure. Oh! You hid the casing in plain sight?" I concluded and peered around the room.

With a smile, Sheryl stood, walked over to my one wall of built-in bookcases, and extracted a specific book. She reached into the empty space behind the book and extracted the shell casing.

"How did you remember which book?" I wondered.

"Simple," she smirked, and handed me the volume. It was the complete works of Edgar Allan Poe.

"Brilliant, Homes," I smirked, and handed it back to her.

"Elementary, Watkins." She returned the casing and the book to their previous positions.

I started to remove the seal on the bottle of wine. "So Sylvia is sending you the information from the flash drive. Could it be those accounts we speculated about?"

"I don't know," Sheryl considered. "Do you have a computer with a printer? I could get my email online, print it up, and we could take a look."

"It's in the bedroom," I said, my mouth suddenly dry. Every time I mentioned the bedroom, thoughts of Sheryl in that nightgown — or even less — popped into my brain.

Sheryl turned red and looked at the floor. Maybe the same kind of thoughts popped into her mind as well. "I'll go take a look," she mumbled and left the room.

"The police still have my laptop, so that machine is pretty old," I yelled as I heard the computer chime and make noises as it booted up.

Sheryl called out from the other room, "I have to warn you, we don't know if this is what we are after."

"If it is, the question becomes, how did it end up hidden in that pipe?" I replied loudly, as I used the corkscrew to open the wine and poured two glasses.

"We also don't know that," Sheryl bellowed. "But in my mind, it points to Jon Kane."

"Because?"

"From what you told me and what I observed, he was being pressured by Ms. Cunningham about Randall's finances."

I stepped into the bedroom doorway with the two glasses in my hands. She glanced up. "Oh! You're here."

I handed her a glass of wine and we toasted and each took a long sip.

With the bed so near I felt the need to talk. "Charles Nederlander is… was… Randall's partner. He would also want to know about any hidden accounts."

"True, unless he was in on whatever scam they had going." Sheryl savored the taste of the wine.

"But who would have been able to get that information? And why kill Candy?"

"Indeed," Sheryl considered as she opened her online email account.

She looked at the computer, and I watched her over my glass of wine. Her face was lit by the glow of the screen, her features focused.

I felt my heart again skip a beat.

At this moment, I could not imagine a more attractive woman. With her intensity and the energy that flowed from her, she was truly spectacular.

"Here it is," she told me, as she opened a document. I came over and leaned to look at the screen, catching the fragrance of some perfume she was wearing. When had she had the chance to put that on? I adjusted my glasses and looked it over. "Looks like pretty intricate stuff. Wait! Is that a list of names there at the bottom?"

"It appears to be," Sheryl said. "Hold on." She pulled her phone from her pocket and pressed a couple of places and held it to her ear.

"Hey, Tommy, it's Sheryl," she said, then paused to listen. "Yeah, how is Marcy and the kids?... That's great..."

She rose and began to pace the room. "No, I've been arrested... For killing Randall... No, I didn't... Not now, right now I'm free... Yeah, Uncle Louie did it again."

She moved back to the screen as she continued. "Hey, remember those accounts we thought Randall had, but we couldn't find... Those may have been why he was killed... I think I have a trace on them... Can I send you a couple of documents and you do that magic of yours?... You're the best!... Okay, I'll get it right to you."

She shut down the phone. Tapped a few keys on the keyboard in front of her, and my computer made a *whoosh* sound as the email was sent.

"Your accountant?"

"Yes." Sheryl picked up her glass of wine. "If anyone can figure out the spreadsheet, it'll be him. Plus, he has a head start from the divorce. Let me print this up."

She pressed a button and my nearby laser printer whirred to life. She had another sip of the wine and then met my gaze.

I shook myself as if from a dream.

"L-let me get dinner," I stammered as I rose.

Sheryl stood as well. "Why is it every time I look into your eyes, I mean *really* look, you always find a need to move away and do something?"

I put my glass of wine down.

"Because I get ideas."

Her eyes narrowed. "What kind of ideas?"

I decided if I focused my eyes on the floor it was the best option.

"Ideas that are damn foolish while the two of us are accused of murder."

"Maybe that's the best time to think about them," she replied and also put her glass down. She took a step toward me and brought her hands to my face.

All at once our mouths met, her warm breath was on my cheek as we pulled each other close.

Our tongues danced, and she moved her hands up and down my back and made little moans in the back of her throat.

She pulled away, and we gazed into each other's eyes.

"Well…" she attempted.

"Well?" I repeated.

"I did have to find out." She smirked and quietly sat down, her breath faster.

"Wha—?" I said, the impact of that kiss not lost on me. "What do you mean?"

"If those previous kisses were an anomaly."

"Oh! Uh — verdict?"

"They weren't." She gazed at me with a sense of wonder. She pushed her hair back and smiled. "Most definitely not."

I felt a need to do something or I would immediately begin to kiss her again. I got up, went into the kitchen and started to prepare our food from the deli.

As I heated soup and arranged sandwiches on plates, Sheryl came to the kitchen doorway, leaned against the frame, and watched me with a smile.

"Do you always run away when a woman kisses you?" she asked.

I looked up and was sure I flushed again. "It's been a while since I kissed anyone — I mean, like that," I said, as I stirred the soup in a small pot.

"Me, too," she said. "After Randall and I broke up, I lost all interest."

"Well, that's a waste."

"What do you mean?"

"A beautiful, and might I add successful, woman like yourself. I would think you would be escorted by a different fellow every night."

She wistfully looked up at the ceiling. "Fellow? No, I shut down. Emotionally, sexually, the works. I thought I would never trust another man as long as I lived."

"And now?"

She ran a hand through her fiery hair in a gesture that I thought was the sexiest thing I had ever seen.

"I'm considering trying again. Maybe with the right man this time."

I put the soup into two bowls.

"That will be one lucky guy," I muttered.

She gave me a sexy smirk. "You know, someone might just get lucky tonight."

She grabbed the bowls, walked to the dining room table, and swayed her posterior suggestively.

This was a side of Sheryl I hadn't seen or was aware even existed. It was as if a switch went on, and when she turned it on... well, it certainly turned *me* on.

I sheepishly brought the sandwiches out and placed them on the table, not quite sure how I should handle this. Was she merely flirting or was she serious?

I was then given an entire show as Sheryl began to eat her sandwich in a very provocative way. She slowly put it daintily in her mouth, took a small bite, then made noises as she chewed and swallowed it. Finally, she closed her eyes in ecstasy as it went down her throat.

My sandwich fell out of my hand, which seemed to have lost all sensation. Possibly because every bit of blood in my body flowed only to my lower parts.

She opened her eyes a bit, and through half-closed lids moaned, "Good sandwich."

I leapt from my chair and took her in my arms as she chuckled deeply.

I pressed my mouth to hers and she put down her sandwich and kissed me back, hard.

Her hand moved down my leg and she began to touch me intimately as I groaned through the kiss.

"I see you brought dessert," she chortled and brought her hand up to my face as our tongues teased each other.

All at once, she jumped and pushed me away.

"Now what?" I gasped.

"Sh!" she hissed, and put her finger to her mouth. "Listen."

I became instantly silent as I heard a quiet scratch at the door of the apartment.

"Quick," she whispered, "get the lights."

I moved to the switch and turned them off, then quietly moved back to Sheryl.

Though darker, the room was lit by the radiance of the street lights which streamed through nearby windows.

"You have a weapon?" she whispered.

"No," I murmured. "The police took my gun, remember?"

"Anything else?"

I slid away, reached into a nearby closet, and extracted an old baseball bat. In the dim light you could see that it was steel with several large black diamond designs on the barrel and black tape around the grip.

Sheryl shrugged. "That will have to do."

I could hear keys jingle as one was inserted in the top of the three locks, which turned and unlocked.

"I'll undo the new lock," Sheryl murmured. "You stand ready with the bat."

I nodded as Sheryl moved to the door with me close behind. We were both hunched in a crouched position, which put Sheryl's rear end almost in my face. I fought the desire to touch it.

Touch it? Hell, I wanted to bite it.

She waited until she heard the key move into the second lock and although whoever used it would not have been able to turn it, she reached up and undid the bolt as if the key had achieved its task.

She stepped back quietly, as only the third lock remained.

The key went in it and turned to release it.

I took a deep breath and held it, stood up, and assumed a batter's stance.

The door opened a little and a hand reached in to feel for the light switch.

I saw an opportunity and perhaps a less violent solution than to bludgeon whoever it was. I gave Sheryl the bat and with both hands grabbed the arm and pulled hard.

The figure of a man fell into the room and made a screech as he came. I slipped past him, slammed the door shut, hit the light switch on, and put my foot to the center of the trespasser's back.

"I have a bat!" Sheryl growled, her voice down two registers. "Lie there or I'll bash in your skull."

He put his hands up to protect his head. "Please don't, please!"

"Turn over," I yelled in my own attempt to sound dangerous.

I removed my foot as the man rolled over onto his back and glared up at us with wild, terrified eyes.

Jon Kane lay on my floor, more surprised than anything else.

"You?" he said. "I thought you were in jail."

28. Imposition

Sheryl Homes

J on sat at Mark's table and stirred honey into the tea Mark had
made for him.

Talk about *coitus interruptus.* We could not catch a break. I
kept the bat at arm's length.

Jon was talking very fast. "I was on my way home from the
conference, but as I entered the lobby of my apartment, the
doorman told me someone was waiting for me."

"So you came here?" Mark asked.

"Like last night?" I accused.

He stared at me in disbelief. "How did you know I was here
last night?"

"Never mind that," Mark bellowed. "Why did you come here
at all?"

"To protect myself," he fretted. "When I heard about poor
Candy, I was certain I was next."

"You believe the killer is after you?" I provoked. "Why?"

He sipped his tea, then pulled a handkerchief out of his breast
pocket and wiped his brow.

"Because I made a deal with Candy to get copies of Randall's
financial records," he confessed. "When I found out Randall was

dead and then Candy was as well, I decided those records *must* be the reason."

"You hired her?" Mark realized.

Jon nodded. "Actually, Candy approached me. She asked if I would be interested in some suspicious accounts Randall owned."

Now it was my chance. "Where did she get the information?"

"She told me she had a source," he said and took another tentative sip of tea. "Someone who had been able to get into Randall's finances and study them. My guess was Charles."

"Do you think Charles Nederlander is capable of murder?" I pursued.

"Three days ago, no. But Randall, then Candy? He might want to make sure that the road to those records is closed."

"Why did you want them?"

"Ms. Cunningham had been pressuring me. She's the company's biggest investor and she wanted to double check what Randall was doing with her money. She was threatening to close her accounts, including her insurance and annuity, which I'm in charge of. Those accounts have paid me a fine commission over the years."

"What did Ms. Cunningham want from you?" I demanded.

"She insisted I find a record of her money *not* provided by Randall."

"Which explains what she spoke with you about at the conference," Mark pointed out.

I gave Jon a hard stare. "And that is what you and Candy argued about backstage in the ballroom."

Jon frowned. "How did you—"

I smirked. "I saw a tall silhouette talking to her, and I just realized it was you. Thanks for confessing."

John mopped his brow again. "Candy wanted more money — after we'd come to a very reasonable arrangement."

"It makes sense of a lot of things," I decided. "Did you give the records to Ms. Cunningham?"

"I never *got* them," Jon whined and took another sip of tea. "Candy had me go through this elaborate ruse where I had to pick up the records by buying a pipe of all things."

"A pipe!" Mark and I bellowed in unison.

"Yes," Jon said, taken aback by this display. "I was to meet someone in the lobby."

"Big man, red hair?" Mark asked.

"No. Some woman met me and gave me one of those elaborate things, like you used in the lecture. And then she told me it was the wrong one."

"What did she look like?" I pushed.

"Tall, tattooed. Nasty attitude."

"Was her name Hypno?" Mark asked.

"We didn't exchange names. But she told me there had been a mistake and the pipe ended up with you."

"'Ended up with me.' She said that?" Mark questioned.

"Her exact words."

Mark frowned. "She brought a pipe for you? We were told there were only three of those and the other was—"

"Sold, yes," I interrupted to shush Mark. "But go on with your story."

Jon looked at each of us and continued, "Well she said what I wanted was in the bowl of the pipe and all I had to do was switch my pipe for yours—"

"A pipe with an 'X' on the bottom?" I asked.

"Yes, she said that was how I would recognize it. I have been trying to switch pipes with Mark ever since."

Mark frowned. "But how did your pipe end up at the crime scene with my fingerprints on it?"

I elbowed Mark in the ribs, but it was too late. You think he would know how to do an interrogation!

"What?" Jon said. "No! I've been carrying that pipe with me ever since."

He reached into his outer coat pocket and pulled out the intricate and overlarge pipe. The shank had come out of the stem and hung loose on two fine wires.

"Oh dear," Jon reported. "I must have fallen on it when you pulled me in the door."

I stared at the pipe in his hand, my mind racing.

He took the stem, pushed it back into the shank, and it seemed to hold.

"What were those wires?" I yanked the pipe from him. "Pipe cleaners?"

"I have no idea," Jon said.

"So your plan was to break in here and switch your pipe with Mark's?" I turned the pipe over in my hand.

"Originally, I waited until Mark was signing books at the booth, then I used the spare key to get into his room—"

"That's right," Mark exclaimed, "there was a copy of all the participants' room keys at the welcome desk!"

"I used it to go up and search your room."

I knew that at this point, Mark had left the pipe in the podium. "And of course the pipe wasn't there."

"I found that out. But I saw Mark's house keys laying out. I guess I panicked. I took the keys with me and had them duplicated at a locksmith around the corner from the hotel."

"I remember, you ran late when it came time to relieve me at the signing booth," Mark revealed.

"That's right. I had to get your keys back in your room," he explained.

"But why did you come here last night?" I demanded.

"I was sure the pipe had to be here," Jon said. "And if I could find it, it might give me something to bargain with."

"Bargain with whom?"

"The killer, of course," Jon babbled and turned to Mark. "If he was willing to kill Randall and Candy for that information, it must be important to him."

"Pretty pointless now." I leaned back in my chair. "The pipe was stolen."

"What?" Jon gulped, shocked.

Mark piped up. "A street mugger knocked us over and took it."

Jon looked from Mark to me and back again. "I don't believe you."

I stood and walked into the bedroom. I could still hear Jon as he said to Mark, "You're lying, right?"

"What do you think?" came Mark's baritone.

I grabbed the sheets of paper from the laser printer and returned to the dining area. "But not all is lost. We found a flash drive in that pipe."

"A flash drive?" Jon exclaimed. "Oh, that's clever!"

"The data was encoded," I told him, "but I have a friend who cracked the code." I put the pages down in front of Jon. "Are these the reports you were promised?"

Jon looked at the documents, then moved his right hand to his inner jacket pocket.

In a quick move, with reflexes that surprised him, I grabbed Jon's arm and twisted it up and away as he yelped in pain.

"What are you reaching for?" I screamed as I used leverage to keep Jon at a disadvantage.

"Just my glasses," Jon rasped, and I released my grip and glanced up at Mark who gave me a look of admiration.

Jon carefully reached into the pocket of his sports coat and brought out a black vinyl case and a pair of glasses.

"Remind me not to make you mad," Mark praised me with a smile.

I returned the smile, then barked at Jon, "Don't reach for anything if I don't know what it is."

Jon nodded, fear on his face.

"Don't know if *I* can promise that," Mark flirted.

I met his eyes and replied in a sultry tone, "In your case, I'll probably know what you're reaching for—"

"This is it!" Jon gushed, too wrapped up in the papers to be bothered with our flirting. "This is astounding. It shows numerous accounts — and there are lists of clients with amounts he — oh my goodness — money he skimmed from them."

I leaned in and my eyes searched the page. Mark leaned over and read it as well.

"Look," Jon said, and pointed at one of the names, "here's Ms. Cunningham — oh, she's been taken for quite a bit."

"So this paper makes sense to you?" I concluded.

"I do have a degree in accounting," Jon huffed. "When you deal with insurance and annuities, it helps to know what you are talking about."

"Well, that will come in handy." I took the pages away from him and glanced at them. "We can turn these records and *you* over to the police."

"The police?" Jon worried. "But I haven't done anything."

I had to laugh. "You stole Mark's keys, attempted to break into his apartment, made a deal with a woman who ended up shot to steal the records of a man who ended up dead. I think Detective DeStadler is going to want to have a long talk with you."

Jon turned pale — well, paler. "No, if word got out about these incongruities — and if I were arrested — it could ruin me."

"Being arrested is better than the murderer tracking you down," Mark argued.

Jon's eyes went from Mark to me. "Let me stay here. I don't want to risk going out again at night."

"Feeling a little paranoid?"

"I'm the link between these records and the murdered parties," he whined. "I need to be protected."

Mark rose and pulled out his phone. "I'm calling DeStadler. If you need protection, he would be the one to do it." He quickly input the number.

The entire time Jon sat with a defeated look on his face, I examined the pages and scrutinized every name on the list.

"Detective? It's Mark Watkins... Yes, sir, Ms. Homes and I are at my condo. However, we received an unexpected visit from Jon Kane... It appears he is afraid that he is targeted to be the next victim."

I focused on the papers in front of me as Mark gave a quick explanation of what Jon had told us. Finally, he put his hand over the phone. "Sheryl, DeStadler wants the translated files."

I gave an exasperated sigh and headed into the bedroom to send it from the computer. Even from the other room, I could hear Mark as he continued to speak on the phone.

"Should we bring Mr. Kane to the precinct?… I see, you've got a search warrant for his place and don't want him in the way?"

I had to snicker at this as I input the email address and sent the files.

"I guess I can arrange a place for him to stay," Mark spoke into the phone.

I froze and popped my head out of the bedroom. I glanced at Mark, and then glared at Jon with a desire to kill.

I had to admit, Mark looked pretty disappointed as well.

"I'll do that, Detective." Mark ended the call and looked at Jon Kane. "Looks like we are roomies for the night. Have you eaten?"

"Not really."

I came out of the bedroom as Mark offered the uneaten half of his sandwich to Jon.

"Is this whole-grain bread?" Jon challenged.

"It's what we have," Mark told him. "I'll make some eggs." Mark went into the kitchen to cook a quick meal.

"Excuse me," I said, grabbed the papers from Jon, and followed Mark into the hallway that was his kitchen.

"He's staying here?" I hissed in a low whisper.

"DeStadler wants us all in the same place." Mark peeked over to see Jon start to eat what had been his sandwich. "They're searching Jon's apartment."

"But I was hoping — I mean, I thought—" I said, and it was my turn to flush red. My voice went even softer. "What are the sleeping arrangements?"

"I figured you in the bedroom, Jon in the small guest bedroom, and I'll sleep on the couch with the baseball bat to make sure he doesn't bolt during the night."

I gave a sigh of frustration. "I guess that'll have to do."

"Anything on the report I can't understand?" Mark said.

I held up the pages. "I've read it from the first name, Albert-comma-Alice to the last name Yeolde-comma-John, but several names jumped out."

I pointed at one of the columns on the top of the second page. "First, this one—" My finger went to "Alexander, Allen."

"Allen had investments with Randall?"

"Apparently, and it looks like Randall got about ten grand from him."

Mark gave a low whistle. "Talk about motive."

"But that's not all, look at this." My finger moved down the column to the name, "Blake, Norman."

"That's the guy who runs the jewelry booth!"

"Yes, who is left-handed and has — or had — a pipe with your fingerprints on it."

Mark frowned. "I don't know, he seemed so… well… jolly."

"He's a big man and might have a lot of muscle."

"I guess so, but Hypno gave Jon Kane the pipe. She works for John Stewart."

"Yes, but we did see her talking to Blake's assistant, Cliff, earlier," I pointed out. "Do you know what 'Hypno' stands for?"

"Hypatia Norris."

"Well, neither Norris nor Stewart's names are on the list. But do you know who else is?"

"You have me at a loss."

I smiled. "Poole-comma-Candy."

Mark nodded. "Wow, he was ripping off a woman he was sleeping with? That's pretty dumb! It would certainly motivate her to be part of the scheme—"

"To get her money back, and maybe some extra — as severance," I insinuated.

"I still don't see why her co-conspirator would kill her."

"Got greedy, perhaps? Once the deal was done, maybe he didn't want to give Candy her cut."

Mark sighed. "Well, this is not quite the evening I was anticipating."

I gave another annoyed sigh. "Yeah, me neither."

He moved his body close to mine and kissed me hungrily.

Jon inserted the last bite of the sandwich into his mouth and froze in amazement at our kiss.

I had to admit, it was a pretty remarkable kiss.

We separated, and with my head spinning, I returned to the table to eat my own sandwich.

Jon finally was able to speak again. He looked from Mark to me and back again. "I thought you two didn't like each other."

"Now, whatever gave you that idea?" I asked and leaned back in my chair with a knowing smile.

29. Dumpbin

Mark Watkins

The morning came too quickly, as it often does. I was in the midst of a lovely dream, which included a bare-breasted Sheryl Homes, who somehow had become the goddess Athena and touched me in interesting ways.

She turned her head as a pounding noise came from an ivory temple, an ancient-looking building with huge pillars and an ornate exterior.

"Ah," she warned, "we have awakened the God of War with our passion."

I looked past her at the temple when the noise came again. There was a muffled voice behind the huge white door, but I couldn't comprehend the words.

"I think you had best answer that," she told me, and with a wave of her hand, disappeared.

I sat up straight on the sofa where I'd slept, as another series of knocks came from my front door. I quickly rose, threw on my bathrobe, and stumbled my way to the door.

Through the fish-eye lens, I saw Detective DeStadler flanked by two uniformed officers on the other side.

"Just a minute," I bellowed, as I tried to be heard through the heavy wooden door. I undid the locks and pulled the door open. "What time is it?"

"8:00 AM," DeStadler said and looked at the officers he brought. "Wait here!"

They nodded and he walked in.

"More bad news, Watkins." He pulled out a paper and handed it to me. "Ballistics can prove that the gun used to shoot Candy Poole was definitely yours."

"Does my bail hold?"

"Not sure. But it is Sunday and you don't really appear to be a flight risk."

"That's good."

"However, if I get pressure from above to pick you up, I will. This is a definitive link to the weapon found in your apartment. I should warn you this will mean a bail increase—"

"How much?"

"A lot."

"What about Sheryl?"

"She shouldn't plan on taking any trips," DeStadler conceded. "Kane here?"

"Yeah, in the guest room." I pointed at the closed door next to the sofa. "I'll get dressed."

DeStadler headed to my guest room, as I opened the door to the bedroom, which almost knocked Sheryl over as she stood with her ear to the door.

"Is he going to arrest you, again?" she worried.

"He can if he wants to," I pointed out calmly. "I want to get some clothes and grab a quick shower."

DeStadler burst through the door.

"Okay, funny man, where's Kane?"

He stopped and gaped at Sheryl, who had, once again, put on one of Susie's nightgowns. This one, however, was silk and though not transparent, it hugged her body tightly and only reached halfway down her thighs.

I was apparently so sleepy I hadn't noticed.

Sheryl quickly grabbed Susie's robe and covered herself.

"What do you mean?" I said. "This is a small apartment. He's in the other bedroom."

"No, he's not!"

I walked past him, through the dining room, and into the spare room. DeStadler was right. The bed was rumpled but empty. I walked over and pulled the closet open, which was filled with boxes of my own paraphernalia — but no Jon.

I bent down and glanced under the bed, just in case.

I stood and turned to DeStadler, who stared at the window.

"I don't understand," I told him. "I slept on the couch. He couldn't have slipped by me."

"Yeah," DeStadler grunted. "When did you last see him?"

"When we all went to bed. He took the printout of those financial reports with him. He said he wanted to try to figure out who had found the files and where they came from."

"Did it occur to you that maybe you shouldn't put him in the room with the fire escape right outside his window?"

I followed DeStadler's gaze to the open blinds where, indeed, outside the window was the metal framework of a fire escape.

DeStadler went to the window. It was shut, but the lock wasn't fastened, which suggested that it was pushed closed from the outside.

"It wasn't cold last night," DeStadler said. "He could've just gone out and down."

"It — it never occurred to me," I stammered.

"How long have you lived here?" He eyed me suspiciously.

"More than twenty years, but I've never used the fire escape."

DeStadler shook his head and pulled out his cell phone as he made his way to the door.

He glanced back at me. "Forget the shower, throw on some clothes. You're coming with me, after all."

I sighed and walked into the bedroom.

"I've gotta get dressed," I said to Sheryl. "You hear?"

"With DeStadler's big voice?" Sheryl replied. "I think the whole neighborhood heard."

She stepped out of the room and I quickly put on fresh clothes, though I put on the same sports coat I had last night, as the pockets already contained my phone, wallet, and that silly pipe Stewart had given me.

I went into the bathroom and patted down my wild hair with water. One of the uniformed officers came over to me.

"Put your hands behind your back, please," the officer said, and I immediately complied.

He tightened cuffs around my wrists and led me to the door.

DeStadler looked over at Sheryl. "Have your phone nearby if I need to talk to you."

"Or arrest me?" Sheryl mocked with a snide tone.

"Maybe."

"Before you go—" Sheryl handed DeStadler a plastic bag.

"What's this?" DeStadler wondered.

"The pipe Jon Kane had in his pocket last night."

He held up the plastic bag, gazed at the pipe, and turned it over in his hand. "How many of these are there?"

"*That* is an excellent question, detective," Sheryl considered as a thoughtful look passed over her face.

DeStadler nodded, handed the bag to the officer who didn't really escort me but stood by if I made a run for it. As if I would run with my hands bound. We went to the hall and got in the elevator.

"I ask you to do one thing—" DeStadler shook his head. "Just keep Jon Kane with you—"

"I don't understand why he ran," I wondered. "It makes no sense. He said he was concerned that the murderer was after him."

"Makes sense in one case," DeStadler said.

"And that is?"

"If he thinks you're the murderer."

I thought about it on the ride down to the lobby.

Yes, that did make sense. As much as any of this did.

I arrived at the police station, yet again, and wondered if I would stay in the nice filthy holding cell or be sent to Rikers.

For someone who led a pretty stable life free of criminal activity, even jaywalking — which is difficult to avoid when you're a New Yorker — I had barely ventured out in the last two years and now I was spending a lot of that time in jail.

If Susie could see this, what would she think?

It was about 9:00 A.M. when I was brought to the precinct with the odd feeling that I could call everyone by name at this point. I was quickly taken to a holding cell by the unsmiling officer.

Remnants of Saturday night's arrests were still in the cell I was given. Several gentlemen were still asleep, one guy mumbled about his mother, and the smell of vomit wafted through the air.

I made myself as comfortable as one can and sat on a hard bench, leaned my head back against the bars, and closed my eyes. I hoped that I could get back into the lovely dream with Sheryl. When I saw her in that sheer nightgown, it had reminded me of the topless tunic she wore as Athena, though not as revealing.

I must have dozed for a few minutes when I felt myself shaken.

"Wha—" I opened my eyes to see a police officer there.

"Your lawyer is here," he said. I was let out of the cell, handcuffed, and escorted upstairs and into yet another interrogation room where Louie DeSoto sat at the table under the watchful eyes of Detective DeStadler and Detective Elvis.

As was usual when Mr. DeSoto arrived, he carried a look of enormous confidence while the two detectives appeared annoyed.

"And there he is!" Louie said, as he rose from his seat.

My hands were freed and I moved to the chair next to Louie.

He faced the detectives and made a broad motion with his arms.

"Do I have to remind you gentlemen that Mr. Watkins has been released by the court on bail or that neither of you have the authority to revoke such bail unless he commits another crime or is an immediate threat to the community?"

"Ballistics shows your client's gun is the murder weapon," Detective Elvis said.

"That's called new evidence," DeStadler said.

"I call it circumstantial. In my opinion, you are just pissed off that your other suspect, who possessed illegally copied keys for Mr. Watkins' apartment, went out through the window. That is no reason to bring him in." He turned to me. "Mark, we are leaving."

Louie started to put files into his briefcase, just as a knock came at the door. DeStadler, with a face like he wanted to eviscerate the next guy who walked in, turned and opened it. A uniformed officer stuck his head in, whispered to DeStadler, and handed him a folder.

DeStadler turned back with a puzzled look on his face. He handed the folder to Elvis, who opened it, took a look, and his jaw grew hard.

Louie had shut his briefcase and wasn't aware of what just happened. He gave me a smile and headed for the door.

DeStadler and Elvis stood in front of it like stone statues.

"Gentlemen, my client and I are leaving," Louie said politely.

"I'm afraid I will have to ask you both to sit down," DeStadler said and indicated the table and chairs.

"There's nothing to discuss. We are leaving," Louie said as he tried to hold his ground.

"I am afraid that a situation has come up that suggests your client is, in fact, an immediate danger to the community."

I slowly sat in the chair.

"*I'm* a danger?" was all I could manage.

"What is the meaning of this?" Louie said as Elvis began to take photos out of the folder and lay them face up on the table.

"We found Mr. Kane," DeStadler said.

The photos were of Jon Kane, his head bloodied, his eyes staring blankly into nothingness.

"The *late* Mr. Kane," Elvis added.

"And as an interesting side note, he was found in the alley at the bottom of your client's fire escape," DeStadler said.

"My building?" I blurted, my mouth agape.

"That's right. His head was bashed in with a baseball bat," Elvis said as a smug look came to his dark face.

30. Kerning

Sheryl Homes

I had been sitting at Mark's dining room table looking at my phone and willing it to ring.

After Mark had left with DeStadler, I stormed around the apartment, fighting the urge to break something, as nothing there was mine to break.

I finally calmed down by lying down on Mark's bed. Okay, I admit it, I put his pillow to my face and inhaled his scent. That totally relaxed my need to break something and excited my other desires.

I finally got out of the bed before I took advantage of myself, and had more coffee.

For the last ten minutes, I had been staring at my phone, and all but jumped out of my skin when it rang.

The display announced: Uncle Louie.

With a far too girly squeal, I hit the button. "Yes, yes, is Mark free?"

My mind was filled with visions of getting him here and having my way with him, whether he agreed to be ravished or not.

I had a feeling he'd be *very* willing.

"Hey, sweetie," Louie's voice came over my phone. "We ran into a snag."

I had to admit, I showed remarkable restraint and did not scream like a banshee and throw the phone across the room in a tornado of frustration.

"What?" I groaned.

"Apparently, they found this Jon Kane character."

"Doesn't that help Mark?" I whined.

"No. He was found at the bottom of the fire escape beaten to death with Mark's bat."

I found I stood up and walked over to the sofa, where Mark had the bat when I went to bed last night. Of course, it wasn't there.

"What can we do?" I said breathlessly.

"Well, Mark's being held based on the idea that he spent the entire night alone," Louie said.

I thought for a moment. "What if he wasn't alone?"

"That would change things, sweetie."

I slapped the table with my open hand. "Mark was with me."

Louie was silent as he considered this. "Are you willing to sign a statement to that effect?"

"I am. Mark snuck into the bedroom at about midnight and spent the night in bed with me."

"Okay! So, this is what I want you to do…"

I was grateful I had brought my suitcase to Mark's place because it gave me the chance to put on my sexy little black dress and a pair of high heels that matched.

I wasn't even sure why I packed that particular outfit in the first place. When I headed to the conference, I wasn't looking to meet anyone. I think perhaps I had planned to wear it to upstage Candy and make Randall's tongue fall out. But now, I needed it for a situation far more serious than upstaging a rival.

I took a cab to Louie's office where a lovely lady, Tina, met me. She was a short woman, a tad overweight, with cropped blonde hair and the look of a librarian, right down to the horn-rimmed glasses.

She took my statement and typed it up for my signature. Then she had to file paperwork, and I stood ready to defend my man, once all our weapons were in place.

About an hour later, Tina and I were riding in a cab to the police station.

"I like your dress," Tina admitted with admiration.

"Thank you, Tina. Do you think it will create the effect Louie is after?"

She grinned. "Most definitely."

The cab dropped us off at the precinct, and Tina and I found Louie standing around in the lobby.

"Hey, look at you, sweetie," he praised as I walked in and gave him a twirl to show off my ensemble. He then turned to Tina. "I owe you, Tina."

"Yes you do," Tina responded. "You know how hard it is to get paperwork moving on a Sunday."

He shifted back to me. "Okay, let me get you up to snuff. They got photos of Kane all messed up and photos of a bat they found a few blocks away. It's an aluminum bat with black diamonds on the side."

"Sounds like the one we had last night," I agreed. "I couldn't find it today."

"I think this Kane guy took it with him as protection. Now, you know what to say?"

I nodded. "I follow your lead."

"Good girl," he smirked. "Tina you got all the paperwork?"

Tina held up the folder of papers with a triumphant smile.

"Okay, it's show time!" he barked.

We went up the stairs and to the room where Mark was being questioned. Louie told me to hang back and stand where I couldn't be seen from the inside when the door was opened.

We stopped outside the door, and he made sure the volume was turned up on a little box next to it. Voices came through the tinny speaker.

"Yes, it's my bat," Mark was saying with a sigh. "Where was it found?"

DeStadler's big voice took over. "A dumpster around the corner from the crime scene."

"I assume with my prints?" Mark said defensively.

"Yours and the deceased. Plus, part of the victim's brain matter. You got an explanation for that?"

"For crying out loud, I didn't kill anyone."

"Look, Watkins, what am I supposed to do? I keep finding items with your prints at places where people are dead."

"I honestly didn't know any of these people before Wednesday. Even Ms. Homes."

Louie pushed his way through the door, and now his voice came over the speaker. "Questioning my client without me, detective? You know that's not a good idea, right?"

"I've got your client's fingerprints on a fancy pipe at a crime scene," DeStadler said. "I've got his gun as the murder weapon at a second scene, and I've got his fingerprints on the murder weapon at a third scene. At some point, I have to assume your client is involved."

"Have you got the TOD?" Louie demanded.

"Time of death was between 1:00 and 2:00 A.M.," DeStadler confirmed.

"I see," Louie said. "Mark, have you told these gentlemen where you were at that time?"

Mark began. "At my condo—"

"Not another word!" Louie snapped.

That was my cue. I moved to the door and stood ready for my entrance.

Louie opened the door with all the finesse of a magician revealing his restored assistant.

I walked in. Well, no, I didn't walk in. I *sashayed* in. I vamped my way into the room and every male eye was riveted to the bitch-goddess who could make their dreams come true.

My perfect little black dress was sleeveless and hugged my bosom and hips like a second skin, to end just as it touched my knees. The color set off my red hair and pale skin. I wore high heels which made me taller and also made my legs look good. I was even wearing a pair of fishnet stockings to complete the ensemble of doom.

As I walked in, Mark's mouth fell open, as well as both Elvis and DeStadler.

I moved to the table and sat demurely as Uncle Louie put a paper in front of me.

"Ms. Homes, is this your statement?"

I gave it a glance. "Yes."

"And it states that between 1:00 and 2:00 AM last night, you were staying at Mr. Watkins' condominium, is that correct?"

"Correct."

"But you were not alone?"

"No, I was not. Mr. Watkins was with me."

"In the bedroom?"

"Yes, he'd crept into the bedroom about midnight." As I spoke, I noticed that there were crime scene photos on the table, so I made a point to give them a quick gander.

"You approved of Mr. Watkins joining you?"

"Most definitely," I said and flashed a smile at Mark that suggested we'd shared pleasures that the detectives could only dream of. "He spent the rest of the night with me until Detective DeStadler knocked on our door about 8:00 AM."

"Hold on," DeStadler bellowed. "Mr. Watkins stated he slept on the couch."

Louie gazed at Mark. "What do you have to say, Mark?"

He took the hint. "I... uh... I didn't want the detective to think anything... um... untoward about Ms. Homes."

"Say what?" Detective Elvis said.

"Hey," Louie countered, "Mr. Watkins is a writer. That's how he talks, okay?"

I spoke up. "I believe that Detective DeStadler saw me in a rather revealing outfit." I cast my eyes down shyly.

It was DeStadler's turn to blush.

"So you see, gentlemen," Louie said, "I have a witness who can vouch for Mr. Watkins' whereabouts at the time of the murder."

"A witness who there is every indication is his accomplice," DeStadler grumbled.

Louie got up and again returned to the door, opened it, and snapped his fingers.

Tina walked in and handed Louie a folded paper with great finesse.

"Thank you, Tina," he said, and the woman gave him a nod and left.

"This is a writ of *Habeas Corpus*, demanding Mr. Watkins' immediate release."

He handed it to Detective DeStadler and turned to Sheryl and me.

"Sheryl, Mark, we are going."

"Don't go far, either of you," DeStadler ordered. His eyes were going over the papers Louie gave him.

Once again, we walked out of the police precinct and I took off the high heel shoes and put on a pair of flats from a bag that Tina, who had been waiting for us, was holding.

"Thank God that's over," I sassed.

"But why did you tell them—" Mark began.

"Ah, ah!" Louie stopped him. "If you are going to discuss anything that might conflict with your statement, I should be out of earshot!"

"Sorry," Mark stressed.

"Uncle Louie," I asked, "will you be able to check on those *other* things for me?"

"Already got a girl working on it," Louie reported.

"A girl?" Tina complained. "Don't you mean Tina, the *woman* to whom you already owe a favor?"

Louie gave a smile. "Ain't she something? I'll call you when I get an answer, but hey! It *is* Sunday, cah-peesh?"

"Do your best," I implored.

With a wave, he turned and headed off in the opposite direction with Tina close behind.

I turned and walked east as Mark caught up to me.

"Why did you say we slept together?" Mark insisted.

"Well, it wasn't a total lie."

He gently took my arm and stopped us. "Yes, it was. If we did, I am sure I would remember."

She smiled at that. "I am sure you would. Quite honestly, if Jon hadn't shown up, it would have been a *fait accompli*."

He looked me over. "Really?"

"Yes, really," I said, and took his face in both hands and kissed him hard.

Then I pulled back and immediately began to walk again. "But now I am perturbed—"

Mark took a moment to catch up and catch on. "Perturbed?"

"Yes, we let ourselves be the mouse in this cat-and-mouse game for the last time. I am ready to solve these murders."

"Just like that?"

"Before the conference ends tonight," I announced, and held up my index finger toward the sky for emphasis.

Mark glanced at his watch. "That is only, like, five hours."

I raised an eyebrow. "Then, Watkins, we shall have to work quickly."

31. Binding

Mark Watkins

We walked into the hotel and up the escalator to the second floor. The place was mobbed with crowds of people in costume. They milled about, all of them talking, which created a dull roar of subdued voices. There was even a waiting line to get into the Marketplace. I was sure the merchants were doing a brisk business.

I talked loud to be heard over the din. "The murders didn't scare anyone away."

"Are you kidding?" Sheryl shouted back to me. "It probably doubled the attendance. Why play at mystery when you can be part of a real one?"

"Hey," a voice bellowed through the crowd, "that's Mark Watkins!"

Another voice rang out, "And look, Sheryl Homes!"

"There they are!" said a third.

All at once, we were set upon by wave after wave of people who wanted their photo with us. Some did selfies and held out their arm as far as they could to get the picture, others used extendable sticks. Several were groups where one person photographed all of them at once.

Sheryl and I smiled politely and took the photos, as we attempted to be good sports when all we wanted was to get out of there.

One of the twenty-somethings stepped away and said, "Wow! I've never had a photo with a real murderer before."

I exchanged a horrified look with Sheryl.

She grabbed my hand and pulled us away, which upset a fresh group of people who expected to pose with us as we scurried down a hallway. We made our way into the secondary lobby where I heard a familiar voice.

There, surrounded by a group of costumed attendees, was Allen Alexander as he pontificated to his crowd.

"I knew he would end up this way," he spoke loudly. "Stealing from me was the first step on a chain that led that deluded man to murder."

"Wow!" intoned a young, well-endowed woman in a form-fitting chain-mail bikini. "You're lucky he didn't try to kill *you*."

"He wouldn't have the guts to confront me face-to-face, *mano a mano*, sweetheart," Allen smirked.

"Oh wow!" the busty beauty gushed.

I ducked my head and Sheryl took us down another hallway. We slipped into an empty meeting room where I closed the door behind us.

"They wanted pictures because they thought we're killers?" she snapped angrily.

"I guess word got out that we're suspects."

She shook her head. "That's just sick!"

"Yeah, and now Allen is making himself out to be a big hero!"

"To add to the myth that you stole his stories."

"On the good side," I attempted, "I always wanted to be a famous writer."

"Me, too, but not an *infamous* one!" She leaned against a large table and sighed.

"How can we investigate?" I complained. "We can't even walk around."

"Not easily."

I muttered, "If we could only be in two places at the same time."

She stared at me and her mouth fell open.

"What?" I asked, puzzled by the look on her face.

"Oh, I've been a fool!" she objected. "I ought to know by this time that when a fact appears to be opposed to a long train of deductions, it invariably proves to be capable of bearing some other interpretation."

There she went with the Holmes' quotes again. "I don't see—"

"Two places at the same time!" she repeated. "The murderer would have to be in two places at the same time—"

"I really don't understand," I admitted. "Didn't we already deduce that Candy helped the killer?"

"But that doesn't explain the fact that Candy was found undressed," she said. "Why would the killer sneak in with a gun, undress her, and *then* shoot her?"

My mouth fell open. "He wouldn't. He wouldn't want to risk her seeing the gun."

"But what if the killer had a partner? That partner could distract her with a rendezvous, leaving the killer to finish off Randall, and then come to the hotel to take care of her."

"If so, perhaps Candy wasn't there when Randall was actually murdered," I hypothesized.

"That could be why they had to eliminate her—" Sheryl snapped her fingers. "Because once she found out that Randall was dead—"

"She would go to the police and ruin the entire plan!"

"Brilliant, Watkins."

"Astounding, Homes."

"So we are looking for a team—"

"Perhaps not! Homes, this could explain why Jon Kane was killed."

Her eyes brightened as she also made the realization. "Because he was the partner — either the killer or the seducer."

"If he was the seducer, the timeline fits," I said. "He was caught on camera going up to the 12th floor at 1:15 AM. Candy arrived back at the hotel at 1:30."

"So Jon could be waiting for Candy to 'celebrate' their new-found wealth."

"And Candy didn't know that the other partner was smothering Randall at the same time."

Sheryl stared up at the ceiling, the gears turning in her mind.

I felt a bit overwhelmed by the possibilities. The days of little sleep, repeated arrests, and the tension as I tried to absorb the data necessary to figure the case out had severely limited my ability to think clearly.

Not to mention the emotional upheaval as I discovered my feelings for Sheryl.

I thought about the different possible suspects: Charles Nederlander had a copy of my pipe and could've worked with Jon Kane. But why would he need to? He was Randall's partner and could've just demanded the information. And why involve Jon Kane?

Winsley Cunningham certainly didn't seem strong enough to carry me to a different room, but with Candy and Jon's help? Could she have been the shooter? Not likely. But how did her cameo end up in Candy's room?

Then there was Norm and Cliff — and Norm was on Randall's list. Could either or both of them have worked with Jon? Then again, John Stewart's partner, Hypno, gave me the pipe with the financial data and told Jon that I had it. And how did our mugger know where'd we be to get the pipe? Only Stewart or Hypno could know what was in it.

John Stewart seemed too damaged by his stroke to be involved, but with the powerful Hypno, she could've been his leg man — uh — person.

Add to the mess, Allen might just be insane enough to do this just to discredit me. What if he found out that Randall cheated him out of money, could that have been an inciting event to push him over the edge?

By this point, my brain felt like it was about to short-circuit.

Sheryl turned to me. "I need a place where I can rent a computer and printer."

I stirred from my reverie. "There's an office place on Seventh Avenue, not far from here. What are you going to—"

"I have a plan," she said.

I swallowed hard. "So far our plans have not worked out very well."

"This one will," she said. "We need a place to assemble the suspects!"

"Assemble the suspects? What are you talking about?"

"I need you to go to the conference welcome desk to see if there is a room that we can use at 5:00 PM."

"What are you going to do then?"

"Reveal the killer!" she said with her now-familiar wicked smile. "Mark, this is what I want you to do..."

I kept my head down as I reached the welcome desk, which was manned by one middle-aged lady in glasses who looked as if she had been there all day.

"Hi!" I said.

She raised her head, gave me a dirty look, then recognized me and brightened.

"Mr. Watkins!" she gushed.

I put my index finger to my lips and glanced about.

She looked at the crowd as if they were bugs. "Oh, yes, the 'fans' have been looking for you."

"They think I'm a murderer."

"Oh, pish! I can't believe that for a minute." She gave a sneer to the people who milled about. "Then again, these folks will believe anything."

She leaned forward from behind the table. "Normally, the conference is pretty much over by Sunday, but with the murders — this is the busiest Sunday we've ever had!"

"I guess that's good?"

"Not when I'm here all alone," she griped. "Candy was a big help, poor thing. Did you get a chance to meet her?"

"Yes," I acknowledged while I nodded my head, "lovely girl."

I decided it would be bad form to bring up the fact that I was drugged by her and it was suspected I shot her.

"But now, it is so busy and I have no help!"

"Only a few hours more… uh—" I glanced to try to read her name tag.

"Alice," she said, as she noticed my attempt.

"Ah, yes!" I confided. "Is there, by any chance, a meeting room that would be free at 5:00?"

She shrugged. "All of them, I suppose. We technically have the meeting rooms until 6:00, but all the events end at 5:00."

"And the Marketplace closes?"

"Yes, the whole thing shuts down and I get some rest!"

I smiled. "Is there a room I can use? I mean, to have an informal… uh… meeting?"

"Well, of course, Mr. Watkins, for you." She looked at a list and then at a tablet computer she had behind the desk.

"Regent is done at 4:00. That might be the best choice," she said and looked up at me. "Are you having an impromptu writer's workshop?"

"Something like that," I agreed.

"How exciting!"

"Isn't it? Thanks."

I grabbed one of the glossy magazines, which listed all the events, and faded back into the crowd.

I worked my way through the filled hallways, and I was surprised to see that the conference had become quite a bit more raucous. There had been a huge influx of younger people and the majority of them in costume.

I walked by two women dressed as a pair of famed super heroines. As I passed them, it dawned on me that they both wore nothing more than a G-string and the rest of their "costume" consisted of carefully applied body paint.

In light of how staid the conference had been the first few days, it certainly was different.

I considered for a moment that perhaps all of our deductions had been wrong. The real reason for the murders was to promote the conference.

I arrived at Regent and peeked in. There was still a panel, with chairs about the room and a raised platform where people spoke. But it was fairly informal and I thought it would suit Sheryl's needs.

At least it fit what she told me she needed before she sneaked out the back way from the hotel.

I pulled out my phone and quickly texted her the room name and the time I had set aside as per her request. I paused for a moment and remembered that I really enjoyed the moment when she input her number into my phone before she left.

It gave me the sense that she wanted to stay in touch. Of course, when she told me the pair of us making love was a *fait accompli,* it had been even better.

She texted me back her approval, and then I started to put her plan into action.

I had to admit I would have preferred to know the entire plan, instead of merely my "assignments." But Sheryl told me to trust her and carry them out.

I looked through the magazine at the conference events until I saw that Charles Nederlander was part of a panel titled: *The Mystery — An Outdated Construct?*

I went through the corridors where I passed a group of young people in jeans and casual clothes, but each one wore a deerstalker hat. They sat around on the floor and discussed something or other that was, and I quote, "dope."

I arrived just as the panel ended and people came out. I glanced in and saw Charles behind the table, where he smiled and shook hands with the other participants.

As I approached, his eyes grew small.

"Charles, I'm glad I caught you..."

He pulled me aside.

"What are you doing here?" he hissed in a loud whisper.

"I was invited, remember?"

"I think it would be best if you were *not* here at all! Candy — and now poor Jon!"

"I had nothing to do with—"

"You really expect me to believe that?" he demanded. "What with you and Ms. Homes stalking about the hotel and accusing me of — I don't know what — to cover your own guilt. I hope you realize I am an attorney and I will—"

I held my hands up. "That's not why I'm here."

He frowned. "What now?"

"I'm here because Sheryl told me there is going to be a confession delivered at 5:00 PM. She thought you might be interested in hearing what actually happened."

The color drained from his face for a moment. "Confession? From the killer?"

"That's what I've been told."

"So you know who killed Candy? And Randall?"

"We will be in the Regent Room at 5:00 PM, and she said it will be worth your while."

He hesitated as if to consider all the ramifications. "I shall... think about it."

Without another word, I turned on my heels and left the room.

I opened my event magazine again and quickly located Winsley Cunningham, who was about to start a panel on *Was Conan Doyle Inspired by Edgar Allan Poe?*

It was just down the hall from Charles and the room had filled up for her lecture. She saw me walk in and a look appeared on her face as if she'd just tasted something unpleasant.

I walked toward her and stopped.

There on her lapel was the green Sherlock cameo!

I quickly put it out of my mind and approached.

"Mr. Watkins," she said politely as I drew near. "My panel is about to begin."

I gently turned her away from the room.

"Yes, but Sheryl Homes asked me to have you meet us in the Regent Room at 5:00 PM."

"Why on earth would I do that?" she snorted.

"Well, for one thing," I explained, as I decided to brazen my way through this, "the police might be interested to know that you own more than one of those cameos and where the other one was discovered."

Her eyes grew wide. Apparently, I'd guessed correctly.

For once.

"That will not be necessary," she replied. "I will meet you there. However, I should state vehemently that I will not be a party to blackmail."

"Nothing of the kind," I soothed. "We just need your insights to get this all figured out."

Her brows lowered and she looked at me suspiciously. "What do you mean?"

"I mean, we will find all the answers then," I conceded. "See you there."

She glared at me as I walked out the door, but didn't follow. I heard her call the panel to order as I walked toward the Marketplace.

My next stop was the jewelry booth of Norm Blake. They were busy with customers as plenty of people bought jewelry and cameos from Cliff as Norm continued to sit and work on his latest creation. He looked tired but happy, and I had to wait for a few patrons to finish before I could approach.

"Hey there, Mr. Watkins," Cliff greeted. "Did you hear about Mr. Kane? Wow, this is the only mystery conference I've ever been to with a real mystery."

I gave him a wan smile. "Guess so. Can I speak to Norm?"

I had to raise my voice above the din.

Cliff nodded and he gently tapped Norm on the shoulder. Norm stood, gave a stretch, took off his glasses, rubbed his eyes, and walked over.

"Norm," I said, "I need your help."

His glasses went back to his face. "Sure, what is it?"

"The police may have figured out who killed those people."

His eyebrows shot up. "Really? Well… that's good."

"But we need an expert to take a look at a cameo they found at the murder scene."

"A cameo? Where?"

"I'm not allowed to say. But if you could meet us at the Regent Room at 5:00 PM—"

"5:00 PM? But I have to break down my stuff. We only have until 7:00 to get it all out—"

"It shouldn't take long," I said.

He shrugged his chubby shoulders. "I guess, if it won't take too long. I can leave Cliff to start packing up."

I nodded, thanked him, and quickly headed to the YE OLDE MYSTERIOUS TOBACCO SHOPPE booth where John Stewart and Hypno also enjoyed the bounty of the increased customer base.

Hypno watched me carefully as I approached, and I tried to remember exactly what Sheryl told me to say.

"Mark," John beamed as he saw me, "nice to see you're out and about."

"Maybe not for long," I told him, and I gestured to Hypno to join us. She gave a dirty look to John, excused herself from a man who compared two pipes, and stomped over.

"What?" she scoffed. "We have customers."

"It's important," I replied. "I am going to be questioned by the police at 5:00 PM at the Regent Meeting Room—"

"I don't see how that concerns us," Hypno maintained.

"Give him a chance," John offered. "Whaddya need?"

"I just need you two to tell them I got the pipe with the red 'X' on the bottom here on Wednesday — not the day I paid for it."

John exchanged a look with Hypno. "I don't see how I could be any help. Hypno actually was the one who gave you the pipe. Besides, we gotta break everything down. We only have until—"

"7:00, I know," I interjected.

Hypno gave a shrug. "I'll go."

John looked at her, surprised. I had to admit I was surprised as well.

"I can talk to the cops," she volunteered. "Maybe it'll help them figure it all out."

"That's great!" I urged, relieved that it worked. "I'll see you then — the Regent Room."

I walked away and moved through the crowds in pursuit of my final participant.

I didn't have long to wait.

"Well, there's the jailbird! They let you go again, huh?" came the voice of Allen Alexander as he approached me.

"Allen, you're just the man I wanted to see."

He stopped about five feet from me.

"Don't try anything," he said, and gave a gesture to the crowds. "There are a lot of witnesses here—"

"I'm not going to do anything to you—"

"No, not where you can be seen. I am really surprised at you, Mark. Who would think that a *putz* like you could secretly be a criminal mastermind?"

I stepped closer and he looked wary.

"You're right," I confirmed. "It's time I came clean and confessed!"

"To what?"

"To everything. The murders, stealing your ideas—"

His eyes brightened. Then he grew suspicious. "Is this a joke?" His eyes narrowed to slits.

"I will be at the Regent Room at 5:00 PM, if you want to find out."

"The Regent Room? How do I know you aren't just trying to lure me there to get me alone—"

"The police will be there. I am going to reveal everything. Be there — if you want."

I turned and walked away. As I moved up a hallway, I glanced back to see Allen watch me with a puzzled expression.

He was hooked.

The game was, indeed, afoot.

It is often said that in war the wait is the worst part. I couldn't agree more.

The wheels were in motion, the players were in position, the flag was ready to be saluted, and I had run out of clichés.

I sat in the Regent Room on the second floor of the Hilton Hotel at 4:45 PM, totally unsure how the next few minutes would unfold. I had no notion of what Sheryl had planned.

I also didn't have any better ideas.

The first to arrive was Charles Nederlander at about ten of the hour. He strode up the hall, chin up, head back, his eyes studying every detail.

He lingered in the doorway. "Just the two of us, then?" he questioned.

"No, we're just the first to get here."

This relaxed him and he took several steps into the room, found a chair near the door, and sat down.

Two minutes later, Winsley Cunningham walked in.

"Charles?" she said, when she saw I wasn't alone. "What does this have to do with you?"

I wanted to shout something dramatic, like "Everything!" However, except for our suppositions, I didn't know if he had anything to do with it or not.

The most hesitant arrival was Allen. He approached the door surreptitiously, although I didn't see him until he peeked around the doorjamb.

"Come in, Allen," I invited.

He stood tall and walked into the room and gave a nod of recognition to Winsley and Charles.

"Why're they here?" he said. "Witnesses?"

"All will become clear momentarily," I said as Norm Blake shifted his large body through the door, followed by the slender Hypno.

"Looks like a party," Hypno said. "This better not take long. I hafta get back to break down the booth."

Norm nodded. "Myself as well!"

"Look here!" Charles said, appearing as if he wanted to take charge. "I don't know why you asked all of us here, but I think you'd better explain yourself right now."

"That won't be necessary," Detective DeStadler said as he walked into the room. He was followed by Detective Elvis and two officers in uniform, a rather tall, thin man and a short, squat African-American woman.

Between the two police officers walked Sheryl Homes with a manila folder clasped in her hand.

32. Rule Line

Sheryl Homes

A s I strode into the room after Detective DeStadler and looked at the assembled suspects, I saw a look of pure relief appear on Mark's face. I am sure he did not expect the police escort.

I glanced at DeStadler, who gave me a nod, and moved to the center of the room.

"Thank you for meeting us, all of you," I began. "This has been a terrible situation. Three people have died due to greed and avarice—"

"Ms. Homes," DeStadler warned her curtly. "When I agreed to this I said no dramatics."

"Hmm?" I said. "Right, right. Sorry."

I started to pace. "In reviewing the clues that we have found, I have convinced the police that someone in this room — perhaps more than one — is our murderer."

"Yeah," Allen piped up, "and the evidence points to you and Watkins. The police have arrested you like four times, right?"

DeStadler gave me a look, as if to say, "See?"

"Be that as it may," I went on. "Please sit down. There are some discrepancies between what each of you told the police and the evidence that has been uncovered."

Everyone found a seat, except the two uniformed officers who stood at the door and Charles who said, "I, for one, find this entire process ridiculous."

"Really?" I told him and opened the folder I carried. "So you were aware that the victim, Randall Lawrence, had secret accounts where he funneled money from your clients?"

"Funneled money?" Charles frowned. "I have no idea what you're talking about."

"That's odd," DeStadler announced as I handed him a page from the folder. "Because Ms. Homes had a forensic accountant go through those accounts. According to him, a month ago a transfer was made into an account *you* own in the Cayman Islands."

Charles went pale. "That was just... business. I didn't know it came from... I mean... it was a deal that we were working on. I just assumed the money was from a legitimate source."

"I'm sure," I chided. "Were you aware Randall kept detailed records of money he 'acquired' from clients through illegal means?"

"I didn't know anything of the kind!" Charles grimaced. "I was merely the legal side of the business. It was my job to handle contracts—"

"You do realize," I pushed, "that if any of the financial reports or forms you signed off on for the IRS are incorrect, you would also be liable?"

"Yeah," DeStadler added, "and they frown on people hiding money."

Charles began to sweat profusely. He ran a hand over his face.

"I believe—" he said haltingly, "—that I will sit down after all."

Winsley spoke up. "I fail to understand why you have us all here! I know I have done nothing—"

"We asked *you* here because we found something of yours," I chirped and gave a nod to DeStadler, who pulled from his pocket a plastic bag that contained the jade silhouette pin.

A murmur went through the room.

Winsley's hand went to her lapel to touch the pin on it.

"That can't be mine," she denied.

"That is why we asked Mr. Blake to join us." I turned to face the red-haired man. "Is there something you wish to tell us about the pin Ms. Cunningham is currently wearing?"

Blake looked from me to Winsley and back, then he peered at DeStadler, who glowered at him.

I drew near his seat to look down on him. "I should tell you, I found this pin in the hotel room where Candy Poole had been shot."

Norm rose from his chair slowly and looked at Winsley. "I'm sorry, Ms. Cunningham, but I didn't know there'd be police—"

"If you know anything, you'd better tell it now," DeStadler growled.

Norm nodded his head. "Ms. Cunningham brought me a picture and told me to make a pin just like it. I was up all night —"

"Really?" I exulted and shot a look at Winsley.

Norm continued, "I told her I could improve upon the design, but she wanted an exact copy."

"Very well," Winsley groused and threw her hands up. "I had him make me another pin! There is no crime in that."

DeStadler stood and leaned over Winsley, towering over her. "So you want to tell me how *this* pin got into the room of the murdered girl?"

"It's all perfectly innocent!" Winsley disclosed. "I had asked Randall to supply me with the details of my accounts."

"Why?" DeStadler insisted.

"My own tracking of the markets gave me reason to believe that Randall was cheating me. However, I also asked Mr. Kane to find out what he could about my finances—"

"Why would you ask him?" DeStadler inquired.

"He told me he had a hacker who could dig into Randall's files —"

I exchanged a look with Mark, who raised an eyebrow. Once again, the mysterious hacker was mentioned.

DeStadler looked down at Winsley. "Do you know who this hacker is?"

"No, Jon was very secretive. But he assured me that he would have the information I wanted by Friday, two days ago."

"Why didn't you tell us about this?" DeStadler challenged.

"At the time you interviewed me, detective, Mr. Kane was alive. However, I did tell you — and also told that annoying Ms. Homes — that I received a phone call on Wednesday night that Randall was giving *his* financial reports to Candy Poole."

"So," I gloated, "Randall had planned to meet with Ms. Poole the night he was murdered!"

DeStadler held up his hand to stop me. "Ms. Homes? I got this." His eyes returned to Winsley. "Go on."

Winsley continued. "Well, Thursday morning I didn't see Candy at the welcome booth, and I was eager to get Randall's reports so I would be able to compare them to the ones I anticipated from Jon, so I borrowed the spare key from the welcome booth to check Ms. Poole's room."

"This was before the body was reported?" DeStadler confirmed.

"Yes. I let myself into Ms. Poole's room, shut the door, and called to her. I had to fumble a bit for the light switch as the blinds were closed and the room was very dark. But when I turned the lights on… there she was, lying there."

"What did you do?" I put in, which got a stern look from DeStadler.

"I am afraid I fell back in surprise and threw my hands up to catch myself on the dresser. I believe that's when I knocked my cameo off. I went weak in the knees and had to lean against the dresser to catch my breath."

"Did you try to help her?" DeStadler interjected.

"It was obvious that she was dead. So, I wiped any possible fingerprints from anything I touched and left as quickly as I could," Winsley said. "It wasn't until hours later that I realized my pin was missing."

"Wait a minute," I pronounced. "You mean you came down and ran our panel, knowing that Candy was dead?"

Winsley nodded. "It might seem cold-hearted, but I honestly didn't know what to do. I mean, the girl had obviously been shot."

"And you went back to that room again?" asked DeStadler.

"Yes, on Friday. Since the police hadn't asked me about the cameo and I couldn't locate it anywhere else, I thought it could be in her room. Instead, I found Ms. Homes and Mr. Watkins." Winsley pointed at me and then at Mark.

DeStadler gave a quick dirty look to me. "We are aware they were there."

"So," Winsley stressed, "I may not have reported Candy's murder, but I had nothing to do with it."

"Yet," I urged, "you had Norm Blake make a duplicate cameo for you."

"People kept asking why I wasn't wearing mine. I decided it would be best if I had one. After all, Mr. Blake is a skilled craftsman."

"I didn't know it had anything to do with murder," Norm blurted. "She told me it had gotten lost when she strolled through Central Park."

"And you, Mr. Blake," I strode over to where the man sat. "You saw Mr. Watkins on Wednesday, the first day of the conference, is that correct?"

"Yeah — uh — yes, he came by my booth," Norm gulped.

"And while he was there, he examined a pipe?"

"Yeah, sure, the Calabash," Norm agreed. "But he had another one, showed it to me and everything."

"And what happened to *your* pipe?" I insisted.

"I don't know. Cliff handled the sales. We either sold it or put it away."

"We will want to check," DeStadler grunted.

I nodded. "Allen—"

"Me? What?" Allen responded, and sat up straight in his chair.

"Of everyone in this room, you have the strongest motive. For years, you have claimed Mark stole your ideas, and I have rebuffed your advances more than once."

"Rebuffed?" he repeated as if unsure of the word. "Look, that was just flirting — no big deal."

"Oh really?" I yanked another page from the folder. "But you also had accounts with Randall."

"He was helping me with my retirement."

"However, you had a few setbacks?"

"Hey, the market changes," he dismissed. "A few ups and downs. Randall assured me that in the long run I would come out ahead."

"Despite anything he told you," she said as she pulled a page from the folder in her hand. "According to financial statements we found, he transferred a portion of your money slowly out of your account. Over time, it amounted to ten thousand dollars."

"What?"

"As it turns out, Randall was skimming the accounts of most of his customers."

"Why, that dirty bastard!" Allen stood up. "I'll kill him—"

Allen suddenly realized what he said and quietly returned to his seat.

"I mean, I'll sue his ass," Allen mumbled.

Detective DeStadler marched over to Allen's chair. "You wanna tell me your whereabouts on Wednesday night around midnight?"

Allen looked up at the policeman as he hovered over him. "I was here, in the hotel."

"Alone?"

His face grew sullen. "Yeah."

"But the question I keep coming back to..." I closed the gap between me and Hypno "...is about that pipe."

"What about it?" Hypno asked, cool as a cucumber.

"It was odd that you selected a pipe that was specifically marked for Jon Kane and gave it to Mr. Watkins." I turned to DeStadler. "Does that seem odd to you?"

DeStadler nodded. "It seems unusual that it had financial data on a flash drive inside it."

"I don't know anything about a flash drive. I thought the red 'X' meant it was a reject." She gave a shrug. "How did I know it was special?"

"Well, somebody knew it was special," I cajoled. "They knew it was so special that they sent someone to steal it. Someone strong and fast."

Hypno shrugged. "People get mugged all the time in a big city."

I couldn't help the smile that appeared on my face. "You're right. But isn't it strange that you knew it was a mugging?"

"Whaddya mean?" Hypno frowned. "People get ripped off, I assume it was a mugger."

"I said it was stolen. I didn't say how," I maintained. "Also it is equally strange, since you were the one who met with Jon Kane and told him that Mark possessed that specific pipe."

"I brought him a pipe, he told me it had to be the pipe with the red 'X'. I told him Watkins had that one. I don't see what that has to do with anything."

I pressed on. "So, Candy sent Jon to pick up a pipe from you, and at the same time, you were unaware of anything special about the pipe he wanted?"

"It begs the question," DeStadler huffed, "of just how you knew Candy Poole."

"I knew her from the convention," Hypno grunted. "She asked me to meet some guy and give him a pipe."

"And you just did what someone you barely knew requested?" I asked.

Hypno shrugged. "She paid for a pipe; we needed the sale. We pride ourselves on customer service."

"So, not a big deal at all," I said. "Let me make sure I follow this. There were three pipes. One was given to Mark, one was bought by Candy Poole and given to Jon Kane, and one was bought by—"

I turned to face Charles. "By you, Charles."

"Yes," Charles said smugly. "And with the things you and Mr. Watkins said to me the other day, I have made sure to keep it with me ever since."

He reached into his jacket pocket and pulled out one of the elaborate Calabash pipes.

He stepped forward and gently placed it on the table.

I made eye contact with Mark who looked panicked. I merely smiled and gave him a wink.

"Mr. Blake," DeStadler took charge, "why don't you call your assistant and find out if a customer bought your Calabash pipe?"

Norm nodded and pulled out his phone.

"That really won't be necessary, detective," I corrected. "You see, I believe that Mr. Blake still has *his* pipe in his possession."

"I do?"

"Yes, because although this was an elaborate and clever scheme, I don't believe Mr. Blake had anything to do with it."

DeStadler crossed his arms. "Do tell?"

Allen stood up. "So let me get this straight, are you accusing one of us or not?"

"I am," I asserted, and put the folder on the table nearby. "Mark do you still have that pipe — the smaller one."

"Uh, yeah," Mark said as he pulled it out of his pocket.

I held out my hand and he gave it to me. I took a firm grip on it with both hands. Then, in one quick movement, I lifted it up, then brought it down to break it across my knee.

The whole room murmured in surprise.

The stem was broken loose from the shank, and the now-loose stem hung from a pair of wires which held the two pieces together.

"What the hell is that?" Mark gasped.

"It is a global positioning system chip," I announced.

"Yeah!" DeStadler affirmed. "That pipe Jon Kane had that we picked up at Watkins' place? Turns out there was a GPS chip with its own power supply in that pipe as well."

"Why would someone do that?" Mark wondered.

"Best as we can tell," DeStadler snapped, "it was used to track whoever had it, wherever he went."

"And with this," I held up the broken pipe, "Mark, you were also being tracked."

"That's how the mugger knew where we'd be!" Mark realized.

"Exactly," I said in triumph.

"But why?" Mark reflected.

I walked across the room until I was nose to nose with Hypno. "You want to tell them or should I?"

Hypno broke eye contact with me and looked over to DeStadler. "I have no idea what this crazy bitch is talking about."

"Very well, then it falls to me," I stated simply. "Where should I begin?"

"I am so outta here," Hypno rose to go, but the two officers blocked the door.

"Oh no, stay. I think you'll find my story very interesting," I hinted. "It's a delightful tale of greed and revenge." I moved to the center of the floor. "It all began a few short years ago when a man named John invested everything he had with a shady financial advisor."

"I wouldn't know anything about that," Hypno grunted.

"Then you'll like this part. You see, John owned an internet security company built on software he'd created. He made investments with Randall Lawrence, but Randall completely mismanaged his investments, as well as skimmed money from the account. Then John's business went through a rough patch, which caused him to lose everything."

"Was he one of the names on the list?" Mark asked.

"Yes, in fact, other than Winsley Cunningham, John was the one that Randall had stolen the most money from."

"I don't see how this has anything to do with me!" Hypno prattled.

"John lost his money, his business collapsed, his wife left him, and he suffered a debilitating stroke."

With a nod from DeStadler, the two officers drew closer to Hypno. She glanced over her shoulder and noticed their approach.

"Now filling in the gaps as best I can, John received physical therapy from you."

"Yeah, I'm a licensed Physical Therapist, but I have more than one patient," Hypno corrected.

"I know. I had a friend look up your license. But here is where it gets interesting. Because as it turns out, you are also a janitor."

She frowned "What?"

I shrugged. "Oh, I guess 'maintenance worker' is more politically correct."

Hypno shook her head. "That's ridiculous."

I walked to the folder and extracted another page. It was a printout of a badge with Hypno's photo on it.

"I have a friend, who happens also to be my attorney. On a hunch, I had him look into all of the people who worked at Randall and Charles' offices downtown. I found it very interesting that Hypatia Norris — rather an unusual name — is listed as part of the cleaning crew."

Hypno stood with her mouth tight and glanced around the room.

"With access to those offices," I went on, "it would be child's play to sneak someone in late at night while you were cleaning. Of course, if that person was a hacker, he would also have to be an expert at cyber security."

Hypno's expression grew very dark.

"Oh, but that's right. Your 'patient' John *is* such an expert. This man who had lost all his money to Randall. How much did he promise you? How big a cut did he say you would get?"

The officers took another step toward Hypno.

"My only question is when did you get Candy involved? Was it before or after you snuck John into Randall's office to hack his computer? Or was it how you got Candy's name?" I once again got face to face with Hypno, both of us standing this time.

In a rapid move, Hypno pulled something from her belt and spun me around. As I gasped, she pushed a catch and a stiletto blade appeared at my throat.

The two officers immediately pulled their weapons and DeStadler reached into his jacket.

"NO!" Hypno yelled. "Guns down or I'll slice this bitch like a pig."

33. Double Dagger

Mark Watkins

S heryl's eyes grew wide, focused on the blade that glinted in the fluorescent light.

"I mean it!" Hypno yelled, with the blade at Sheryl's throat, which drew a muffled noise from her.

DeStadler removed his empty hand from his jacket and gave a wave to the officers, who lowered their weapons.

"Okay," DeStadler warned. "Think it through. There's no way out of here. Give me the knife, and nobody gets hurt."

"Clear the doorway," Hypno barked and pulled Sheryl toward the entrance as an officer stepped aside and cleared a path.

"You can't get away," DeStadler exclaimed.

Hypno sneered and pushed her way through the door with Sheryl.

The officers, DeStadler, and I rushed the hall as Hypno pulled Sheryl to the elevator bank and hit the down button with her elbow.

"Stay back," Hypno yelled.

The elevator door slid open. It was empty.

She dragged Sheryl in and the door shut.

I bounded to the nearby stairs and rushed down them. DeStadler shouted something after me, but I couldn't understand him. I took the stairs two at a time, with my hand on the rail to make sure I didn't fall. My knees still ached from all the running and falling I'd done, but I pushed past it, as adrenalin coursed through my veins.

I reached the mezzanine level and burst through the door.

Even though the conference was officially over, the lobby was still completely packed with people in costume as they continued to party. They stood in colorful packs and their voices jumbled into a loud, ambient noise.

I tried to get through them to reach the elevator, but the crowd was impassable and I couldn't make any headway. I saw the light go on over the elevator and the door slide open, but I couldn't see if anyone got off through the crush of people.

Finally, I turned a different direction, then shoved my way through the crowd with loud apologies as I went. I sought to get a glimpse of the tall Hypno.

There was a movement to my left, and I caught a flash of fiery-red hair, and I turned to see Sheryl being pushed by Hypno. She had Sheryl's arm twisted behind her back, and I could see the glint of the knife held low at her back.

They moved through the crowd, and no one could see the weapon as she forced Sheryl on through the room. They worked their way toward the closed door of the Marketplace.

I tried to draw closer, but my path was blocked over and over by Sherlock wannabes, fanciful elfin or Japanese Anime persona, and numerous other characters from fantasy and fiction.

By the time I reached the closed Marketplace door, there was no sign of Sheryl or Hypno. I quickly yanked it open, as a guard in uniform rushed over to block my path.

"Sir," he said, "it's closed! They pulled everyone out."

"Emer… emergency," I wheezed. "Call the… police."

I lunged under his arm and into the room.

He didn't pursue. I hoped he'd follow my request.

I turned and ran for the tobacco booth. Well, where it had been. Several of the booths were already gone and the pipe and drape that they were made of had been removed, and there were now large open spaces.

I was surprised that there was no one there. With all of the vendors who had to leave by 7:00 PM, I thought the place would be busy with teams of people as they packed. But it was as empty as a ghost town.

I suddenly felt vulnerable. I had pursued Hypno with no weapon of any kind. What would I use against a knife-wielding adversary? My cell phone?

I was, after all, an out-of-shape writer, not a martial arts expert.

Notwithstanding, I turned the corner to huff and puff as I went and headed straight down the aisle toward the booth's location.

Just a dozen feet ahead of me was Hypno with Sheryl's arm twisted behind her. They both had their backs to me. I increased my gait to catch up.

The next few moments seemed to happen in slow motion.

Hypno turned to see me heading straight for her, released Sheryl, and pushed her out of the way so she fell to the ground. She held up the stiletto, which glinted in the light. A gleam appeared in her eye, as she braced her arm in preparation to gut me.

I was moving too fast to stop, but I knew she was left-handed. So as her arm straightened to make the deadly thrust, I rotated my body sideways and aimed my left shoulder at her right shoulder.

I saw the blade slip past my shirt, and her arm slid past my chest. The knife stabbed into the fabric of the right side of my sports jacket, which had opened from my rotation.

The blade missed my wallet and cut into the cloth just as my left shoulder rammed into Hypno, which knocked both of us to the ground.

It was a hard hit on the concrete floor, as Hypno took the brunt of the fall from my body as I landed on top of her.

With little awareness of how much it hurt when we hit, I rolled off her, not sure if Hypno still had the knife. I was confident she was adept at how to use it.

I stopped rolling as I heard a clatter on the floor nearby. I followed the sound and looked to see that the knife had gone flying out of her hand when we fell.

Lucky.

Sheryl rose to her feet, as Hypno leapt up, even after the bone-clattering fall. She glanced about for the knife, then moved into what looked like a fighter's stance to face Sheryl. Obviously, she had hand-to-hand combat training.

Sheryl, however, planted her feet firmly and in one quick move, straightened her arm so that the flat of her palm made contact with the bridge of Hypno's nose.

She did this while she yelled, "Hee-ya!"

There was a loud *crack*! Hypno stopped and stood there for a moment, a look of dull surprise on her face. She wavered on her feet. Then, her eyes rolled up into her head and she went down like a sack of potatoes.

Sheryl ran over to me as I struggled to catch my breath and stand up. I only got as far as my knees.

"Ohmigod, ohmigod, are you hurt, are you bleeding? Talk to me, Mark," she exclaimed as I gasped.

"I—I—I'm fine," I croaked. "Miss… missed me."

"Well, I won't," a deeper voice said.

We both looked up to see John Stewart, who glared down at us with a gun in his left hand. Well, his good eye glared. The other one still peered off in the distance.

The gun was very similar to my own — probably the same year, model, and make. A silencer extended out and added several inches to the barrel, aimed dangerously in our direction.

"So you figured me out," he chuckled. "Who thought you could?"

"How did he get here?" I panted.

"Hypno called him from the elevator," said Sheryl.

"That's right. Now, the two of you are going to help me get her into the car."

I looked at all the bins which laid about the half-packed booth.

"What about your stuff?" I asked, and realized how incredibly stupid my question sounded.

"Don't need it anymore. I can buy anything I want. I have all of Randall's money." John waved the gun at us. "Help her up."

We both bent, grabbed an arm, and struggled to haul up the unconscious Hypno from the floor. We got under her armpits and carried her.

"Clever plan," Sheryl goaded John. "I have to give you that. Take Randall's money and point the police at us."

"What can I say?" John bragged. "The police always look at the spouse — or ex-spouse — first. It took some planning, but I almost got away with it."

"I think I can see how you did it," Sheryl confessed. "But I'm not sure of the details."

"You two move ahead of me, so I can watch you," John ordered. "Head for that curtain with the exit sign."

"It was your idea to steal from Randall," Sheryl grunted as we carried Hypno. "It was revenge for him losing your money."

"No, revenge for stealing from me. I always thought he didn't just make bad investments. Hypno helped get me into Randall's office, and I hacked his computer. It was all encoded, but that was easy. That's when I found his 'special' records and saw how he ripped everyone off, including me."

"But you couldn't actually open the accounts to transfer the money."

"I could hack through his reports, but the triple-security on the accounts was too much for even the best hacker."

Sheryl went on. "That's when you and Hypno came up with the plan to force Randall to give you the passcodes."

"I came up with the plan, but Hypno was happy to help. She's quite a lady."

"How did you get Candy involved?"

"Saw her name on the list. Hypno and I tracked her down, showed her the secret accounts, and how her boyfriend — well, ex-boyfriend at that point — ripped her off."

"You convinced her if she helped, you'd get her money back."

"With a cut of the whole take."

"Was it merely a business arrangement?" Sheryl wondered. "I mean, getting her to make a play for Mark—"

He gave his off-center smirk. "She was a firebrand. She thought seducing Mark would be fun—"

"Thanks," I sneered. "I'm glad I could be so entertaining."

"Come on, Watkins," John leered. "She knew about your wife, that you'd been alone. She figured it would be a thrill to have a woman like her chase after you. She was under the impression that after she drugged you, you'd be used as her alibi. She didn't know we were setting you up to be the patsy. We considered using Allen Alexander-"

"If you had, I would've paid to help you," I offered.

"Candy said no way she would even pretend to make a play for that guy, even if to only drug him. Plus, you were a better choice. When we found out you had a gun and everything, the plan fell into place."

We reached the curtain under the exit sign, another part of the elaborate pipe and drape.

"Hold up!" John said, and he moved from behind us and pulled the curtain aside. He gestured us to move in with the gun. The hallway beyond was dirty, dingy, and not well lit. It was as if the moment you left the public spaces, the hotel became a dark and sinister cavern.

We passed through the curtain. He followed us into the gloomy hall.

"Keep going straight. This is a hallway nobody uses."

"What was Candy's relationship with you?" Sheryl inquired, as she tried to keep him focused.

"Hypno likes girls as well as guys, and Candy was surprisingly creative. She was a lot of fun for both of us."

"So why kill her?" Sheryl asked. We were both panting hard from the weight of Hypno as we dragged her.

"She decided to cross us. She made copies of the financial reports I gave her and put them on a flash drive, which she hid in the pipe marked with an 'X'. It was a deal she worked out with Jon Kane."

"She was hedging her bets, in case you didn't pay up."

"Yes, but we figured it out and Hypno — in a smart move — gave that pipe to Watkins instead. After he touched the display."

"The display pipe... I forgot I'd held it," I said, as the realization sunk in.

Stewart gave that grotesque smile. "There were actually four pipes! Though we had planned to use the pipe with the 'X' to leave at Randall's."

Hypno's head lolled to the side and a soft moan escaped her lips.

"Until I left it on the podium," I concurred.

"We gave Candy the display one wrapped up with plastic so it wouldn't get new fingerprints."

"Which she took to Randall's," Sheryl guessed.

"Yes. Randall had asked her to come pick up reports he had faked for the Cunningham broad. Candy brought the pipe as a gift."

"They had planned to meet, which is why Randall let her in," Sheryl reckoned.

"And it was very convenient that your ex-husband already had the handcuffs and leg irons in a drawer at his place. Kinky bastard."

Sheryl flushed red at this but went on. "Candy knew where to find them, from previous 'play dates.'"

"Gotta hand it to her. She batted her eyes, made a few lewd suggestions, and got him trussed up like a turkey on

Thanksgiving. I needed to go uptown and get Mark's gun. All Candy had to do was let me in."

"I still don't understand why you killed her," Sheryl quizzed.

"She didn't want anyone to get hurt. Not Randall, and not Watkins."

"Drugging me was okay?" I whined.

Stewart ignored me and went on, "She was fine with cuffin' him and stealin' his money. She felt he deserved that."

"So, between threatening to smother him and firing that shot near his head into the wall—" Sheryl said.

"Oh, you know about that?" Stewart chortled, pleased with himself.

"—Randall gave up the account numbers and the passwords."

"He cried like a baby and gave me everything I asked for."

We continued past bins of trash that were lined up on the right side of the hallway and moved toward a big open room that had several filthy windows, which let in dappled sunlight.

"Gotta hand it to you," Stewart praised. "Pretty clever that you figured out a lot of it."

"Where did the money go?" Sheryl said.

"I transferred it to accounts of mine offshore. Once I took care of that, I sent Candy uptown."

"So she was gone by the time you suffocated Randall."

Stewart seemed to revel in the memory. "That was a joy I didn't want to share with anyone. The bastard who ruined my life sucked his last breath — or tried to — with me pushin' that pillow on his face. I felt him die."

Sheryl kept going. "Then you came back to the hotel—"

"Yes, where Hypno was having some fun with Candy."

"Which is why she was naked."

He gave a lopsided shrug. "One last 'dance' shall we say? I let myself into the room, Hypno threw on some clothes and dragged Mark out as I — well, let's just say I took care of the problem."

"Leaving your silhouette on the wall."

Stewart stopped. "What's that?"

"There was blood spatter on the wall. It showed a big person— left-handed."

"Nobody bothered me about it."

"Then you had Hypno return the gun," Sheryl said, "while you went back to Mark's room and left that incriminating email—"

"He didn't even have a password on his laptop. Piece of cake."

Hypno was beginning to hold her head up herself and blinked rapidly as we reached a large garage-style door in the big room, obviously one of the hotel's many loading docks.

"What about Jon Kane?" Sheryl asked.

"With Candy gone, Hypno told Kane that Watkins had the pipe with the records, and that fool spent the weekend following you like a puppy. Deflected suspicion from us and kept him out of my way."

"And when Mark paid for the pipe, you gave him the smaller pipe with the GPS so you could track us."

"I was coverin' all the bases. I wanted to make sure that the police couldn't prove that there was more than one pipe with Watkins' fingerprints. I tracked you two and Jon Kane on my phone. I knew when Mark was arrested, I could track when he was released, and I saw you two come back to the ballroom at the hotel."

"Which is why you were outside the door when we came out. You weren't going to any lecture."

"It was a good thing I did. I saw you with the other pipe."

Sheryl went on, "So, you got Hypno to be our mugger."

"Got the pipe back, didn't we?" he smirked.

"After we copied the files."

"That I didn't plan on. I figured if Kane or the cops had got that drive, by the time they broke the encryption, I'd be long gone. Don't know how you did it so fast."

We reached the garage door. Stewart hit a red button and it began to rise.

"So why kill Kane?"

"Can you believe that creep tried to blackmail me?" Stewart snorted. "Recognized my name on that financial report and put two-and-two together. He wasn't as dumb as I thought. He called me up and demanded I split the take with him or he'd go to the police."

"So you agreed to meet him outside Mark's condo."

"I knew he was at Mark's place 'cause of the GPS in the pipe *he* had. Told him to go out the fire escape. He probably figured since I had the stroke I wasn't much of a threat. Hypno took care of him. Snuffed the loser with a baseball bat he brought to protect himself — with gloves on, of course."

Hypno had regained consciousness, planted her feet on the floor, and pulled her hands free from both Sheryl and me.

She stumbled over to John Stewart, who helped her stand straight. She was still a bit groggy and said, "Which one clocked me?"

"The broad," John said as he kept the gun pointed at us. "Got you good. Pretty sweet move."

"I'm gonna kick her freakin' ass," Hypno said, her lip curled in an angry sneer.

Stewart glanced out at the street. "No time. Someone cleared the Marketplace floor."

"Wha'?" Hypno forced herself to focus.

"Nobody was in there when I brought the car around. We gotta get outta here."

Hypno looked sullen and pointed a wobbly finger at me. "He made me lose my knife."

John smiled that creepy half-face smile of his. "I'll buy you a dozen. Let's go."

The door was open fully and a car waited on the other side. Apparently, when Hypno headed upstairs for the 5:00 meeting, Stewart had brought a car around for a quick getaway.

They only needed to step down from the loading dock, into the nearby vehicle, and they would be off.

"Here," Stewart said, and handed Hypno the pistol, which she also took in her left hand. "Cover 'em while I start the car."

"The police have copies of the financial data. They will track the money down," Sheryl notified the pair. "You'll never get away with it!"

Hypno glared at Sheryl and shifted the pistol toward her.

"Actually," I said loudly with my hands up, "I think you've gotten away with it very well."

Hypno gave a smirk at me, then carefully took a bead on Sheryl. "You two are the only ones who know the truth. Without you, we are home free—"

She zeroed in on Sheryl, aimed the long barrel of the pistol at the middle of her chest. Sheryl's face turned to me, and I saw genuine fear in her eyes.

I had to do something. It was instantly clear to me. Here was a chance at happiness, another chance at love, and this psychopath was about to take it from me.

Her finger tightened around the trigger.

I grabbed Sheryl and pulled her behind me.

"Mark, no," she said.

The grin of a barracuda appeared on Hypno's face as a wild look was in her eyes. "I'm disappointed in you, Watkins. You know this gun. If I aim right, the bullet will go right through you and kill her anyway."

She shut one eye and brought her other hand to the grip, as she assumed a shooter's stance.

I closed my eyes and turned my head in anticipation of the shot.

"THIS IS THE POLICE," came a voice over a megaphone. "PUT YOUR WEAPONS DOWN AND PUT YOUR HANDS UP."

Hypno yelled a very unladylike string of curses, enough to make a sailor blush. With no concern about us, she jumped off the loading dock and ran to the car, the pistol in her hand.

Sheryl gave an exhale of release, turned me around, and pulled me into a hug.

"That was—" she gushed.

"I know—"

"The *stupidest* thing I've ever seen!"

"I thought I was going to lose you," I said as I held her tight.

"I'm not so easy to get rid of," Sheryl reassured as she hugged me back. She suddenly pushed me to arm's length. "But, honestly, what the hell were you thinking?"

Immediately, several police cars pulled up with lights flashing, and a team of men dressed in SWAT gear came from up the street with very impressive guns. Hypno cursed as two officers grabbed her and threw her down on the ground. A team surrounded her and confiscated the pistol.

In the car, John Stewart held up his left hand and slowly got out. They quickly pushed him face down to the ground.

Detective Elvis strode up the loading dock stairs. He had on a bulletproof vest with the word "POLICE" on both the front and back. He took off his black helmet. "You two all right?"

Sheryl released me, after a quick peck on the cheek, and pulled out a small silver device from a hidden pocket somewhere in her black dress. "I recorded the whole thing! I have his confession right here."

It was the first time I ever saw Detective Elvis smile.

And it was beautiful.

He drew closer and took a hard look at me.

"You okay, Watkins?"

"Just a little light-headed," I told him.

I looked over at Sheryl and she had blood on her left arm. "You're hurt!" I said and pointed.

She looked at the fresh blood and gave a shocked, "Oh!" She rubbed it, but there was no wound. "It's not mine."

"Where did it come from?" I asked.

Sheryl's eyes grew large. "Mark, you're bleeding!"

"Yeah, you are," Elvis pointed at my right arm.

I looked over and saw that my jacket sleeve was saturated with blood, almost down to my wrist. There was a tear in the fabric halfway up my arm.

Sheryl gave another little "Oh!" of concern.

"It would seem the knife didn't miss me," I gulped, and carefully opened the tear to see how badly I was hurt.

"Your sleeve's a mess. That's a lot of blood, man," Elvis said.

"Just a flesh wound," I offered gallantly as I looked through the rip at the slice in my arm, which did indeed bleed profusely.

At which point I fell slowly to the ground, as I heard Sheryl shriek.

But, images flashed in my mind.

Before me was Suzie in her hospital bed. The final bed she would ever lay in. Tubes went up her nose, in her arm, and under the covers to parts I didn't want to think about.

She looked up at me and gave me a weak smile. "We've had a great marriage, while so many of our friends split up."

"It's all because of you," I told her.

"No, you're a good man to be married to." She forced a smile. "It looked easy because it was easy. Once I'm gone—"

"Please don't say that, Sooz," I said, the tears falling.

"I want you to find someone," she told me, her eyes wide and imploring. "And I want you to make her as happy as you've made me."

Then, there was darkness.

34. Golden Ratio

Sheryl Homes

T he next few hours were the toughest for me. An unconscious Mark was rushed to the hospital, and I rode in the ambulance.

They got us into emergency, and I was ordered to a waiting room and told to be patient. I am not good at patience, but it did give me a chance to go over my notes and put the final pieces together.

Mark had lost a lot of blood, but I was told he would pull through, and I insisted I be there when he woke up. So they put me in his room, and I did a lot of thinking.

This had been quite an adventure, but now, was I really thinking about a relationship with a man eighteen years my senior? Sitting in the hospital, I knew that someday this was how it would end. With me holding a death watch over this man.

That is if we could even make it work.

On the other hand, had I been really living? With the divorce, I had gone into my protective shell and lost all interest in men and sex. Meeting Mark had reawakened my desires, as well as my dreams of a real relationship.

I would seriously be a fool not to take a chance if it could be a success.

Lewis

But I was afraid — so damned afraid. To open myself, physically and emotionally, seemed so scary.

"Hey there," came a whisper from the bed.

I jumped, and with a strangled cry, I moved out of the chair to the prone form of Mark. "You're awake!"

I couldn't stop the tears that fell down my face.

"Hope you'll forgive me if I don't get up," he croaked.

I ran my fingers through his hair. "You lost a lot of blood. Good thing there were EMTs nearby. They said you could've bled out."

"Didn't even know I was cut," he apologized, and looked over at his right arm. It was wrapped in gauze. He then looked at the pint of plasma which hung with an IV and went into his left arm.

"Thirty stitches," I said and adjusted his pillow. "It's going to leave a scar, but they say you'll be fine." I couldn't keep my hands off him, and I kept touching his hair, his arm, his face.

"A scar. Won't I be manly?" he joked.

"You tackled Hypno and jumped in front of me when she had the gun. That *is* pretty manly—"

"Thanks."

"If manly means idiotic—"

He gave a shrug. "Do what you're good at, I always say."

Just then Detective DeStadler walked into the room. I immediately rubbed my eyes to stop the tears, but it had probably made my eyeliner run so I appeared like a raccoon.

"He awake? I'm gonna need a statement," DeStadler ordered.

"In that case," Mark groaned, "I'm unconscious."

This got a chuckle from the detective, who sat in the chair I had vacated.

"Went through that digital recording you made," DeStadler told me. "Good job. You got him to confess to everything."

"Thanks," I replied.

"We checked on that gun he had. Same make and model as Mark's. When the forensic guys looked in the barrel of Mark's gun, they found scratches that could only be made by the same silencer. Both the silencer and his gun were illegal."

"Wait a minute," Mark grunted. "I still don't understand." He looked at me. "How'd you figure it out? And how did you get DeStadler to come with you? And that SWAT team—"

I had to smile. "A bit of investigation to pull together my suspicions, some help from Uncle Louie and my accountant, and a lot of laying it out for the detective."

"You didn't lay it *all* out for me," DeStadler mocked jovially. "The financial data is what made the difference. Using the account numbers, our guys and her accountant were able to track down where the money ended up. He put it through a lot of back doors and blind alleys, but we were able to trace it."

"What will happen to the money?" I wondered.

DeStadler shrugged. "It will be returned to all the people that Randall Lawrence stole it from in the first place."

"Even Allen Alexander?"

DeStadler nodded.

"Well, I guess it couldn't be a perfect ending," Mark griped and gazed up at me. I shivered. It was one of those looks that felt like a caress. "I still don't see how you found Stewart."

I exchanged a glance with DeStadler and spoke, "I ran the names on the list through a search engine, see what turned up. However, I got lucky when I picked the correct name first."

"But John Stewart's name wasn't on it," Mark recalled.

"That's because that isn't his name," DeStadler chuckled. "It was his alias."

"What?"

I leaned a little closer. "Remember how I mentioned that the sign at his tobacco booth had the words too close together?"

Mark looked chagrined. "Vaguely. What about it?"

"For some reason it stuck with me. I recalled that one of the names on the list was 'John Yeolde', and when I looked him up, I found a man with a background in internet security. I was able to trace some old press releases, and when I found a photo, I realized he was the same man who ran the tobacco booth."

My point became suddenly clear to Mark. "So all the time we thought it was *Ye Olde Mysterious Tobacco Shoppe*—" he started.

"But it was actually *Yeolde Mysterious Tobacco Shoppe*. He'd had that sign made with his real name. I can only assume he created 'John Stewart' and got the business cards with that name when he came up with the scheme."

"I guess the strategy was predicated on us actually being at the conference."

"No," I corrected. "He planned to do it anyway. But he was clever. When he saw you were going to be there, he was sure you would be the perfect person to set up for the crime."

"How could he know I would come by his booth?"

"Candy was his point man — uh woman."

Mark's mouth dropped open. "That's right! She suggested I visit the Marketplace."

I nodded. "And I am sure that if you didn't go to the booth, she might have brought you the pipe later."

"To make sure my prints ended up on it."

"So as far as getting us on board," DeStadler told us, "your lady friend here came to the station with printouts she'd made from looking this guy up and highlighted information from the financial records—"

"Which is why you needed to rent the use of a computer and printer," Mark deduced.

"Exactly!" I announced. "I realized we had cast too wide a net and we needed to focus on the details."

"Once I saw the evidence, and that cameo from Ms. Cunningham, Elvis and I were willing to back her up," DeStadler said. "I got Elvis to cover the outside of the hotel with the SWAT team, in case anyone made a break for it."

Mark considered this for a moment. "Besides the name, was there anything else, Sheryl?"

"I had seen the forensic photos of Jon Kane, when Louie and I got you out. I realized from the blood spatter that it was a left-handed person with a lot of strength. Yet, because of his height and the damage done to him, I was sure it had to be someone shorter than our shooter. It had to be a team — a team that did not include Jon Kane."

"So," DeStadler agreed, "we reviewed the videotape of the elevator from the night of the murder. This Hypno broad went upstairs about the same time as Jon Kane. Candy arrived a few minutes later. Then we noticed that John Stewart showed up about fifteen minutes before Candy was shot, carrying a shopping bag—"

I interrupted, "Which we deduced contained the pillow, as well as your pistol."

"We had also expanded our search of the surveillance footage of the back stairs of the hotel. With this new information, we took a look at the night of the murder. About 3:55, Hypno walked down with the *same* bag as Stewart, but with less in it. That's when we think she returned the gun to your apartment."

"After John shot Candy," I said.

Mark seemed to process the information. "So she returned my gun while Stewart — or Yeolde — wrote the fake email."

"Since she didn't steal the gun from your apartment, she didn't know to leave the magazine separate," I pointed out.

"And then with Jon Kane," Mark said, "Hypno already knew where my apartment was, and Yeolde told Jon to go out the fire escape and meet in the back alley."

"Yeah," DeStadler agreed. "We think he took the bat for protection, and she got it from him and killed him."

"Wow!" Mark marveled.

DeStadler continued. "Once Ms. Homes brought us the information about Ms. Norris being on the cleaning crew at Randall's offices, we tracked down arrests for both fraud and prostitution in her past."

Mark considered this. "Probably why Yeolde thought she'd be the perfect partner."

"Probably," DeStadler mused. "But the *coupe de grace* was the pipe Jon Kane had that you turned over to us."

"Remember," I recalled, "when he pulled it from his pocket, the stem was loose from the shank?"

"Yeah, and there were wires that you said might be pipe cleaners," Mark recalled.

"I had our computer crime guys go over it," DeStadler said. "They found the GPS chip with a small power supply."

"Which is why you thought there was the same thing in the smaller pipe I had," Mark acknowledged.

"It was the only way I could deduce the mugger — who we now know was Hypno — could find us," I told him. "So, between what I'd found—"

"And what *we'd* found," DeStadler added, "we got a much clearer vision of who actually orchestrated the murders."

Mark shook his head, as he tried to absorb it all. "So, you let Sheryl question the suspects to get Hypno to show her hand?"

DeStadler shrugged. "It wasn't regulation, but I figured you two deserved a break after all you'd been through. I also had Elvis clear everybody out of the Marketplace, in case there was trouble."

"Right," I added. "That explains why there was no one in there when we arrived."

DeStadler nodded. "Elvis saw Stewart head out — we know now to get the car — and he quickly cleared the place. We didn't know he had a gun."

He stood up from the chair and straightened his tie. "But you both handled yourselves well. I mean it. When you get out of here, come by the station and give us your statement."

"As long as I know you aren't going to handcuff me or throw me in a holding cell," Mark said, "I'll be happy to."

"Don't worry. I will make sure any charges against you will be dropped," DeStadler declared.

"So," Mark said, and reached out for my hand. "Maybe we aren't such bad detectives after all?"

DeStadler smiled. "I don't want to encourage you, but you two make a pretty good team. Although, I would say there is, probably, one detective between the pair of you."

"It was elementary, my dear DeStadler," Mark said.

I gave him a dirty look. "Amazing!"

"But do me a favor," DeStadler begged. "Don't get blamed for any more murders, okay?"

"That will be *our* pleasure," I agreed.

DeStadler gave a smile and strode out.

"When can we leave?" Mark asked.

"You're on pain killers, and they want to keep you overnight for observation," I expressed. "Once they release you, you're coming home with me."

"Really?"

"I have to nurse you back to health." I ran my fingers through his hair again. "Besides, I did tell DeStadler we spent the night together, remember? You don't want to make a liar out of me, do you?"

I bent close and brushed my lips to Mark's, and we fell into a passionate kiss, as the machine that counted his heart rate began to beep wildly.

35. Endpaper

Mark Watkins

T wo weeks later, on a bright May morning, Sheryl and I sat at her kitchen island and stared at each other over toast and coffee. We both wore pajamas and enjoyed a lazy Sunday. Her eyes gleamed and she wore a satisfied look.

"Last night was amazing," I said, unable to stop the smile on my own face.

"I have to admit I am surprised."

"By what?"

"It just keeps getting better!" She gave a contented sigh.

I nodded. "I thought it was pretty damn great the first time."

"After all that 'foreplay' when we solved the crime? Oh, yes, I was *quite* ready."

"I was sure we couldn't improve, but…"

She gave a smirk. "Who says I can't teach an old dog new tricks?"

"Who are you calling old?" I pulled her into my arms and she giggled as I kissed her neck.

"Don't start anything," she laughed. "We don't have time!"

I let her go and she got on the other side of the island to be safe. "You know what we have to talk about."

She nodded. "I know. We've been avoiding it."

"It is a serious commitment," I pointed out, and I reached across the counter to take her hand. She interwove her fingers in mine and gave a squeeze.

"Are we really ready for it?" she worried as doubt crept into her eyes.

"It's not too late to change our minds."

There was a buzz at the door, and we both glanced at the intercom, and then each other. Finally, Sheryl walked to the box and hit the button to open the outside door.

"I mean, it's not like we know everything about each other," she stressed, as she walked over to the door and undid the locks.

"I agree. And some people might say it's far too early in our relationship," I reasoned, as I grabbed my coffee cup and walked over to her.

"I know. But I think — it feels right."

There was a knock and Sheryl opened the door. Jeff Moss strode into the room like a freight train.

"Hey, sweetie," he said, and gave Sheryl a peck on the cheek.

"Hi, Jeff."

He paced over to me and gave me a quick hug. "Hey, babe. How's the arm?"

"Fine, fine," I said as he walked over to the table. Sheryl and I followed as he put his briefcase in the middle of the island. "Can we offer you anything?"

"Toast, coffee," Sheryl said. "I think we have a bagel."

Jeff looked at Sheryl, hopeful. "Can I smoke?"

Sheryl grimaced. "Ooh! I rather you didn't."

Jeff lifted his hands in a pose of surrender. "Gettin' harder and harder to find folks who let me smoke. Next writer I sign up better have a two-pack-a-day habit."

He turned and opened his briefcase in one fluid motion.

"So," I asked, "what's the word?"

"I've got the contracts," Jeff approved. "The publisher is really excited about this."

"We were just discussing it," Sheryl admitted.

"All you have to do is sign the papers, and we are good to go," Jeff said.

"So," I brooded, "the publisher was willing to commit just from the outline?"

Jeff opened his arms. "C'mon, babe. You are both proven commodities. Plus, you happen to have an agent who is a genius. To have *both* your names on a new Sherlock Holmes novel? It was like shooting fish in a barrel."

"Hmm," Sheryl wondered with suspicion. "Are we the fish or the barrel?"

"Who cares? The point is, there is already buzz online about this book."

"Great," I protested. "All we have to do now is write it."

"The easy part, I'm sure." Jeff pulled out several stacks of papers from his briefcase. "So, here, sign away."

"Oh, Mark, you sign first. I'm going to open some champagne." Sheryl walked to the cupboard to get glasses and a bottle out of the fridge.

Jeff handed me a pen, and I went to the final page on the multiple copies and signed my name on the correct line of each.

"You two will get an even split," Jeff insisted. "Let me tell you, the publisher is paying you a very nice advance. To be honest, one of the biggest I've seen in years."

"And you getting your ten percent doesn't hurt either, I'm sure," I mentioned.

"I think I will be able to catch up on a few things," Jeff smirked as Sheryl put champagne flutes in front of us and popped the cork.

I poured the three glasses as she took the four copies of the contract and quickly added her signature to them.

We each picked up a glass.

"To the newest writing team: Homes and Watkins!" Sheryl proclaimed.

"What's wrong with Watkins and Homes?" I taunted.

"It flows better the other way," Jeff corrected.

We toasted and each took a sip.

Jeff looked at me and then at Sheryl.

"You guys look good," he smiled. "No, I mean it, both of you look really good." He thought about it for a minute and then added, "Happy."

"Thanks," I told him and walked over to Sheryl to take her hand in mine.

Jeff smiled. He downed the bubbly and set his glass down. "Okay, gotta go. I'll have checks for you by the end of the week."

He put two copies in his briefcase, left one for each of us, and I escorted him to the door. He left as quickly as he had entered.

I returned to Sheryl and refilled my glass.

"You sure you're okay with this?" Sheryl worried, with a glance at the contract Jeff left for her.

I smiled. "I told you, I'm more than okay. I'm excited about doing it."

I gazed into her eyes.

"Even though you've never collaborated before?" She twined her arms around my neck.

"Well, I wrote the Sherlock Holmes books for Susie. I guess you'll have to be the one I write new ones for." I pressed her lips to mine.

"And with," she said and nuzzled my neck.

We were still at the passionate stage of our relationship, and I could feel myself quickly become aroused as I kissed and touched her.

"I would like to suggest a collaboration we could work on right now," I said with a suggestive wink.

"Do you think it will be a success?" Sheryl replied coyly.

"If the past few weeks have been any indication, I believe we will both be pleased."

With the champagne flutes in our hands, we made our way to the bedroom to continue the interplay for our mutual benefit.

In what I hoped would be a long partnership.

Books From Mindbender Press

Paranormal Mystery
Fire In The Mind
Seduction In The Mind
Reunion In The Mind
Haunted In The Mind
Devotion In The Mind
Asylum In The Mind
Specter In The Mind
Vengeance In The Mind
Echoes In The Mind
Infection In The Mind
Justice In The Mind
Ritual In The Mind
Vanished In The Mind

Horror
The Muse
Kept In The Dark
The Vanishing
Digger

Romantic Suspense
A Study In Murder
Murder By Misdirection
Vanishing Act

NYPD Wizard Detective
The Wizards Of Central Park West
The Vampires Of Greenwich Village
The Werewolves Of Washington Square

About The Authors

Debra Snow and Arjay Lewis are a husband and wife writing team.

Debra Snow is an author, entertainer and professional belly dancer who has traveled the world and performed at casinos, cruise ships as well as local television.

In 1990, while performing at the Taj Mahal in Atlantic City she met magician and writer Arjay Lewis. It was a match that has lasted ever since.

While Arjay developed his short stories, scripts, and novels, Debra acted as his editor, proof-reader, and cheering squad.

Arjay's books started to be published in 2017, and his novel *The Muse, A Novel Of Unrelenting Terror* has won 14 Awards. He has 8 books published in the *In The Mind* series of paranormal mysteries.

In 2018, Debra took her hand to the keyboard and began her first novel featuring mysteries laced with romance. Together they created the male and female narration used in *A Study In Murder.*

Today Debra and Arjay are partners in Crime... Fiction.

FREE NOVELLA

A DOCTOR WISE PARANORMAL PREQUEL

A history of strange deaths, a psychic trying to master his abilities. Can a graduate student with mental powers uncover the secret of a haunted house?

A tragic car accident claimed his fiancée and unleashed strange mental abilities with which Leonard "Len" Wise has only recently come to grips. He has been asked to do a reading at Scudder House, a location of mysterious sounds, strange happenings, and a dark history.

With his mentor, Doctor Fritz Kohl, to help him, Len must reach deep to rise up to his full potential.

Hidden in the Mind is a prequel to the Doctor Wise series of paranormal mysteries, and gives you unique insight into this man and his bizarre experiences.

If you like sympathetic heroes and supernatural surprises, then you'll love Arjay Lewis's novella.

Free Novella

A street magician is murdered, a knife sticking from his chest. Can a NYPD rookie use her unique talents to find a killer?

Prophecy "Pro" Thompson is a female African-American, NYPD uniformed officer. Pro and her partner find a street performer stabbed through the heart and Pro decides to work the case in her free time.

During her investigation, Pro meets magician Jamie Tobin, a charming Irishman who tries to amaze her but becomes more interested in romancing her.

If you enjoy a kick-ass female protagonist, and a story mixed with crime, romance and comedy, you will love this fast-paced novella by Debra Snow.

This novella introduces the new series *Murder By Misdirection*, coming in June 2019.

http://www.debrasnow.com